OVERTURE ix
  The Sound of Silence

CHAPTER ONE 1
  Blues in the Night

CHAPTER TWO 13
  Mad World

CHAPTER THREE 27
  Running Up That Hill

CHAPTER FOUR 33
  Don't Stop Believin'

CHAPTER FIVE 47
  Church of the Poison Mind

CHAPTER SIX 63
  Easy Lover

CHAPTER SEVEN 77
  Girls Just Want to Have Fun

CHAPTER EIGHT 89
  [Offbeat]

CHAPTER NINE 99
  Message in a Bottle

CHAPTER TEN 113
  It's Only Love

CHAPTER ELEVEN 125
    Eternal Flame

CHAPTER TWELVE......................... 141
    Crimson and Clover

CHAPTER THIRTEEN...................... 161
    Close My Eyes Forever

CHAPTER FOURTEEN 175
    A Hazy Shade of Winter

CHAPTER FIFTEEN 189
    You Give Love a Bad Name

CHAPTER SIXTEEN 209
    Invincible

CHAPTER SEVENTEEN................... 225
    Let There Be Rock

CHAPTER EIGHTEEN...................... 241
    Orion

CHAPTER NINETEEN 253
    The Loneliness of the Long
    Distance Runner

CHAPTER TWENTY 269
    On the Turning Away

CHAPTER TWENTY-ONE 281
    The Edge of Seventeen

OUTRO 299
    Fumbling Toward Ecstasy
    Breathe. Love.

Acknowledgments

A book is like a magical key into an author's innermost thoughts and creative imagination. It is a unique assembling of the author's own perspective on life, its ups and downs, side splitting funny parts and heart wrenching challenges. The story of the Sky-bound Misfit has been brewing inside my imagination for many years. Writing a book takes time, focus, and commitment from the author and the author's support crew. I have so many to thank for the support I have received along my pilgrimage towards the completion of my first novel. In particular, I would like to thank my husband, Ken Thompson, and my children, Devon, Zarya and Liam for gifting me with the time to write. I could not have written this book without their love and support. Others kindly helped with feedback. Becky Leonty and Janet Gallagher graciously volunteered their time as my continuity readers. My teen daughter, Zarya Powell-Thompson gave me invaluable advice on my cover design and synopsis. Andrew Powell, my brother, advised me on my Québécois slang. My parents, Penny and Bill Powell, supported me with so many other undeniably important pieces that go into writing and publishing a book. I thank you all!

This novel is a work of fiction. Although based on the author's life experiences, this story is a product of the author's imagination. Characters, places, and events are either fictitious or used fictitiously. Any resemblance of characters to actual people is a coincidence.

For all the sky-bound misfits out there

OVERTURE
The Sound of Silence

July 1, 2018

O*hmmmmmm*. The sound of the universe. That is what I heard as the air failed to catch me. Wind, water, the cawing of a crow, a train in the distance, someone else's desperate yell. Sounds become one big jumbled hum when you're travelling breakneck speed. They say that an object stops gaining speed when it reaches a certain velocity as it is pulled by gravity through space. I must've hit the river just before this took effect.

The river embraced me, and time faltered. There were no smells. I saw black. I couldn't breathe. A faint roar pricked at my consciousness as if from a long distance away.

Then my mind suddenly sharpened, and I was overwhelmed by a sense of panic. I frantically grabbed for something, for life I suppose, but everything rushed passed me, over me and under me. The river's roar became a beating thunder in my head, hammering fear into every inch of me. My lungs burned with the lack of oxygen. My instincts scrambled for a solution. I reached out desperately for help but found none. My lungs ached. I surfaced briefly but couldn't stay afloat. The current was too strong, the river too wild.

Then my world dimmed. I was losing the battle. My consciousness faded. For a brief moment before everything went black, I thought I felt something... no, someone, touch me. Then I slipped away and fell through time.

I landed with a shock, where it all started, in 1985.

My name is Francesca MacKenna, aka "Frankie", and this is my story.

PART 1
Death of the Third Person

CHAPTER ONE
Blues in the Night

May 1985

My life began in a pub. Standing there on a windowsill, a twelve-year-old kid in a world full of adult decisions, frozen in time one minute and reborn the next. On the sixteenth of May, 1985, sometime shortly after six in the evening, I officially began my journey toward living in the first person. No longer would I be a simple materialization of my parents or the projection of their world views and desires: "Frankie, the famous clarinet player!" Or "Frankie, the politically correct peacekeeper!" Or "Our Frankie! The future UN Secretary-General!". On that day the smallest of small coincidences managed to happen, and the way I experienced life was changed forever. With a whiff of urinal soap, "Frankie" was orphaned, and "I" was born.

Here's how it happened.

❜

The pub was a true relic, bubbling with historic pride, located in a string of old neo-Gothic buildings in Montreal's French east end. Until it had been sold a few years before, it had been in Frankie's family for over fifty years. Metal-grate steps led up to a thick timber door surrounded by grey stone walls. An old iron lantern hung to the left of the door, "1840" etched in the stone beneath it. The inside architecture reflected that of the door: timber walls and ceilings held in place with impressive log beams. As was typical in these old buildings, the warped wood-planked floor had demanded that the more permanent furniture, such as the bar, be altered by a carpenter to match the uneven deck. Old cast-iron column radiators, with long-broken thermostats, were located at each end of the bar and on the far side of the stage. To release the excess heat, a huge bay window, with a sill deep enough to accommodate the rears of at least three adults, lay slightly ajar, even in the most frigid of weather. Throughout the winter months, the back door would be propped open a crack. Beyond the door at the back of the pub was a narrow alley of stone-brick walls and iron staircases that spiralled down from the top floors of buildings, past back doors to the street. This particular building represented the breath, heart, and the soul of Montreal, not only because of its physical and historical mystique, but because, within its walls, it had been transformed into a typical French-Irish pub. Carved wooden letters hung above the bar: *L'Irlandais*.

Frankie sat, fiddling absently with her long auburn braid, in the wooden crook of the pub's huge bay window. Her right leg dangled off the edge, her foot resting on a big terra-cotta vase filled with colourful South American flutes of various shapes and sizes. Books and jazz magazines, along with paper and pencils, lay by her knees, scattered on the sill in her own organized chaos. Her dad had promised to help in the preparation of her next class presentation if she agreed to sit through his jam sessions at the pub this week. He was practicing for next week's spring-fling battle of the bands. His band would be playing jazz with a Celtic twist. Anywhere else, the mixture of the two might have raised eyebrows, but this was Montreal, where great melodies are made with hearts and souls, period. She looked up at him and his clarinet almost admiringly; the instrument protruded from his mouth so naturally, almost as if it were surgically attached. She glanced at the other musicians—piano, fiddle, alto sax, bass, and drums. Their trumpeter was missing, and they never found anyone to play the trombone bit, but they would make do. Frankie looked back at her dad, and her imagination began to twist and turn. Her dad's clarinet began to melt away and metamorphose into the long, sophisticated silver trunk of a soprano sax. The edges of her eyes lifted into a dreamy grin. He started to play, and the sax snapped back into a clarinet. She frowned a little. Frankie was bored. But she also knew that whether she agreed or not to his "deal," she would still be sitting, waiting, through it all, so she'd agreed. Her presentation would be on Oscar Peterson.

Oscar Peterson. Born and raised in Montreal. A Canadian jazz icon. Frankie's dad's hero. Frankie repositioned herself, pushing her research melange to the side, and picked up a flute from the vase beneath the windowsill. It was a fat one with a deep whistle. It came in two parts. She removed the end pieces and held the body up to her eye like a telescope. Her world narrowed into a circle with one main actor in the middle—whoever she chose to aim at. This time, her prime subject was a little brown mouse with a white splotch under its chin. Pierre, the bartender, had used all the tricks in the book but poison to rid the pub of mice, but he just could not out-smart this one. Frankie smiled; she was glad that a little city wildlife had been spared. The mouse ran along the edge of the wall a few feet to her left, up the foot of a coat stand, into a coat, resurfaced at the coat's collar, and then, with an acrobatic jump, came to rest on the thick wooden frame of a Guinness advertisement. It sat there, above a depicted glass mug filled to the brim with creamy black stout, glancing around the pub as if anticipating an exciting show. A fat house spider dangled on its thread, motionless, in front of the slogan "Hold it." Frankie thought that if she were a mouse, she might think live people shows were interesting too, if not exciting and often confusing. Peering through her flute telescope, she felt a bit like that mouse, a spectator in ultimately boring but possibly interesting circumstances.

She shifted her telescope to the right. The musicians had moved the tables to the side, and they sat in an informal circle facing each other. Her dad was changing the reed in his clarinet. His soft, tanned complexion contrasted the stark winter whites of the other musicians. Although of East India origin, he had been adopted at birth and grown up with Irish Catholic traditions. He had never gotten around to exploring his Indian roots much, beyond reading a few books. In his own words, he was a self-proclaimed "agnostic Irish-adopted Indian Anglophone-Quebecois Canadian Montrealer, but above all, a jazz musician."

Frankie's mum also had Irish roots, but they stemmed back to one of the many Irish orphans who had been adopted by French-Canadian parents in the 1850s. Frankie's dad had told her a tongue-in-cheek story about how her mum's great-great-great-grandfather had suffered a fatal reaction to British imports in Ireland during the potato famine. Although Frankie's dad's joke passed right on over Frankie at the time, his main point was that the guy's wife was left alone with three kids, and this Frankie thought to be an intriguing piece of family history. Strong and brave but struggling to survive, Frankie's mum's great-great-great-grandmother, who was commonly known simply as

"Ma," argued her way into a job on a ship heading for the Americas. In exchange for her services as the head cook, Ma and her children received free passage and food. So, equipped with only the clothes on their backs, together with a friend's promise that Canada was the land of opportunity and an address for a Catholic convent that would give them shelter upon arrival, Ma gathered her kids together and left her home for new beginnings.

Only one member of the family survived the trip. Kenneth Maguire, Frankie's mum's great-great-grandfather, a wily orphaned seven-year-old, arrived in Montreal into the fortunately warm and patient arms of French-Canadian adoptive parents. Along with many other orphaned Irish children who arrived in Quebec at that time, Kenneth retained his surname. Frankie's mum considers herself Francophone, but her surname (Maguire—pronounced in French "Mah-gee-r") reveals her family history.

Frankie's thoughts wandered onto the last parcel she had received from her mum, exactly two years ago on this date. It had been posted in Nepal. It contained a letter and another "traditional" blouse. She hadn't seen her mum since she was five. Frankie now owned nine "traditional" blouses from nine different ethnic groups across Asia. Her mum still hadn't found herself, even after years of wandering through so many faiths (Hinduism, Jainism, a variety of Buddhisms that Frankie couldn't remember the names of, and the most recent—Taoism), but she promised to come home when she succeeded at becoming an *uncarved block*: "My chains are society's, Frankie, but my path is for you. You are my guiding star! Teach me how to release the chains, to become once again like a child, an uncarved block, and I will come home... *Je t'aime, Frankie!*" The last letter they had received was shortly after Frankie's tenth birthday. Complicated. That's what Frankie's dad called her mum.

9

"*Colisse* Pierre, you gotta do something about these spiders!" Frankie lowered her telescope and tuned in to the voice. It came from a group of three men sitting a few feet away at the near end of the bar. She had seen them before. They never sat with the musicians. Always in their own corner, in their own language, separated. One was fishing a spider out of his beer.

Pierre smiled, and, referring to the spider in the famous story *Charlotte's Web*, he attempted some humour. "*Excuse-moi*, but at least Charlotte's a cheap date, eh?"

"Who the hell is Charlotte?" A tall man with a bulging belly, the kind that has been trapped by a belt, looked at the spider on the rim of his glass with disdain and pushed the glass toward Pierre. Pierre motioned to the spider and then flicked it off the glass.

"*Tabarnak*, he's given them names!" All three men doubled over the bar in laughter, one of them blurting out in between gasps, "She's an English whore is what she is. Hangs 'round where she's not wanted and spoils people's beers!" More laughter, then Trapped Belly added, "Just like that crazy Paki *tapette* with the clarinet sticking out of his face."

"Eh, cool it there!" Pierre said sternly and pointed down at the bar "In my pub, there are no language wars."

Trapped Belly turned toward his friends and replied, more to them than to Pierre, "*Et pi?* Check the neighbourhood we're in, *mon ami*. Does it look like an invitation for square dancing to you?" His friends laughed into their beers but said nothing.

Frankie rolled her eyes at his use of the word *square*, often used by frustrated Francophones to describe Anglophones. That was some pun coming from such an ignorant shithead.

Trapped Belly had spat his joke in the direction of Frankie's dad. Frankie looked back at him. He was flipping through some music sheets, expressionless.

Tolerance. That is what he was always preaching to her about: "Whatever happens, Frankie, you must be the one to show *tolerance*." Smooth, mature, I-didn't-hear-it tolerance was what she saw on his face at that moment. Maybe he hadn't heard the comment. A mix of feelings stirred in her: embarrassment, anger, sadness, resignation. And then tolerance.

Frankie glanced back at the mouse and the spider sitting atop the framed Guinness advertisement. Although she generally liked people, animals, insects, and plants had proved, in her experience, to be far less complicated. When she observed animals, she could come to understand them. Their behaviour was honest and predictable. The mouse and spider had no hidden motives for sitting on top of the frame; they were there for either food, shelter, or as a means to get somewhere else. Or, in this case, perhaps some light entertainment.

People, on the other hand, were really confusing. People's behaviour did not necessarily reflect their intentions, thoughts, or feelings. This was especially evident in the differences between what people said and what people did. Trapped Belly's comments could have stemmed from his dislike of immigrants from that huge, all-encompassing place in the East called "Pakistan" (which only reflected his ignorance about her dad's place of origin), or they could have reflected his resentment against Anglophone Canadians or a reaction to an election or a new language law, or they could have just been a desire to show off in his drunken state in front of his friends. But, after what happened a short while later, Frankie concluded that people generally did not know themselves, as animals did. And in this way, Although people could be amusing to watch and interact with, animals were much more evolved and balanced in the sense of reliability. They enjoyed your company or they did not. They wanted to play or they didn't. They meant harm to you or they did not.

Frankie's mum was another example. In her letters, she described how much she missed Frankie, how much she would like them to be together, and how much she loved her. She wished that her "path" would bring her home to her soon—as if her "path" had a power of its own that just wouldn't release her, that had kept her prisoner for the past four years. Frankie pictured her mum trapped in the top tower chamber of a huge shadowy castle called the Path, her aging, bony fingers wrapped around rusty iron bars, gazing down helplessly at the world below. A recluse from her family and friends, she would wander around in her lonely tower, expecting to find her Self somewhere in the shadows. Frankie wished that her mum, rather than the "path," had been the one in control. If her mum had been a mouse or a spider, perhaps she would have had more control over the physical whereabouts of her body and mind. Animals, at least, didn't follow conceptual paths at the expense of their loved-ones. Frankie wished people could be as simple and straightforward as that mouse on top of the Guinness ad. *Mais, c'est comme ça*. They're not.

Frankie peered through her flute telescope again. The spider in the frame had disappeared from in front of the slogan. But the mouse still sat there, alone on its people-gazing podium. It sniffed the air, then proceeded to clean his groin. She shifted the flute back to watch the circle of musicians. They were playing an improvisation game. Her dad had picked the melody this time, and the others were joining in attempts to complement it with their own unique melodies.

Frankie remembered when this pub had belonged to her parents. Before it became L'Irlandais, it was known simply as Melodies. Her dad was addicted to the concept of *melodies*. Melodies this, melodies that—everything in life could be reduced to a melody with many variations. Over breakfast just that morning, as he'd skimmed through the *Vancouver Sun*'s employment section, her dad had said to her, "Frankie, you know Montreal. It's like a huge colourful orchestra that can't make up its mind about which melodies it wants to play, but it's exactly that indecision that makes the place so beautiful and unique."

Frankie wished he would hurry up and finish his current melody so she could just complete her Oscar Peterson assignment and get home in time for the latest episode of *MacGyver*. She stood up on the windowsill and stretched, hoping to make her impatience a bit more obvious.

Then it happened.

9

Frankie had relaxed and now leaned casually against the window frame. She brought her flute telescope back up to her eye and began to observe the musicians. Her telescope's spotlight circle blocked out all but its perimeters. As she searched for her dad, her flute trapped another object in its sight: the beer left in her dad's glass was really fizzy. Unusually fizzy. This fizz was quite unlike the foam that appears after pouring or shaking a beer. The fizz was coming right up from the bottom of the glass, creating a miniature tornado that dissipated upon contact with the surface. Then the glass disappeared from the spotlight she held it in.

At the far end of the bar, a suppressed quiver of laughter escaped from one of Trapped Belly's friends. Frankie let the flute drop from her eye and watched the drunken three. Trapped Belly had just returned from the bathroom and had a mischievous look on his face. He winked at his friends.

Frankie tensed, as her whole body felt the concept of "Uh-oh."

The group of musicians had finished their jam session. Pierre was among them taking orders for the next round. And her dad, completely distracted in conversation with his neighbour and utterly oblivious to the storm happening in his glass, emptied the last of it into his mouth.

The first sign of his distress was the look of confused astonishment on his face. His eyes were wide and tense, his mouth half-open but silent, and an embarrassed flush sprang to his cheeks. Then his hand seemed to forget it was holding a glass. The glass broke on its way past the table's edge to the floor. The shatter penetrated Frankie like a fire alarm. But instead of taking action to extinguish the fire, she just stood there, on the windowsill, frozen in time, peering at the world through the eyes of a stunned mime. For exactly two seconds, the world around her also stood motionless. Then someone shouted "Oh! Holy *merde!* He's choking!"

Frankie felt like her world was being sucked up by that tornado in the glass. The pub began to spin around her in a rush of people-panicked bubbles, all trying to reach her dad at once. And she stood there, frozen in the eye of the storm, unable to help her dad escape the fate that was about to change her life forever.

The first person to reach Frankie's dad was the culprit himself. In two adrenaline-charged leaps, Trapped Belly had his huge bear-sized arms wrapped around her dad in the Heimlich, all the while shouting "oh *merde*, oh *merde*, oh *merde*, cough it up! *Sacrement*, you're not allowed to die before you get your revenge on me!" To Frankie, it looked awfully like he was trying to finish her dad off by squeezing the life out of him.

Then everything went silent again. Frankie stared out from her mind's eye. She saw the flushed, panicked faces of people shouting directions at each other. She saw Trapped Belly and her dad in their strange embrace. A woman stood at the bar and clutched a phone to her ear, listening and nodding intensely, as if the words coming through the receiver were a prophecy bent on saving the world. But Frankie heard nothing. Then a melody. All the noises in the pub had blended into one single melodious tune. Frankie floated outside the melody and wondered when the climax would rouse her.

For a moment the melody faltered as the source of her dad's misery shot through it. Frankie watched as what seemed to be soap was ejected from her dad's oesophagus. It landed in the puddle of beer and broken glass with a padded thump, leaving a path of slippery relief in its wake. The pub began to breathe again. Gently, Trapped Belly released Frankie's dad from his life-saving embrace and eased him into the closest chair. Then he thanked God and collapsed into the chair next to him.

But Frankie wasn't paying attention to Trapped Belly or to anyone else in the pub. Only her dad existed at that moment. She studied him from inside her trance. He was trying to catch his breath. He was really, really trying. The wheezing sound he made began to flow along with the melody in her head. What was wrong? Something was wrong. Then it hit her, and she heard her Self scream: "My dad! It's perfumed soap! He's allergic!"

But it was too late.

Just like that, Frankie's dad's agnostic Irish-adopted Indian Anglophone-Quebecois Canadian Montrealer jazz musician life was extinguished by a misused lemon-scented urinal puck.

Frankie's vision wobbled, and her world went dark. Her perspective was yet to be born again.

⁌

That fateful night would mark the death of Frankie's third-person being. No longer would Frankie be a simple extension of her parents' wants, needs, and worldviews. When Frankie's eyes finally reopened, she was involuntarily be reborn into a new life. *She* became *I*.

CHAPTER TWO
Mad World

My sense of smell returned first. A whiff of sweet perfume, roses, mixed with cigarette smoke and... peppermint? Toothpaste? The smell nagged at something in me. In my mind, smoky peppermint breath began to materialize, forming words—or one word.

Frankie

Frankie

Frankie

Frankie

I could hear my name being delicately hurtled at me from a distance; echoing down a long tunnel and into my brain, then rattling around my frontal lobe before finally settling somewhere in me that felt like everywhere. My name summoned me, every part of me, from the unruly hairs on my head to the rough calluses on the palms of each hand and down to the end of each overgrown toenail. In acknowledgment of the new sensory information, I opened my eyelids just a crack and sneaked a peak around the room. Floor-to-ceiling pale green flooded through me. Purple lilies stood attentively in a vase on a low steel table at the foot of my bed. My eyes drifted to the left and stopped at a large square hole in the wall that accommodated a wire-meshed window. A pigeon paused on the window's cement sill, peering in at me inquisitively. Below the window sat a well-worn wooden school chair, empty, waiting.

The room seemed awfully strange. The last time I'd had my eyes open, which I was sure was only a blink away, it had seemed I was stuck up in the rafters of my dad's old pub, like Charlotte in her web, observing my world from a distance.

A vision flooded through me: watching, as if with spider's eyes, through my flute telescope, a life that wasn't mine but that mattered to me even more than my own, being decided on by forces outside its will. And then, in an instant so unpredictable and fast that it seemed surreal, strange, wicked forces had reached out, curled themselves around my heart, and snatched part of it away. But unlike Charlotte, who saved a life by wrapping the world in her web of wisdom, I just hung there, stuck, caught in my own web, paralyzed, unable to change fate, my world imploding. Frankie, me, hanging there, frozen like a mime, in the third person.

How surreal.

I blinked.

It seemed more like a bad dream than a memory.

Definitely a bad dream.

"Frankie, *ma p'tite chouette,* we're so glad to have you back with us! My name is Nurse Jocelyn." A smiling, chubby-faced nurse cupped my face with warm hands. Her big blue eyes leaped into my own with an intensity that promised to catch me before I dared fall back into my comfortably unconscious oblivion. I had been asleep for five days now, she told me. Everyone was very worried. Everyone. There was something that was off about that word. It should mean more to me, but it felt oddly empty. I opened my mouth intending to ask about it, but nothing came out.

"*C'est quoi, Frankie?* What is it, Frankie?" The nurse looked genuinely concerned.

I tried again. Nothing.

Nurse Jocelyn continued, "Frankie, nod if you can hear me."

I nodded.

For a moment the nurse's smile faltered, her yellow-hued teeth only just peeking through plump fuchsia lips.

Nurse Jocelyn looked at the doctor, whose mass of curly white hair and bushy black eyebrows seemed swept in waves from one temple to the other, had just shocked my line of vision. "No verbal response, but she does follow me with her eyes as I speak, and she is able to nod."

The doctor shone a light into my right eye, tensing his curly eyebrow as he studied my reaction. He scratched his bearded chin, his mouth tightening into a thoughtful grimace, and commented to the nurse, "Could be post-traumatic stress disorder. She's sure been through a lot." Switching off the light, he took my hand in his hefty warm paw, gave me a friendly, dimpled smile, and said, "Try not to worry, Frankie. You'll be right as rain in no time. We have a specialist on the way."

"Are you thirsty, Frankie? Orange juice sound good?" It was the nurse again. As I couldn't speak, I just nodded and stared at her, willing her to read my eyes: "What am I doing here?" She stroked my cheek, swept a few stray hairs off my face, and clipped them in place on the top of my head with a bobby pin, then went to find some juice.

Apparently I had a disorder. But what kind, I was unclear. Something to do with traumatic posts. The bushy-eyed doctor had told me that my dad had died. I couldn't believe it. It didn't make sense. The whole scenario was what nightmares were made of. To think was exhausting. Sleep took over.

In grade 4, we learned about the third person in school. *Elle est.* She is. Used to describe someone other than me. I could only remember that night in the pub in the third person. It was not *me* watching. It was some other girl. It couldn't have been my dad choking. And it was definitely not him swelling up and suffocating on what I would later remember as twisted lemon-scented piss-pot ethics. It was not real. Just some wild story told in the third person.

That first morning, as I lay semi-comatose in my hospital bed, drifting in and out of the conscious reality that had been defined for me by smiling strangers in white smocks, I decided that all events on and before that night in the pub belonged to my third-person life. They were pieces of someone else's existence, another storyline. As I slept, tossing and turning to dreams that seemed surreal, in my sterilized hospital cot during that first week, my life before the sixteenth of May 1985 became a myth. It became a creative innovation chiselled together by the mischievous gnome in my unconscious mind. A fantastical story that I'd twisted here and there until it became so unreal to me that I no longer identified with its narrative. There had to be a reason for me being in this hospital, listening bilingually but unable to speak, but I soon became quite sure it had nothing to do with my dad. In fact, I had no idea about what the reason could be. By lunchtime on that first day, I had become as confused as a lab rat in a maze.

❢

My experiences throughout the next few days were similar to those of a bug under a microscope, a frog in an aquarium, or, well, a rat in a lab. Paralyzed and pinned in place by forces outside my willpower, I was virtually dissected, philosophically discussed, and theoretically defined—all in the name of help. But, as most of this discussion went on outside the confines of my pastel walls, I somehow managed to be, all at once, the epicentre of knowledge and terrifyingly clueless.

The great anomaly (and, sometimes I thought, excitingly challenging symptom—not for me but rather for my doctors) was my mind's reaction to the so-called event that I was sure had not or could not have happened. Although I could hear and understand everyone in both languages, except for the word *Pappa*, I had forgotten how to speak. And even though I could move my head, the rest of my body remained still. Most intriguing of all: I absolutely refused to admit the possibility that my dad could be dead. To the nurses' despair, I repeatedly asked for "Pappa." Perhaps he had finally snapped and run off pilgrimaging other people's religions with my mum. I refused to believe he was dead. Definitely not dead. With these terribly annoying symptoms, I had managed to attract the curious minds of doctors and their students from all over the province. Interestingly, all of them assured me that I would be right as rain in no time because I was in the hands of specialists.

Nurse Jocelyn snapped her fingers next to my head, "Frankie? Frankie, ça va? Are you paying attention? Sweetie, it's important that you answer the doctor's questions as best you can so he can... so he can help you as best he can, OK? *Comprends-tu?*" She filled her smile with as much honey as she could muster, "Yes... I know you understand. You're a smart girl! Now, remember, two blinks 'yes' and one blink 'no,' OK?"

The current consensus was that my disorder was not about traumatic posts at all but was more likely *ASR*. Wow, what a relief. The diagnosis had drifted in from the hall through a crack in the door a couple of hours earlier. I was still waiting for an explanation.

A tall blond doctor with a protruding chin and sharp blue eyes stood next to the nurse on my right, equipped with nothing but his white lab coat and a well-rehearsed you-can-trust-me smile. Two interns stood on my left, armed with pencil and pad, minds charged and ready for possible-antidote scribbling. Nurse Jocelyn had introduced this latest crew as "*le therapist.*"

This particular morning had been filled with questions concerning my feelings about strangers in photos from someone else's album.

I tried closing my eyes for a few moments. Maybe they would all disappear. It had worked in the pub.

They didn't.

Nurse Jocelyn held up a photo. A woman's face. The woman in the photo had hair the same colour as my own, but it was short and swept back across her head in a false gelled perfection. Her cheeks were flushed, and she was smiling.

The doctor looked from the photo to me and took a slow, thoughtful breath as he took in my reaction. He relaxed his face, a controlled masterpiece, then said, "Frankie, what emotion is this person feeling?"

I looked at the photo. A woman smiling. Yes, she was definitely smiling. Her mouth curled up at the sides, painted lips parting to reveal bleached teeth, which had the effect of pushing her pink-powdered cheeks upward and causing some wrinkles around her nose and eyes. She was looking straight into the camera through light brown eyes that looked like tipped over half-moons, courtesy of her smile. Her whole face was participating in a perfect smile. But her eyes were off. Something was not right. Something missing. Yes, it was that sparkly inner shine that is released through the eyes when a person is truly happy It was that that was missing. This smile belonged to a model; it was not honest happiness.

The doctor continued, "One blink for sad, two blinks for happy, three for angry, four for scared, and five blinks for none of the above."

I looked at the doctor and gave him five forced blinks.

He smiled.

The interns' minds possessed their pencils with a brief intensity, then relaxed, patiently waiting for more input.

The doctor shared a glance with Nurse Jocelyn.

Next photo.

A young girl and her mother were on their knees in a grassy field of wildflowers. They were dressed in black, which was an odd contrast with the carefree, multi-coloured variety of flora that surrounded them. They had their backs to the camera and were hugging each other. I couldn't see their faces. They knelt before a gravestone.

The doctor studied me.

I waited for the question.

The interns studied me.

I waited.

Nurse Jocelyn studied me.

While they thought about what to ask, I wondered about my own mother. Where was it that she last wrote from? Bangladesh? Nepal? Somewhere in India? I wondered what she would have said about the last photo, the one of the smiling woman. Probably would've said she needed a douse of some Asian religion or at least a pilgrimage of some sort. My dad would've said she needed a clarinet. That thought almost made me laugh. I smiled instead.

The interns shared a glance.

Nurse Jocelyn cradled me with her big blue eyes.

The doctor kept his composed gaze steady on me.

"Frankie, does this photo make you feel like smiling?"

I shook my head for no. No, nothing funny going on in it.

"What about crying? Does it make you feel like crying?"

What? I looked at it again. Nope, don't recognize anyone. Nope, definitely don't feel like crying. I shook my head again.

"OK. So, it doesn't make you feel like smiling or crying. Does it make you feel angry?"

Angry? This time my no was preceded by a clenched jaw and an overly dramatic wide-eyed iris roll. *I'm twelve, not a moron. Get on with it!*

A silent hmm revealed itself in a mutual, not-quite-conscious tensing of the eye muscles in each of my four guests. The doctor was the quickest to catch himself and resume his you-can-tell-me-everything-sweetie professional mannerism.

"OK then, that will do for now, Frankie. Thank for your time. We'll let you rest while Jocelyn fetches your lunch." The doctor patted my leg and flaunted his PhD-winning smile. "Hang in there, sweetheart. See you later this afternoon."

Jocelyn came over and took my face in her hands, "*Tu es merveilleuse, Frankie.* You are wonderful. These doctors are the best of the best. Don't you worry. You just hang in there, OK?" She kissed my forehead, embraced me with her eyes for a moment longer, then turned toward the door with an upbeat, "What you need is some music!" She returned a few minutes later with a small boom box. She set it on the table next to my bed, plugged it in, and pressed play. Tears for Fears's "Mad World" was first up. I think Nurse Jocelyn was trying to tell me something.

While Nurse Jocelyn had been fetching the boom box, the small posse of doctors that had been in my room a few minutes earlier had reassembled for their habitual note-sharing session outside my room. I wished they would fix that broken hinge in my door. It gave a slow, un-oiled, creaky squeak until it was almost shut but never managed the whole journey. So, as it was, I was graced with barely audible mumbles from the hallway that were consistently laced with my name along with some other keywords, most of which I didn't understand.

But there was one word in particular that crept up so often that I was beginning to figure out its meaning. Or at least I thought I was.

,

Denial. That was the word. That was my "disorder," my problem. That's what they called it. Denial. Like it's a loose screw. If only they could find the right size screwdriver, then I would learn to accept that event that did not occur and consequently regain my power of speech. Denial was being caused by the loose screw, and they were the handymen. Lucky me. All that was missing was the right screwdriver, and I would be right as rain in no time. I couldn't wait.

And I still hadn't got an answer as to why I was being kept in this hospital, away from my dad. Where was my dad? He wouldn't really have left me, like my mum, would he? Did he really finally crack? When I passed out in the pub, did he think I had died? Did he start to run, thinking he had lost me, and just not turned back to check again?

A memory pricked at me: the nurse sitting on the edge of my bed on that first day when I woke up, comforting me with her whole being, supporting me with the sheer strength of her willpower and telling me with complete conviction that my dad "*est avec les anges, Jésus-Christ son protecteur, Dieu son sauveur.* He has joined the angels, with Jesus Christ as his protector and God his saviour. *Il n' est plus avec les vivants, Frankie, il est mort.* He is no longer among the living, Frankie, he is dead." As Nurse Jocelyn said this, her eyes had turned a teary pink. She had cupped my shoulders gently, one in each hand, and hung on to me with a gaze that promised I would be OK, that everything was shit now but things would definitely improve. I had looked at her, considering her words carefully. As they reassembled themselves in my mind, I remembered a conversation I had had with my dad.

It was just after spring break. I was sitting on the floor in my bedroom re-reading one of my mum's letters. She had written me a story. That was her way of communicating with me, always in stories. This one was about a goddess called Saraswati. My mum had included a card with a painting of Saraswati on the front. The goddess sat on a rock next to a river, surrounded by mountain flowers, with a peacock at her feet and a banjo in two of her hands. She had four arms. In her other two hands she held a book and a pearl necklace, her only piece of jewellery. No weapons. I remember thinking it strange. Saraswati was unlike the goddesses in previous stories my mum had sent. She seemed... simple and peaceful. Apparently, according to my mum's story, Saraswati saved a wise old sage from an evil demon by transforming herself into a powerful river, distracting the demon with her magical flowing beauty while at the same time carrying the old man to safety on her waves.

My mum wrote, "Today, Frankie, as I followed my feet along the shores of that same legendary river, I imagined I was being lured through life by the most beautiful and wise ascetic in all of India, Saraswati. The veins of India, she has no home, no temple. Her wisdom is her wealth. It is within her. It is *my* life force. I am her. She is me. *Tu comprends, ma chérie?* I am her. She is me." No, something in me had been quite sure I didn't understand. As usual. So I had asked my dad. As usual.

My dad had become quite a scholar in the area of Asian religions since my mum had left, but this time he just answered, "I don't understand either, Frankie. But what I do know is that your mum's Saraswati has a lot to do with my own choice of religious beliefs." He shot me a slightly flustered I-will-only-go-so-far-at-explaining-this glance and said, "Personal gods, as Einstein might have agreed, are a comfortable creation of our imagination. Your mum is… sort of like taking a holiday, you know, away from reality."

I released a relieved smile. It was impossible. How could my dad be with God when he didn't believe in him? They got the wrong person. My mood lit up, and I tried to speak, to tell Nurse Jocelyn that it was OK, it was all just a mistake. My lips moved, but I could only manage a strangled groan. I tried to shine my message through my eyes, to send it telepathically, but she didn't get it. Looking back now, I see how distorted my thoughts had become as I tried desperately to change my dad's fate. Nurse Jocelyn just looked at me with sad eyes, stroked my cheek with a warm hand, then left to find the doctor. This is about the time that I became the epicentre of discoverable new and improved knowledge.

The door hinge squeaked. These guys never knocked. Fed up with being cared for so thoroughly, I dropped my eyelids, feigning sleep.

,

Rubber-soled footsteps squeaked across the antiseptic linoleum floor around the end of my bed to the window. The chair acknowledged some extra weight with a creak that travelled down its old wooden spine and into its back legs.

Silence.

A few minutes ticked slowly by.

I could be patient, but it's not an easy task keeping your eyes so still under closed eyelids while you're awake and feeling curious.

Another squeak from the chair.

Then, "Hey, ummm... Frankie? You awake?"

Damn, my curiosity must've given me away.

"Frankie?"

The voice was gentle. I vaguely recognized it. As if it had disturbed me once before, a long time ago. A gurgle of emotion started to bubble within me, somewhere close to my heart. A hand touched my leg softly, settling itself on my shin. Fine. He wins. I opened my eyes.

Oh no. Shock hit me hard. I hadn't seen this face since I was little.

"Uncle Seb? Oh. Oh no. No, no, no, no. Oh no." My words returned so naturally. They had been waiting there, locked up in me, but now the key had arrived.

"I'm so sorry, Frankie" His eyes looked haggard. He looked at me, into me, trying to connect on a deeper level. Seb's green eyes and soft bone structure reminded me of Mum. If it weren't for his dark brown hair, they could've been twins. "Oh, Frankie..." He came closer, took my hand in one of his, then released it and decided on a hug instead. "He's gone, Frankie. He's gone."

CHAPTER THREE
Running Up That Hill

"He's gone." That's what Seb had said. My memory of that moment, of those first words, uttered in my first-person life, and of the unfortunate truth that they held in them, will always remain as sharp as the colours that follow the clearing of a thunderstorm.

"He's gone." Those two words struck me with such unexpected force, such surprise, such speed, that initially I almost didn't understand them. But then just as quickly, they lost their value as simple words and became a whole concept. Those two short words transformed into an experience with a history that had been intimately interwoven with my dad's. In that moment I remembered everything.

My dad was no longer with me. He could only be remembered.

It was to that realization that my whole being reacted. It was then that my arms began to tremble from beyond my awareness. It was then that my hands clenched so powerfully into fists that blood was drawn on my palms by my neglected fingernails. It was then that my teeth cut through my top lip as I bit it. My whole body seemed to react in mutual convulsions to this terrifying new reality that had just become my life. The chaos of that night in the pub gathered like hot lava within me, bubbling just under the surface of every pore in my body, and then erupted like a deep sea volcano from somewhere so remote inside me that I couldn't consciously locate its origin.

The tidal wave that rode on the force of that inner eruption carried not only memories of my dad but also a huge, mixed up replay of every traumatically significant event in my life. My mind swelled like a silent killer wave filled with rippling flashes of all the someones now gone from my life. My dad had been my everything. He had been the glue that kept my life together. Everyone else who had loved me had disappeared long ago. I curled up into a ball on my bed, with my face buried in my knees. My tears had soaked through my sheets and were now working their way through my pants. My family consisted no more of "us"—now it was only "me."

As I sobbed, I remembered the love in my grandmama's plump warm embrace, a perfect complete love, around my scrawny four-year-old body. She had had a special warmth.

I remembered my granny's telltale wink as she lured me into some secret joke she had planned for my grandpa. Her sense of humour remained with me always.

I remembered my grandpa's ebullient storytelling about magical gnomes and protective spirits. I would sit next to him in the grass, spellbound, hanging on his every word. My grandpa's cat, Taniwha, had been named after one of those protective spirits. Taniwha would stalk my toes from under my grandparents' creaky staircase, sending me screaming for help with terrified laughter every time. He was more of a tricky gnome than a protective spirit.

I remembered my dad, saving me from his child-eating cat, yet again.

I remembered my mum's easy smile and curiosity for life.

I remembered my mum before her sadness.

Then there was the crash. The fatal patch of black ice, waiting to trap unsuspecting drivers in its invisible death cloak, that took all three of my grandparents away from me all at once.

Then my mum's silence.

And my dad's love.

My mum's sadness. And her distance.

My dad sitting with me, under our big oak tree canopy, him on my rope ladder and me on the swing, talking me through it all, keeping memories alive. And sometimes, just sitting, the two of us, without speaking, my thoughts following the breeze through the leaves above us, his thoughts following his breath down through the shaft of his clarinet and into the music that materialized. Remembering on our own terms.

Then there was my mum's first letter, left for our attention in between the toaster and an eggcup.

And her second, from Thailand. Then the third. And fourth. And the others.

And throughout: my dad's love. Swinging with me. Laughing with me. Crying with me. Helping me keep memories alive. My melodic shield against sadness. Just the two of us.

My emotional tidal wave became the hospital's five-star main attraction over the next forty-eight hours. But as the wave finally retreated back into the ocean that was my life, so too did my loyal medical observers retreat back into the attempted objectiveness of their own worlds. That, to my relief, no longer required the presence of my physical being.

Now that I had accepted my dad's death, I was handed over to the prepare-to-be-discharged staff. My arms and legs worked. My brain worked. I had regained my speech, in English anyway. Nurse Jocelyn assured me that my French would come soon too. She handed me a Kate Bush tape and said, "Kate always gets me through tough times. Hang in there, Frankie. The hill looks big now, but you'll make it. You're a strong kid." Then she gave me a big hug and signed me over to my long-lost uncle and only available relative, Seb.

Seb. He stood there, silent, thoughtful, waiting, framed by my hospital door.

It had been a month since my dad died.

Today would be my new beginning.

PART 2

Innocence

CHAPTER FOUR
Don't Stop Believin'

June 1985

Seb. The long absent brother of my mother that I hadn't heard from in years. He had never been a big part of my life. The last time I saw him, he was a wildly busy twenty-something student with zero interest in kids. Until a few days ago, his name had only been rarely mentioned since my grandparents died. He had just vanished. Like my mum. Into the abyss of soul-searching wonder. So I assumed anyway. The impression I had, going into our new forced relationship, was that of "What a jerk."

Yet.

He had this charm. Or maybe it was his charming lame sense of humour. I'm not sure if he had changed or if I had just never noticed it before because he had never spent much time in my life until now. Somehow, though, through just being himself, he could make an uncomfortable situation feel almost enjoyable.

♩

I spent the first couple of days trying hard to ignore him and his unhinged sense of humour. He would speak, and I would look tiresomely away, but not before I was sure he caught my eye roll—that was especially for him, and he should know it. I wanted control over our relationship, and I had it. He spoke, I eye-rolled. There was no way he was getting in. He hadn't been in my life for years, and now I was expected to greet him with smiles and honey. Not happening. Uh-uh. Never. No way.

Seb almost broke through my armour on the second day, but I held strong. I sat at the table, stone-faced, as he served a meal that he had just spent two hours making. He'd put Journey in the tape deck for the hundredth time. I cringed as the song "Don't Stop Believin'" came on for what felt like the trillionth time. Trying my best to act oblivious to his cooking effort, I glanced down at my dish, and my eyes widened in horror. My taste buds screamed with anticipated assassination. *What the hell is that?* My bowl was filled with gooey green mush. Seb had decorated the top with slices of tomato as if that would somehow make it look more edible.

"Saag paneer." Seb was grinning. I couldn't tell whether it was amusement or pride etched in his smile. I desperately hoped that it was amusement and he'd momentarily shout, "Just joking!" and produce a pizza from behind my ear.

Noticing my hesitation, Seb added, "It's... Uh... Indian? You know, *saag paneer?*"

I thought, *Oh shit, it's pride. No getting outta this. I'm going to have to eat it.* "Ah. Oh. Yeah. Saag paneer. OK, then. What is, uh, what's in it?" Then I added under my breath, "Did you drain the swamp?"

Seb smiled patiently and handed me a piece of bread. "Here, something to dip."

I almost smiled but caught myself. Seb was obviously trying to make me comfortable by cooking an Indian dish. Little did he know, my dad had never learned Indian cooking, and the only thing I'd ever tasted that was Indian was naan bread and some kind of curry that a friend had made for us after my mum had left.

I put my spoon in the bowl and moved the mush around a bit. There were some whitish rubbery lumps in there. My stomach tightened. I lifted my spoon to my mouth and forced it in.

My taste buds imploded with the bittersweet taste of fenugreek. I remembered the taste as my dad loved fenugreek. But this much of it was utterly shocking. My eyes started to water as I forced myself to swallow it.

Seb looked at me, puzzled, as he lifted his own spoon to his mouth and took a bite.

He paused for a second, not swallowing, just holding the food in his mouth. His face had started to turn pink. He got up from the table and, trying to maintain his usual laid-back demeanour, walked nonchalantly over to the sink and spat it out. Standing over the sink, facing the window, he started to laugh.

He turned toward me and said, "*Merde*. I'm so sorry, Frankie." He looked at the pot of green goo on the table and his laugh grew. "*Tabarouette.* Cooking is just not my art! Should listen to my buddies. They keep begging me to stick to omelettes!" Now he was holding his stomach laughing. He caught his breath and asked, "Pizza?" then roared with laughter again as he went to find the phone book.

I looked at him, amazed, as he laughed himself over to the phone. I just couldn't hold it up. This guy was weird. And weird appealed to me.

Seb officially broke through my shield on our third day of get-to-know-you. As we did the dishes together after a delicious and thankfully quite plain omelette he had made, a putrid whiff of sulphur wafted up from a familiar undisclosed place. I blushed slightly. Seb looked at me, his green eyes twinkling, and said, "Hey, Frankie, you want to hear an old bush song about farts?"

"Wha—?" I felt my cheeks turn from pink to crimson.

Big smile on his face, he looped his arm in mine and bellowed out the tune with a slightly French accent as he danced me around to the room.

"Oooooh, whe-en the grizzly farted, the black bear sighed, and the black bear said, 'Oh blimey!', and the grizzly said, 'Well, it's your own old fault, you shouldn't stand behind me!' Ha!"

Seb's ridiculous jingle took me by surprise, my guard crumbled completely, and when he had finished the song, I broke out in stitches, laughing along with him.

I had to face it. This guy was OK.

9

Seb's unique charm was reflected in his choice of living quarters. His home was located on Ile des Voyageurs, a little island on Rivière des Prairies, not far from Montreal. According to Seb, some older inhabitants had chosen the name for the island twenty years ago after they had become its first permanent residents. There were no more than fifty houses on the island, of which most had been transformed from cottages to full-time homes within the past two decades. The houses certainly had character. My first impression of Seb's place was that he must be living in a *cabane* à *sucre*, as it really just looked like a prettied-up shack in the woods, bathed in mystique and surrounded by sugar maples. He'd even tapped the trees. It was comfortable though. Quiet. Very different from the downtown town house I had lived in with my dad.

As I walked around the island on my second day, I counted forty-seven houses. There was only one road, one big potholed loop that started and ended at a bridge that linked the island to the rest of the world. The other way off the island was by train. There were two train bridges, one that led to Montreal and the other to Laval.

I spent the summer exploring the island. Seb's property reflected the special charisma of the island as a whole. It looked to me like an old rural village that had been recently revamped into a shiny new oldness. Seb had carefully preserved the character of his house, from the cedar shingles on the pitched rooftop to the timber plank walls and the stone chimney. And his neighbours had given likewise care to their own dwellings. The properties all lined the riverbank, and between each were wooded groves. The middle of the island rose up slightly in a treeless rocky hill. Someone had put time into keeping it cleared of large growth, and there were wildflowers all over it. Sitting on top of the hill, I felt like a flower queen, surveying her dominion. From various spots on my hill, I could see a few of the houses quite clearly. At night, if people didn't take care to shut their blinds, I could see right into some of them. *I Spy* quickly became an interesting pastime on evenings when I found myself bored at home.

Ile des Voyageurs wasn't a rich neighbourhood, but it was certainly a much loved one. It was definitely somewhere that could grow on me. I liked the anonymity of the place. I had never been much of a social butterfly, and people here seemed to be fine with that.

The inside of Seb's house was as expected. Cottage style, but with a permanent-living, durable feel to it. With the exception of the stone countertops and porcelain bathroom tiles, almost everything was made of wood. The whole place had a charming rustic character. It breathed authenticity. The bedroom I came to call my own had two of those peaked windows that stuck out from the roof like a set of square eyes with triangular lids. Seb had brought over my bed from my dad's place. It was against the wall in between the windows. A desk had been placed at the end of it, just below the window. There were built-in closets along the opposite wall. It was a small room, but it had potential. I was glad that Seb had brought over my bed. It didn't look like much, with stickers and drawings all over its creaky wooden frame, but it had been mine since forever.

There were photos hung on the kitchen walls. Grandmamma with my mum, sitting by a lake. Seb and three friends in full hockey gear, posing with medals around their necks. One photo in particular intrigued me. It was of Seb and a friend, sitting on the front step. Both looked exceptionally thrilled in the photo, as if they were sharing an inside joke that no one else would ever know. Their eyes sparkled with the secret.

Seb came into the kitchen and noticed me staring at it. "That's Pete. You'll meet him soon. He's actually renting a room from me. But he's not home much. He's a CO, uhh, conservation officer. Works up north. Usually only home for a few days every month." I looked from Seb back to the photo, and he continued, "Pete helped me renovate this place. He's a great carpenter in his spare time. He built the chair you're sitting on." It was an oddly shaped chair. It seemed carved to fit a specific body shape that wasn't mine. "He likes to personalize his chairs. That one's mine. I like armrests, and I'm shorter. His is this one, bigger, with a slightly reclined back—his preference. And the other two are random designs for random bums—that's the way he puts it, anyway. He's kinda quirky." Then, putting on his best British accent, he continued, "Please, do choose your preference, me lady." He motioned to the chairs, gave a little curtsy and a silly smile.

Seb wasn't home much. His job as a lawyer working for legal aid meant late nights. Often he wouldn't get home before eight in the evening, which left me with a lot of time for exploring the neighbourhood.

,

It was a quiet place. From my spying ground up on the hill, I could see that most homes contained older couples. I only spotted one yard with kids in it, and they were much younger than me. At first I didn't observe much interaction between neighbours, which left me thinking that people on this island must be here to escape something that they don't want anyone else to know about. This storyline intrigued me. A mystery's always more fun than boredom, especially when you have your own spying ground.

I borrowed Seb's binoculars, found a double-margin notebook and pencil in the kitchen's junk drawer, and got to work.

By August I had quite a book written. Most of my notes were just wild guesses, scribbled beside my doodles in the margins on the left, but here's what I knew for sure.

The older man and woman in the stone house danced together most nights in their PJs before going to bed, yet slept in separate rooms. Married? Siblings? Loud snorer? Who knew? I liked to think they were old Russian ballet lovers who had finally escaped horrible relationships elsewhere to run away hand-in-hand and live the rest of their lives together on a tiny island in nowhere in particular.

Then there was the middle-aged guy in the redbrick house. He either had a lot of friends who were girls or a lot of girlfriends. He also had numerous visitors who came and went by boat. Everyone visiting him arrived in nice cars and shiny clothes. I couldn't see through his windows though. They were too small. I called him Al Capone.

The house with the little kids looked well lived in. The yard was not as tidy as the others. There were toys all over it, and the dandelions had claimed control. The mother of the little kids looked tired. She had a glass of wine every day on the patio about half an hour before her husband returned from work. And she also had frequent visits from Al Capone while her husband was out.

There was a very athletic middle-aged couple living in a log house with big windows. They lounged around stark naked most evenings. On some nights they were doing more than just lounging. That house made me blush. I tried not to peek in on them.

Seb's neighbour, a single woman in her sixties, tended her garden every morning from eight till ten, disappeared from view for the rest of the day, and then worked on some kind of project in her living room every evening from sundown to eleven. Like clockwork, I could depend on her schedule just as I could depend on my watch. However, this evening she seemed to have deviated. She wasn't in her living-room.

"I thought I felt eyes on me." Her voice emerged out of thin air behind me.

My heart jumped into my throat. I dropped the binoculars and almost fell off my sitting rock. The woman stood there with her flashlight, shining it on me. I felt like a trapped burglar. She had been so silent. How long had she been standing behind me? I thought, *Ah! I've been caught!* I tried to greet her, but my words got stuck with my heart in my throat, and I just sat there, the ultimate depiction of a deer caught in headlights, staring at the dark shape holding the flashlight, frozen and wide-eyed.

She switched off her light and settled herself down on the rock beside me. Now I could see her more clearly. She had curly grey hair that was pulled back out of her face with a headband, which made her curls pop out wildly all over the place above her ears. Her face was round, with flaring cheekbones, a crooked, witchy nose, and all-knowing owl eyes.

"Oh my, relax child. If I wasn't of legal age, I might be sitting up here doing the same thing." She laughed, but somehow it didn't make me feel less caught. "This island sure does keep its secrets." She smiled wryly. "Well, between most of us anyway." My words remained caught, but my heart began to settle back into place.

"I'm Ani."

Silence.

Ani continued, "And you must be…Seb's niece?"

More silence.

This was my prompt to speak.

"Frank—" I coughed out. "Umm, Frankie, uh, not Frank."

Ani smiled warmly and stuck out her hand for me to shake, "Well, Frankie, welcome to the island of well-kept secrets." Then she winked. "I won't ask about yours, if you don't ask about mine."

❜

I spent most of August over at Ani's. She was an artist. Her living room was full of tools and boxes of coloured unspun wool. She made pictures, copies of photos and paintings, by felting wool. It was quite amazing. She'd made whole mountain ranges, with glaciers and rivers and wildflowers. She had even made portraits of famous people. On her living room wall hung Elvis Presley reclined on a couch, wearing nothing but his birthday suit. I blushed when I saw it. She said she had imagined most of that one.

I was especially taken by her copy of Salvador Dali's *Swans Reflecting Elephants*. That one had been my dad's favourite painting. My dad had hung a copy of it in our living room. And Ani had recreated it in felt. I couldn't take my eyes off it. She noticed me admiring it and commented, "Reality is a reflection of our perception. It's a good lesson in life, that painting."

Ani had been some kind of Norwegian diplomat earlier in life. The walls in her main entrance were packed with framed photos taken during her world travels. There were photos of the Great Wall of China, vibrantly coloured seaside villages in Norway, old castles in Ireland, mountains and glaciers in the Rockies, zebra grazing on the Serengeti plains in Tanzania, Balinese dancers, and rural villages on islands in the Pacific.

There was an old guy in one of her photos, with a pig tusk pierced through his nose. He was standing there completely naked but for a gourd tied onto his precious part. He was holding a pair of new hiking boots that Ani said had been a gift from her. He wasn't wearing anything on his feet. The photo had been taken in Papua New Guinea. The guy was some kind of village elder. He looked to me like a character from that comic strip *B.C.*, like someone from the caveman age who had been inadvertently transported through time and hadn't figured it out yet. I felt embarrassed for him—a naked caveman icon, for all to judge and giggle at. A strange choice of wall art, I thought.

Ani was a strange bird but definitely interesting.

She spoke with a slight accent and liked to dress her sentences up with flair, which added to her enchanting charisma. "This island that we live on"—she looked at me and paused for effect—"it allows my inner recluse to flourish," she said, putting her hands on her heart, then just as quickly removing them and motioning grandly to the world around her. She exclaimed with passion and conviction, "I've been popular and rich and loved! *Herregud!* Have I lived!" And with a wink she continued more matter-of-factly, "Now I just want to shine quietly through my art." Her gestures were anything but quiet. Her body spoke volumes, even before her mouth joined its line of thought. Time paused and listened when she spoke. But I got what she meant. The island certainly had an inspiring character. Though Ani didn't seem like the type to shine quietly.

9

Seb's roommate, Pete, arrived home on the first Friday in August. I had returned from Ani's to find him standing in the kitchen making supper. Tall, blond, blue eyed, and rough around the edges. He obviously didn't mind facial hair. Last year, in History class, I had done a project on the Viking expeditions to Newfoundland. If I was to draw a picture of what I thought a typical Viking looked like after a month on a boat, I might've drawn Pete. Although thankfully not smelly, he was quite scary-looking. I almost turned and hightailed it. But then he smiled, and the whole room warmed up.

"Well then, look at you. You must be Frankie!" He put down the potato he'd been peeling, wiped his hands on his jeans, then placed them on my shoulders and squeezed gently in a "let's break down those barriers quickly and get on with it" gesture. Handing me the carrots and a knife, he motioned for me to get chopping. That would be my first cooking lesson of several to come. Which was great with me as I'd begun to gag on Seb's precooked omelettes.

Seb came through the door early that Friday. Seeing each other, they simultaneously laughed and then hugged. Seb ruffled Pete's hair, which seemed a bit comical as Seb was a head shorter than Pete, and he exclaimed, "Gained a couple of pounds of shag there!" and laughed louder. "Just trying to scare the bears off—all part of the CO do." COs apparently had perks, like not having to ever groom.

We spent that Saturday fishing in the river behind Seb's place. We must've caught a hundred perch and thrown back ninety-seven, but that was the first weekend where I felt truly happy again after my dad died. We roasted our catch over the fire pit in the backyard. Those three poor fish were very small and very bony. We were really only eating them because we hadn't managed to catch anything bigger. Still brutishly unshaven, Pete sat at the picnic table next to the fire and carefully picked the roasted flesh from the bones and arranged it on crackers, on top of sliced cucumber and little heaps of sour cream.

"Mademoiselle, s'il vous plaît, un hors-d'oeuvre?" Pete bowed and extended the plate of neatly arranged appetizers to me. "Only you could turn bony perch into a delicacy, Pete. Oh, and look—" Seb pointed to some dark spots on the piece I was about to put in my mouth. "Mmmm, that one comes with caviar!"

I paused, said, "Uh-huh," and almost looked, then rolled my eyes and ate it.

Pete's face was a block of stone, "Sorry, Seb, that was it with the fish eggs." If the twinkle in his eye hadn't given him away, I may have gagged the fish right back up.

Seb and Pete had this honest, silly, magnetic charm about them, and I found myself entirely absorbed in their ping pong banter. These guys weren't my dad, but I could feel a future with them. They brought back my smile.

,

The following week zipped by. Having Pete home during the days made the house feel more alive. I woke up to the smell of fried breakfast and the sound of Seb and Pete's happy banter. Seb normally left for work at 8:30 a.m. and returned around 8:00 p.m., but this week he had been arriving home by 4:00 p.m.

While Seb was at work, Pete taught me how to whittle a stick. My first projects were a walking stick and salad spoons. By Thursday we had moved on to bows and arrows. Pete was an avid hunter. He hunted with both bow and rifle. Being able to catch one's own food intrigued me. Doing it with a bow, well, that was the coolest thing ever. By the weekend, we had somewhat functional bows and a few arrows too. We'd have been hard-pressed if we had to depend on them for survival, but they were perfect for knocking tin cans out of trees and off garden furniture.

And that's just what all three of us did all weekend. These guys were definitely growing on me.

Pete went back up north on Monday. Seb went back to his regular work hours. The house was quiet again. I returned to my philosophical explorations of "reality" with Ani. There were three weeks left before I would start at my new school.

It was a strangely happy summer that had had a heart-wrenchingly bad start. The island had become my limbo place—a place in between places. A little vacation from life's woes.

CHAPTER FIVE
Church of the Poison Mind

September 1985

School was not my thing. But not because of the obvious reasons. Learning came easily to me. Besides team sports, I excelled at everything and was top of my class in English, math, music, and art. My teachers adored me. Academically, I succeeded without much ado. I couldn't help it. Academia just came effortlessly to me. Although not inclined toward team sports, I somehow won school running races without having to train for them. This may all seem like a blessing, but it wasn't. When it came to making friends, well, that's where my failure was. In elementary school, I'd been nicknamed Super Freak. Until grade eight, I had felt like the scary alien in the room that everyone was curious about but avoided just in case.

The week before school started, I decided that my new beginning in life would include a "new me" at my new school.

9

At 8:30 a.m. on September 3rd 1985, I stood in the concrete courtyard of Beats High School and looked up at the U-shaped five-floor monstrosity of a school. Beats High was a fine arts school located in downtown Montreal, across the street from McGill University's main campus and not far from the train station. It was the same train that linked Montreal to Laval and stopped on Ile des Voyageurs between the two. Beats High occupied the old High School of Montreal building, a charismatic neoclassic beaux arts style structure. It was quite magnificent. Back in May, my dad had enthusiastically shared with me that Oscar Peterson had attended school in the same building. There were other famous names too—Maynard Ferguson, Christopher Plummer, Norma Shearer, among other icons from the world of the arts and beyond. The building had quite a colourful history.

Beats High went from grade seven to eleven and had an English and French side. It also shared the building with Beats Elementary School. In total, from kindergarten to grade eleven, there were over 1200 students. As I stood in the courtyard admiring the building, kids sat, stood, ran, laughed, shouted, played ball in front of me, behind me, and all around me. This would be my first day in grade eight and the official launch of my *new me*. I fiddled insecurely with my headband. My long girly braids were gone, replaced by my new Madonna 'do. In truth I didn't listen to Madonna much, but her hair was *in*, and I desperately needed some *in* ingredients in me. I now sported a shoulder-length wavy do, pushed back with a bowtie headband behind teased and hairsprayed bangs. On my ears I wore big silver hoops, and my wrists were adorned with twenty fluorescent jelly bracelets. The rest of me donned waist-hugging acid-washed jeans, with a tucked-in Culture Club T-shirt on top. Standing there, alone on my first day, in a sea of movement,

I was both awestruck and panic-struck. If terrified wore a wig, it would've looked like me on that first day.

My dad had arranged for my switch of schools earlier in the spring. Like him, I was a natural clarinet player. He thought I would be happiest at a fine arts school that offered more advanced music classes. I wasn't as passionate a musician as he was, but I went along with it because it made him happy. And I wouldn't exactly miss my previous school anyway. The second thing I accomplished at my new school was to personalize my choice of instrument. When asked by my homeroom teacher what instrument I played, smiling sweetly, I replied, "Soprano sax." I had never lied to a teacher before. With that lie, the *new me* in me felt a little thrill.

My first accomplishment was to make a friend as I struggled to find my homeroom in a building of a thousand rooms. I studied my orientation letter. Room 03. With Mrs. Potter. I stood motionless just inside the front entrance, or what I came to know as the Foyer. Kids of all ages moved around me as if they knew exactly where they were going. I couldn't imagine ever remembering where anything was in that insanely huge place. I tried to get the attention of a passing teacher by tapping his arm and adding an "uh-hello?," but he didn't hear me, and then he was swallowed by the crowd. Panic moved through my veins and began to materialize in my knees. My inherently annoying inclination toward shyness wasn't helping. I needed to find my voice or my knees would soon tremble me through the floor. That's when my saviour appeared. Drowning in a sea of panic, I was suddenly thrown a life-saving float named Sam.

Sam shouted from through the crowd, "Hey! You new here?" I looked around, wondering if it was really me she was speaking to. Yup, it was me.

"Yup" I nodded.

She came bouncing through the maze of busyness. Her light brown eyes sparkled as she introduced herself. "I'm Sam!" Before waiting for my response, she glanced down at my orientation letter and exclaimed, "Cool! We're in the same homeroom! Come on, let's go!" Then she grabbed my hand and led me quickly through the crowd.

We ran down the main hallway to the closest stairwell and down into the basement. As we ran, I shouted, "I'm Frankie! Nice to meet you! Why are we running?" She glanced at me and laughed. I couldn't help but laugh too. Sam had a lot of energy. I soon learned that, when teachers weren't watching anyway, running is just how she got from place to place.

Sam looked a lot like me before the *new me*. Although of Taiwanese descent with black hair, she had long braids, was skinny, and was completely cosmetic-(and hairspray-) free. She had a smile that encompassed her whole face and expressed "come on, let's play!" I learned later that Sam's parents were ultra conservative and strict. They had worked very hard at conserving Sam's childish innocence. Her cuss words, for example, were curiously disguised— sugar instead of shit, and gosh rather than god. But, unlike me, Sam was not shy whatsoever. The moment our eyes met, I knew I'd found my missing half. I also knew I could leave the hairspray out of my morning routine.

Sam had been a student at Beats since grade five and knew of hidden passageways and secret rooms in this old building that very few other students had discovered. One such place was an old deserted swimming pool. Only a handful of kids knew where it was and how to access it, and all five of these kids were in my class. They were *the secret pool club*. By ten in the morning on my first day, I had been introduced to them all.

Amir, Matt, Raph, and Dave. They were a funny bunch, always teasing each other and full of laughter. Amir especially drew my attention. Until now, I had never met such an attractive boy. Matt, Raph, and Dave hadn't bloomed yet—the three of them were scrawny, short, and little-boy-like. Amir was the exception. He was tall and lean, with large almost black eyes and long fawn-like eyelashes. He had this noble nose, the kind I imagined Caesar must've had. His skin was like dark creamy chocolate. He smelled like vanilla. His hair was an ebony mass of silky tight curls. His lips were sensually heart-shaped. His fingers were long and elegant, and I thought that he must be a piano player, although later discovered that he also played clarinet, at which point I briefly considered switching instruments back to the clarinet just so I could sit beside him in band.

As we sat in class on that first morning waiting for our homeroom teacher, Amir looked at me with those big deer eyes and said, "Hey, it's Frankie, right?" I couldn't answer as I had swallowed my voice box, so he continued, "Uhhh... do you have a pencil I can borrow?"

I felt like everyone else in the room had disappeared. I looked at him slightly dazed and said, "Sure."

"OK, is it in your pencil case?"

I said, "Oh... yup... here you go. Choose one," and I handed him my whole pencil case. Earlier in the summer I had started exploring my body and had discovered my pleasure parts. Amir's presence made my pleasure parts tingle.

During lunch hour on that first day, we ran up the purple stairwell to the large landing in between the fourth floor and what must've been the attic. The stairs above this landing led to a permanently locked door. As the fourth floor was the top floor with classrooms, this landing had very few visitors besides us.

Matt won the race up the stairs and arrived on the landing with a victory cheer. Then he shouted to Sam, who was third up, "Rematch!" and sprawled himself belly down on the floor with his arm out in front of him in arm-wrestle position. Sam rolled her eyes. "You're never going to beat me Matt, give it up."

Although small and gangly, Matt was an attractive kid, with "kid" being the key word here. He looked like he had East Indian in him. A bit like me but darker. "Awe, come on, you scared?" Matt was determined. He couldn't keep losing to a girl.

"Yeah, trembling," Sam retorted, paused, and then laughed.

Looking at Matt's defeated expression, I interjected, "I'll arm wrestle you."

Raph and Dave let out a poorly controlled chuckle. Raph had an Italian air, with brown hair and matching eyes, and Dave was a blue-eyed Scandinavian blondy. Raph added his two cents. "Go for it, Matt. Maybe you can just keep wrestling through the girls until you finally beat one." And the three boys who were not Matt doubled over with laughter.

"Holy mother of moly, grow up." Sam rolled her eyes dramatically, "The only one of you who's managed to beat me is Amir."

I lay down on the floor in front of Matt and put my arm out. "Ready to go, Matt, or are we gonna keep clucking like chickens?" My shyness was already subsiding with this group. It was hard to be shy around kids who wanted to hang out with you whether or not you were a shy, awkward nerd, if that makes sense. We looked at each other for a moment, then put our elbows together and clasped hands.

Sam got down on her knees beside us and hit the floor with her hand three times. "One! Two! Three! Go!"

Matt was quite strong. I took a moment to test the waters, keeping my arm still at a ninety-degree angle, then letting him push me over a bit, then pushing him back over a bit. We were both doing our share of grunting. He gave me quite a fight. I pushed him almost all the way over. I had him at that point. But I felt for Matt. If I won, he'd be incessantly teased. I let him push me back up to the centre where we "struggled" for a bit, and then he pushed me over and won the match. He jumped up and danced around the landing, hollering his victory song to the high heavens. "Na, na, na, na. Na, na, na, na. Hey-ey-o, go-od-bye! Na, na, na, na. Na, na, na, na. Hey-ey-o, go-od-bye!"

So of course the other boys immediately challenged me. That victory song was just too much to bear. Raph and Dave lost miserably. Amir was from a whole different planet when it came to strength. And it didn't help that my muscles went to jelly, along with my mind, as soon as our hands touched. He defeated me on the first push.

❦

By mid-September, I was permitted into the *secret pool club* as member number six. Prior to this, I had never been part of any club or group or team. The closest I had come to being part of a club was occasionally jamming with my dad's band. I had always been the outsider, or perhaps better put, the one left out, the *shy freak*. This changed everything. I was absolutely thrilled. I was a member of a secret club.

The initiation process for full-membership was quite straightforward. If I could pick the lock to the pool room, I would be accepted as an equal member of the club. The following Tuesday, we had library time and I spent it flipping through survival books, trying to find tips on picking locks. Sam described the lock on the pool room door as one of those massive old padlocks that is sometimes used on cabins in the woods. I thought it should be quite easy to pick (according to a *MacGyver* episode I saw once, anyway). I didn't find what I was looking for. But I knew who could help me.

After some consideration about what my story would be (for a "school project," of course), that evening I called Pete at work. The conversation went like this:

"Hey, Pete! How are you?"

"Hi, Frankie! What a pleasant surprise. I'm doing well. How are you?"

"Fi-i-i-i-ne..." I drew the word out as I thought about my approach. "So, caught any deer lately?"

"Nope. A few grouse and a fat rabbit, but the deer are too smart for me this season."

"Ah... too bad." I had hardly said hello, and I was already losing my nerve.

"How's your new school?" Pete continued with genuine curiosity.

"Go-o-o-od." My mind was stuck on my question like an anchor. Small talk failed me. And lying just wasn't part of my rapport.

"So-o-o-o... anything in particular on your mind?" He was on to me. Might as well just get to the point.

"Have you ever been, like, locked out of a cabin in the woods and, li-i-i-ike, had to pick the lock?"

"Uh-h-h... maybe." I could picture Pete's right eyebrow rising, as it did when he was curious but skeptical.

"Wow, so cool! So, how might have you have done that?" Slyness was not my forte.

"Why, you planning to rob a bank?" He laughed.

"Yeah." I laughed. "That's it! You got me!" I forced more laughter out. "So, any tips?"

"Nice try, Frankie." I could imagine Pete smiling as he said this, "Come on, what's goin' on?"

Argh! "OK, fine! I need to know because it's part of an initiation thing at school."

"And?" He added this tentatively. It was followed by a few moments of silence, then I lost my nerve completely and came clean about everything. Pete let me speak, and I spoke until every last bit of information, including my feeling of loneliness at my previous school, was out on the table for him to scrutinize.

But to my surprise, he didn't judge me. Instead he responded with, "You'll find what you need in the tool shed behind the house. There are jars of nails on the shelf just inside the door. You'll need a long one. The hammer is hanging on the wall next to the nails. Use the hammer to bend the nail in half, to a ninety-degree angle." Then he told me exactly what to feel for with the nail inside the lock as I picked it. And he finished with, "I'll deny all of this." Pete was the coolest.

,

The next day during lunch hour, I stood in an empty dead-end hallway together with the other pool club members. There were only two doors in the hallway. One led into the drama classroom and the other into an old abandoned shower room. Raph stood in the junction of the hallway and checked that no one was coming. He signed an "OK" confirmation with his fingers and quickly joined us as we entered the shower room.

When the door closed, we were in complete darkness. Sam said the light hadn't worked for as long as she could remember. Matt produced a flashlight from his pocket and switched it on. Upon initial inspection, the shower room looked like it had only one entrance. It was dark, had a musty odor, and was covered in old cracked tiles. Definitely spooky. It wasn't welcoming but absolutely intriguing. It was a perfect horror movie murder room. I wasn't surprised that other students stayed away from it. Matt shone his light at the far corner of the room, and a hallway materialized before us. We followed Matt to the door at the end of the short hall. It was a big heavy door without a permanent lock on it. When the pool was closed off, the door had been fitted with a latch and pad locked shut. The lock was as Sam had described. Big and old. Perfect for easy picking. And, to my utter pleasure, I discovered I was a natural at picking big old locks. I followed Pete's tips and managed it within a minute. According to Dave's watch, fifty-seven seconds to be exact. Pride had never tasted so sweet.

Entering the pool room was like entering a world filled with secrets from past lives. Matt found the light switch and flipped it on. The room came to life. The pool itself was a typical rectangular hole in the ground, far from Olympic size but big enough for short laps and lined with blue tiles. It had four access ladders, and a couple of books lay open on the floor in the deep end. The rest of the room was much more intriguing. Along the walls around the pool were stacks of old wooden well-used desks, chairs, sporting equipment, and musical instruments. There were even filing cabinets filled with old student records. I peeked into boxes and drawers, exploring the innumerable treasures. What I found was ancient field hockey equipment, wooden lacrosse sticks, a partly deflated basketball, an old trombone, a broken clarinet, a drum set, and boxes upon boxes of dated textbooks. There were hearts with initials from past generations etched into desks forever more. There was still a reed on the broken clarinet. Someone had etched "Chris" onto one of the hockey sticks. The place even smelled like history. It had that dusty library-basement smell, of old furniture, leather-bound books, and mouse droppings.

During the fall, we met in the pool room at least three times a week. It's where we shared secrets and gossip. It's where we had thumb wars, played cards, wrestled, laughed hysterically about everything and nothing, and where the boys quietly read comic books while Sam and I read romance novels. The only part of the club Sam and I were excluded from was the Dungeons & Dragons meetings. D&D meetings were strictly "boys only." That was the deal. We were "in" as long as we didn't meddle in the boys' imagination-time.

So of course Sam and I made it our goal to meddle as much as possible.

The pool room was the perfect arena for meddling with peoples' imaginations. Our creativity was incessant when it came to pranks. Our most successful one, when it came to how powerful a reaction we got, was the time we dressed the boys' D&D figurines in little doll's dresses that we had made during Home Economics class. We dressed the little figurines up in flowery tube dresses and set them out strategically in an open trombone case in the pool room, together with some of Sam's old dollhouse furniture, to make it look as if they were playing house. Amir laughed. Dave swore at us and then laughed. Matt shook his head gravely and told us we had destroyed the sanctity of D&D. And Raph didn't speak to us until their revenge three days later when they replaced our sugar with salt during our cooking class and then watched with muffled hilarity as our Home Economics teacher sampled our cake. Pranks were fun, but mostly we just eavesdropped on the boys' in-between conversations as they played D&D.

9

September raced by, as did October. The 1st of November was rainy, grey, miserable, and thankfully a Friday. We had spent most of the morning in band class with a sub. Band must be the worst class ever for subs. Especially if the sub wasn't the type to arrive with a whip and be ready to use it. And most did not as that would be illegal. Predictably, less than halfway through, the teacher stormed out in tears after realizing that half the class had switched instruments and were playing awfully just because, at which time, of course, some cheekier students locked the door after her and then, convulsing with laughter, disappeared out the window into the courtyard and onward to freedom.

The rest of us suffered through Principal Baldo's wrath. In both his personality and physical appearance, Mr. Baldo (aka "Baldi") was the epitome of arrogance and dullness. After ardently banging on the door to be let in, he stood erect in front of the class with a sour look on his face that said, "I'm always disappointed, but exceptionally so at this current moment." He stayed silent, glaring at us, for the longest minute in the world. Above a permanently crinkled forehead, his stringy hair was combed from one ear, over his bald spot (hence his nickname) to the other ear, held in place with...Brylcreem? Gel? Egg whites? Sam and I had a bet going but never managed to discover the answer. He always wore brown dress pants, held up with suspenders, over a white, sweat-stained, long-sleeve collared shirt. He had his hands in his pockets. His bloated tummy stuck out comically from his ultra-straight army admiral posture. I wondered if he had to wear suspenders to keep his pants from falling down over his flat I-spend-my-entire-life-sitting ass. After he was satisfied that his glare had summoned everyone's deepest insecurities, he launched into a forty-five-minute ceaseless lecture on morals and honour. If there was a world cup for driest person, Baldi could've easily won against sandpaper.

That Friday morning had sucked. By lunch hour, our evil ways had been sandpapered out of our brains. We sat in our chairs, instruments on our laps, trying not to fidget, thoughtless and numb, when the lunch bell finally rang. We were exhausted, demeaned, bored, hungry, and couldn't wait for the weekend to start.

Sam and I arrived in the pool room before the boys. It was a D&D day.

We sat behind some filing cabinets, reading our books and eavesdropping on the boys. They were sitting in a circle in the pool, with their figurines and dice on a mat in the middle. There was surprisingly a lot of talk about girls.

They never discussed girls around Sam and me. It hadn't really occurred to me that they noticed girls much at all, in a romantic sense anyway, before we heard them talking among themselves, without girls around. Tammy was the highlight in their conversation. Tammy had bloomed early and was blessed (so the boys thought anyway) with humongous boobs that bounced around in rhythm with the perfect curls on her head whenever she moved. Neither Sam nor I had started menstruating yet and were both as flat as dimpled pancakes. This talk about bouncy boobs deserved an eye-roll at best and was downright insulting if anything. I mean, why is it that boys make girls all about boobs when girls get finally them? I was glad that I didn't have any. My brains still counted for something.

We almost got up and gave them a piece of our minds. But curiosity kept us in check. We listened intently.

"Did'ya see her in English this morning? When she tripped on the chair and almost went flying? Oh my god, her boobs, like, bounced all over the place." That was Raph.

"Yeah, I'm telling you, they're getting bigger." Matt.

"D'ya think she knows that they, like"—Raph chortled—"bounce?"

"Of course she knows, you fool. You, like, goggle at her all the time. If you're not careful, you're gonna lose your eyeballs on the floor. They're just gonna roll right out of your head and across the floor to her feet." They all laughed.

"She's a person, you know. Cool your hormones." That was Amir. He's so cool.

Then Dave intercepted, "C'mon, seriously, Amir, you don't goggle? They're in our face every day! And she wears those super flimsy T-shirts, even in the rain. Her nipples are like weather-forecasters. I can always tell when it's cold out by looking at her." More laughter.

"She's like that porn star in that magazine you brought. Ya know the one. Uh, Bunny something?" Matt to Dave.

"Yeah, she is kind of. Maybe without the zits." Dave.

Dave jumped up, climbed out of the pool, and walked over to one of the desks. He opened it and pulled out a pile of magazines. He was standing quite close to us, and we could see him clearly from our hiding spot. We sat still as statues and held our breath. Then almost choked when we saw what kind of magazines he was holding. I was sure we'd be discovered. But, absorbed in his dirty mind, Dave was oblivious and climbed back down into the pool. We sat there, momentarily stunned.

"Oh no. No, no, no. I thought you were gonna bring those home! If we get caught with those my mom will send me back to Africa!" Amir said, only half-jokingly.

Amir's voice had broken the spell. I looked at Sam with wide eyes. She silently mouthed, "How did we miss this?" I shrugged. I took off my shoes and motioned for Sam to do the same. Then we crawled very quietly on the tips of our fingers and toes from the filing cabinets to some boxes that were closer to the pool so we could get a better look.

Dave opened the magazine that showcased, presumably, Bunny the porn star, who Tammy resembled. We couldn't see much, but what I can tell you for sure is that she was definitely top heavy.

They all studied the picture, including Amir.

"Yup, you're right. They do kind of look the same," said Amir. He immediately lost points on my coolness scale.

"No way! Look at her. Bunny is..." He thought for a second. "Triple A perfect. Next to her, Tammy is just a kid with boobs." That was Dave.

The bell rang. Startled, the boys jumped. They scrambled out of the pool, returned the magazines to the desk, and hurried out.

Sam and I glanced at each other. I looked down at the romance novel in my hands. I smiled mischievously. "I've got a great prank, Sam. This one's going to highjack their imaginations like never before." We shared a wicked smile and began to conspire. By the end of the day we had come up with a plan that would butterfly its way into the future in ways that we hadn't predicted.

CHAPTER SIX
Easy Lover

November 1985

On the weekend of my thirteenth birthday, with help from the boys' naughty magazines, Sam and I contrived our first anonymous erotic short story.

The bell finally rang on the afternoon of that nails-on-chalkboard, cringe-worthy first Friday in November. Sam was coming over for a weekend-long sleepover, as we had plans to celebrate my birthday together on Saturday. I had never been a fan of big parties, or small ones to be honest, so we decided on keeping it very small, with just Sam, Seb, and Pete.

Before heading home, we made a quick stop in the pool room and borrowed some disturbingly enticing research material from a certain hiding spot that we shouldn't have known anything about.

We sprinted down University Street, through the McGill metro station, down McGill College Street, through Place Ville Marie to Central Station, and caught the 3:45 train just as the gates were closing. The conductor gave us an impressed smile and shook his head in amused confusion. "Always out of breath, never missed one yet." We collapsed in our seats, breathless, and laughed.

The train was of the old and creaky variety. Even at full speed it went "bump-d-bump-d-bump-d-bump-d-bump." Personally, I thought it was quite soothing and often fell asleep to the rhythm. It could make for quite the orchestra at times though. As it slowed down, it sounded more like "creak-squeak-bump-d-bump-d-creak-squeak-bump-d-bump-d-creak-squeak-bump-d-bump-d-screeeeeeeeeeech!" until it came to a full stop seemingly against its will. We used to joke that the whole thing must be held together with conductors' belts and elastic bands. One thing I really appreciated about this train was that the boarding doors were open at all times on both sides of each carriage, which made it easy to jump on board if you were having a lazy morning and caught it as it was pulling away from the station (very convenient). The seats were, well, like the kind you get in yellow school buses—useful, but... well, they were useful. As long as the person behind you kept their knees off the back of your seat, they were also somewhat comfortable. Sam and I sank down in our seats, with our knees up against the empty seats in front of us. The 3:45 Friday train was always rather empty, and there were only three other people in our carriage that day. We took out our research material and sifted through the pages, gobsmacked and wide-eyed.

"Oh my gosh! Is she... Is she..." Sam's question got stuck in her throat as the image sank in.

I whispered back, "Yup. She's kissing his thingy." Might as well just say it.

"Ewwww! That is so so sooo gross! Holy crapiolla, looks more like she's trying to swallow it! Why would someone do that?" Sam was extra innocent. Her parents had managed to keep her mind especially pure, mainly by filtering out most potential friends from her life. I had been the lucky one they had allowed in, surely on untold conditions.

"OK." I closed the magazine for a minute. "Let's look at it from a researcher's point of view. Our mission here is to gather information for the perfect prank. And perfect it's going to be. That means we've gotta understand what the boys see in the ladies in these magazines. We've gotta think like them, get into their brains, you know?"

"I think thinking like them is going to make me barf," Sam said, her forehead and eyebrows scrunched up doubtfully.

I opened the magazine with two women embracing on the front cover. They were wearing string bikinis that they might as well have not bothered putting on. The magazine was full of nude women kissing and touching each other in a variety of secret places. "If you take the penises out of the picture, look, it's not as bad."

Sam's curiosity got the best of her. Her cheeks flushed pink as she checked out the picture. "Yeah, I guess... it's kind of...uhhh, interesting."

I dug my notepad out of my bag and wrote, "Have you ever touched yourself?"

"What? No! What?" Sam instantly turned redder than a ripe tomato.

"You have! Haven't you?" I whisper-shouted back.

Sam took the pen and wrote, "I look at myself. All of myself. In the mirror. Pinky swear not to tell anyone!"

I wrote back, "Pinky swear. Anyway, I've looked at myself too. It's not a big deal. It's my body. Have you touched yourself too?"

Sam's red tomato cheeks ripened tenfold. She smiled embarrassingly and nodded.

I smiled broadly. "So have I," I wrote. Then I whispered, "Good then, we've already done our basic research. Now we just have to figure out what the boys like to imagine when they think of naked girls. And then we can write our story." My smile turned thoughtfully mischievous.

Our stop was approaching. Feeling a little flushed, I put the magazines, notepad, and pen back in my bag. Writing this story was going to be so much fun.

9

We arrived home around 4:45. Pete was in the kitchen making sushi rolls. He was full of surprises when it came to food. He was cutting smoked salmon into thin slivers. At least in wasn't raw fish. Along with hunting, Pete fished up north and smoked most of what he caught. Sheets of what he said was dried seaweed lay in a pile next to his chopping board, about to be irreversibly included with our meal. Yuck! I had never eaten sushi before, but I'd heard about how awful it was from Raph, who had been forced to try it once. Sam and I gave each other a worried glance.

Pete noticed our hesitance, grinned in amusement, and said, "Well, you can be thankful we won't be serving it on top of a naked lady as is traditional in Japan." His smile spread farther across his face in a "see, it could be worse, and watching you eat this will be my thorough pleasure" expression. Little did he know, the sudden shock in our eyes and colour of guilty embarrassment in our cheeks had much more to do with the mention of naked ladies than it had to do with the thought of eating sushi off them. But that did give me an idea.

We disappeared out of the kitchen and up to my room. Since I started at school, I had begun to let go of the past, not in a forgetful way, but rather in more of a moving-on way. I now thought of my bedroom as *my room* rather than as the guest room, just as I referred to Seb's place as *my home* rather than as Seb's place. In September, with Seb's help, I had finally personalized my room with a bright spring-green paint job and tonnes of pictures that I had ripped out of various teen magazines, depicting my favourite celebs. Molly Ringwald, Rob Lowe, Alyssa Milano, Andrew McCarthy, Emilio Estevez, Culture Club, and Cindy Lauper were sticky-tacked to my walls. And a special spot on the slanted ceiling over my bed was saved for a ridiculously large poster featuring Corey Hart in his leather jacket and sunglasses, looking down on me with his sensually puffy lips. That one kept falling down on top of me as I slept. Waking up with him on top of me was like… Well, I liked to think that Corey just wanted to snuggle.

We spread our research out over my bed. Sam's cheeks were no longer the colour of overripe tomatoes. She had adapted to naughtiness quicker than I thought it would take her. She combed through the images with pure scientific curiosity now, as if they contained coded information from another planet.

"Hey Frankie, look at this one. Do you think that feels good? It looks a bit painful to me. I mean, isn't that wax hot?" Sam had big question marks in her eyes. I looked at the picture. The caption above it said, "Precious Pandora Turns Up the Heat on Massive Muscle Mike." A naked woman with long, wavy blond hair sat on top of a bare-chested muscular man and dribbled wax from a burning candle onto his chest.

"Yeah. That's kinda strange. I wouldn't touch hot wax. He must have skin like leather. Weird." I kept flipping through the pages of another magazine. It was the one without men.

There was a picture of two women sitting next to each other, embracing. "Voluptuous Boob Duo" was scrawled across the page above them. Their boobs were the size of cantaloupes. Jutting out above tiny waists and skinny legs, their breasts made them look awkwardly top heavy, as if they could easily topple over with a strong wind. Their nipples were covered with tiny leaves, and their lower private spots were hidden by the position of their entangled legs. They had their cheeks touching, side by side, and their tongues sticking out between their plump red lips, as if reaching for each other. They were looking sensually at the camera. "Hey, Sam, do you think these ladies are really into each other? Like, lesbians? Or is it just for show, like for boys?"

Sam looked over at the page I was holding up. "I dunno. Maybe both? They definitely have humongous boobs, that's for sure. And boys do like boobs."

I shrugged. "Yeah. Big boobs." I paused to think. "Hey, sushi gave me an idea. What about writing a story about boys eating lunch off a naked lady with huge boobs?"

Sam's eyes widened and then filled with sparkle. "Gosh, yeah! Or she could eat lunch off one of *them*."

My own eyes twinkled. "Yes. Let's do it."

So that night, through many giggles and outright fits of fall-over laughter, we wrote the story. It went like this.

Hi there, sexy boys,

Maybe you've heard of me. My name's Precious Pan-

dora, and I like to keep things hot. Do you like heat? Because heat is what I've got. I've got tonnes of heat just for you, and you, and you, and you. Can you feel my heat? Would you like to? Well, keep reading because you're about to.

Now close your eyes, boys. And just Imagine. Imagine my soft skin on your fingertips. Imagine my long silky hair tickling your muscly bare naked chest. Imagine my big voluptuous boobs bobbing around as I move, my nipples poking out every time you breathe toward them. Just thinking of your breath against my body makes me all goose bumply and hot. I like to dream about your breath and your fingers.

Last night I dreamed that I ate poutine right off your naked bodies. You were lying down, with your massive muscles all twitchy and waiting for me. First I covered you each in fries, your favourite ones, from the Dep. I covered your muscly chests, your bellies, and around your bellybuttons, and I kept going down, down, and down, until I reached your toes. Then I sprinkled cheese all over the same parts. Now, we all know that a good poutine always comes with melted cheese. Luckily you were all so hot that we had no reason to worry. The cheese melted perfectly as it hit your hot bodies. Sizzle, sizzle. Next came the gravy. It was warm, not too hot, just right like body heat. I poured it all over each of you.

Now came the eating part. I was starving and so skinny because I hadn't eaten for days. I love poutine, and I love boys. I plumped my lips out and kissed each of you on the mouth and the neck, with my tongue sticking out a bit. Can you smell my vanilla perfume? I can smell your man-smell, like sweat and stuff, but the good kind of stuff. Then, with my big humongous boobs bouncing all over your bodies, I licked every last fry off each of you. I might have mistaken parts of you for fries... You tell me. You were delicious.

Thank you for the meal, Matthew, Amir, Raphael, and David.

Yours truly,

Precious Pandora xxx

It was 9:40 p.m. by the time we completed the letter. It was now folded and contained within a bright red envelope with a pink heart sticker holding it closed. We lay on my bed looking up at Corey Hart and listening to Philip Bailey and Phil Collins sing "Easy Lover" on the radio in the background.

"I think we should sneak it into Matt's locker just before lunch. Matt can't keep anything to himself, he'll *for sure* tell the others *right away*. I can go to the bathroom during English class and do it then. They always take *ages* to get to the pool room. We can go straight there when the bell rings and hide. Oh my god! I can't wait to hear their reaction!" I laughed and looked at Sam.

A huge smile lifted Sam's cheeks. "Holy sugar shit, this is so-o-o-o wrong, Frankie! My parents would kill me. I love it!" She laughed, her smile so big that her eyes were no longer visible between her eyelashes.

We spent Saturday in stages of birthday celebration. Sam and I woke up to the smell of pancakes and bacon. Seb and Pete had decorated the kitchen with multi-coloured balloons and shiny ribbon. There was a new chair at the table. It had my name engraved on its back and had different-shaped butterflies engraved here and there all over it. It was absolutely beautiful and suited me perfectly. Pete had tailored it for my smaller bum and had built in a footrest to accommodate my shorter legs (the table was a bit tall for me). It was the most comfortable hardwood chair I had ever sat on. There was also a thick leather-bound book in my place at the table with a big purple bow plastered to it. Imprinted on its cover was "Frankie's Business." I almost cried. Then I laughed. Then I did cry. And then laugh-cried some more. Losing my dad had felt like losing everyone in the world I loved and who loved me. I hadn't heard from my mum in years and had stopped expecting to hear from her. On that morning, I felt love again for the first time since I lost my dad. I gave Seb and Pete the biggest hold-on-forever hug I could muster.

The rest of the day consisted mainly of eating, chatting, eating, laughing, eating, chatting, a bit of target practice, laughing, more eating, a bit of spying, more laughing, a visit from Ani, who brought over a triple-tiered black forest cake, more laughing, and more eating. By the time Sam and I got to bed that night, we were so stuffed that we couldn't imagine being able to eat again before Monday. Yet, like our frequently exercised 'dessert tummy', we proved on Sunday that we also had one reserved for leftovers.

9

On Monday morning, our plan went as smooth as smooth as it could go. I excused myself from English class to go the bathroom and slipped the envelope containing our sexy letter into Matt's locker. At lunch, we easily made it to the pool room well before the boys. We returned the magazines to their desk and hid in our usual spot behind the filing cabinets. The boys had planned for a D&D game, so wouldn't be expecting us. We heard the door creak open about ten minutes after we arrived. There was a rumble of voices, all talking at once.

"Eh, douchebags, who forgot to lock the room?" Matt asked, as if he'd never make such a stupid mistake.

"You're the douchebag! Now shut up and let me have it!" That was Raph.

"Stop it, Raph!" Raph must've tried to grab it from Matt.

"Did you read it all?" Raph again.

Matt must've nodded because Dave then added, "Then stop being a twit and hand it over!" There was a rustling noise. Dave must've grabbed the letter.

"Hey, guys, relax. Put it on the floor so we can all read it," said level-headed Amir. They were now in the pool.

"What if your mom finds out, Amir?" Dave sniggered.

"What if it's *about* your mom, Dave?" It was Amir's turn to snigger.

There was more rustling of paper. Then complete silence.

And more silence.

And more silence.

Then, "Oh shit... shit." Raph.

Then, "No shit." Amir.

And then, "Nope, no shit there. *That*, baby, is the real thing. Wowweeeeee!" Dave.

Then Matt chimed in, "D'ya think Tammy wrote it?"

That comment was accompanied by the sound of a head slap. "Ouch! Hey!" Matt.

Then, "Tammy never even acknowledges our existence, dumbass." That was Amir.

"Then who d'ya think...?" Raph asked.

"Dunno. But it's not bad... But she lost me at the vanilla perfume. It would be like smelling my mom," Amir said.

"Argh! Amir! Stop bringing your mom into it. You just totally screwed up my fantasy." I could almost hear Dave's eyes rolling.

"Poutine and big titties... Wow, just wow. That's what I call a *Happy Meal*!" Matt chortled.

After a few more comments thrown back and forth, Dave took the story and placed it in the drawer with the magazines. There wasn't much time left for D&D, so they took out the cards for a game of War.

The last comment spoken before the boys left the room was made by Dave. "We could, like, sell this. I totally know kids who'd buy it."

When Sam and I heard Dave's comment, the light bulbs in our heads started flashing like inspired pink neon signs. I looked at Sam and could see my excitement reflected in her eyes. She reflected my thought back to me: "We could totally do this." Our smiles slowly curled across our faces as they connected with our conspiratorial thoughts.

That week we spent our lunch hours in the food court at McGill metro station. There were some tables in a weird poorly lit location behind the stairs, near the bathrooms. Very few customers choose to sit there. It was the perfect place for teen plotting. Our brains were exploding with ideas and questions. Should we release weekly or monthly stories? Should we make them like parts, or should they stand on their own? How would we distribute them? How much should we charge?

"First things first, Frankie. If we get caught, I'll spend my best years stuck in my attic being home-schooled by two of the most boring parents in the world. How are we going to keep this secret?" Sam looked thoughtful rather than doubtful.

"We have to do it anonymously What about…" I thought for a second. "I dunno, what about having boys give their names and money to, maybe Dave, and then Dave could leave it somewhere for us to collect? We could do it all by letter, so he wouldn't know who he's dealing with."

"No, I don't think we should involve the pool club. They'd be onto us pretty fast," Sam said, rightfully.

"Totally. So maybe we could put a box somewhere and get the boys to leave their names and money in it?" I pondered.

Sam thought for a moment. "Hey, yeah, at home we have one of those metal money boxes that locks. You know, the kind that people use to collect money at the entrance to dances and stuff? It locks with a key, and it has a slot on top so you can shove money into it without opening it, like a piggybank. My mom used it once at some event. I don't even know why she keeps it. She'll never know it's missing."

The wheels picked up speed in my head. "Perfect! Listen, we can put the box under the stairs on the landing at the top of the purple stairwell, maybe on Fridays 'cause the janitor doesn't work then. The boys can put their money and names through the slot, and we can pick the box up after school."

The engine had started and our planning purred along smoothly from that point on.

,

Here's how we did it.

We started with another story. This time we made it all about one reader rather than about the four boys. The reader was the co-star in our story. The story featured a tanned brunette with big brown starlet eyes and, of course, huge boobs. We made her out to be a magical booby fairy that had the ability to make the reader's deepest desires come true. We wrote the story as a beginning to the next story to come, a part one of two. We finished it with:

"To get your personalized version of what happens next and for future stories to come, write your name and locker number on a two-dollar bill and drop it in the money box that you will find on the 4 ½ floor landing—purple stairs—most Fridays. Your story will be delivered to your locker the following week. $2 per story. Tell your friends. Be discreet."

Once again, we delivered it to Matt's locker, knowing we could rely on him to spread the word. Matt was one of the most enthusiastic kids I knew, and his enthusiasm always spilled out through his mouth in an ebullient avalanche of sharing. He would serve our purpose perfectly.

CHAPTER SEVEN
Girls Just Want to Have Fun

Our business launch succeeded without much effort. Matt did exactly as we expected he would. On the first Friday, we opened the box to find eleven $2 bills with names on them. Almost all the boys in our class had put their names in the box. The next Friday, six boys from the French side had also included their names, along with twelve from our class. The Friday after that we were overwhelmed with a total of twenty-six names, of which a few belonged to boys in grade nine. By the beginning of December, we had made over a hundred dollars off boys' sexually fascinated imaginations.

With so many requests, we didn't have time to completely personalize each story, so instead we just changed the names of the starring characters, along with a few other details. So "Tim" would star in his own story, with a porn star who had a name that we thought Tim would like. And if Tim had any special proclivities we knew of, such as an obsession with a specific sport or physical feature, we'd try to twist it into the story. All boys were fascinated with boobs, as far as we were concerned, so as long as we kept the main focus on boobs, we were sure the story would be appreciated.

By mid-December, we had been running our little black market business for a month. Sam sat on the top step of the 4½ floor landing, with the box open in her lap, counting the bills.

"Thirty-six. Oh my, pollywog excrement, Frankie, this is too much for us. I think we need to go on sabbatical or something," Sam exclaimed with faux seriousness.

I looked at the pile of bills in Sam's hand with an incredulous wonder. "Wow. Thirty-six. That's seventy-two buckaroos. Crazy. Christmas vacation starts in a week. Let's write a story for these guys on the weekend and then take a break."

Sam handed me two of the bills, gesturing to the names on them. "Grade sixes are too young, d'ya think?"

I looked at the names. "Yup, we gotta give those ones back. Now, grab the money, honey, and let's go shopping!"

Neither Sam nor I had ever had much spending money available to us, and at this point in time we were possibly the wealthiest kids in our class. Beyond a few bags of fries bought at the local Milton Street Dépanneur, we hadn't yet spent much of our loot. After our last class of the day, which happened to be the first of three classes we'd have on sexual ethics, we retrieved our incredible wad of cash from where we'd hidden it in the filing cabinet in the pool room. We left school that afternoon with $158 in our pockets and the biggest Christmas shopping smiles ever.

,

After spending a few dollars at the arcade, we headed for the Mad Pranks store at McGill metro station. McGill metro was and still is at the heart of Montreal's underground city. Everything you need for survival can be found there without ever having to surface into the frigid winter weather. It is a maze of underground shops and entertainment and connects to other underground shopping mazes via tunnels and metro stops. We'd received permission to stay in town after school and go to the five o'clock showing of *Jewel of the Nile* at Cineplex Centre Ville, which, in the 1980s, was located in the basement of McGill metro station. But first we were going to buy prank toys and props for the pool room.

The Mad Pranks store could've easily doubled as a museum of pranks through time. It had everything from tasty-looking trick candy to props to costumes and wigs to fully loaded prank kits equipped with assembling instructions. Although it was a small store, the shelves were stocked with every prank toy and prop imaginable. On the ceiling were paintings of famous pranksters. Charlie Chaplin was depicted throwing a banana peel on the sidewalk in front of a hopelessly unaware pedestrian. There was a painting of Abraham Lincoln running around with a broom on fire, which was a result of his own practical joke backfiring, so to speak. And my favourite was a comic characterization of Virginia Woolf and friends wearing turbans and caftans, with dark paint on their faces, trying to convince the British Navy they were Abyssinian princes sent by the Emperor of Abyssinia, which the Navy fell for wholeheartedly. Bob, the store clerk, was brimming with stories about famous pranks played throughout history. We usually didn't buy much, but Bob always seemed exceedingly happy to see us, maybe because we were such enthusiastic listeners. Each time we walked in, he had a different toy or prop to tell us about. We would listen and laugh and laugh and listen and laugh some more. If we hadn't had time constraints, we could've easily listened to Bob's stories for hours.

This time we were on a mission, though, and had only twenty minutes to make our purchasing decisions. When we entered the store, Bob was nowhere in sight. We assumed he was in the storage room unpacking more exciting props. We always looked forward to new stock, as new props were always accompanied by exciting Bob stories. We had a basic plan for what we wanted. Sam produced the list from her pocket.

Sam looked at the list and smiled conspiratorially. "OK, so, first things first—fake blood and bones!"

"Over here. Got 'em! Oh my god, Sam, check these costumes out. They are so, *so* perfect." The costumes hung on the wall. I searched through them. They were all medieval warrior costumes. "This one's mine!" I held one up to myself and looked in the mirror. It consisted of a fake chain mail vest, a leather belt, and an off-white cotton shirt. The vest had slits up the sides and hung almost down to my knees. I put the costume on, fastened the belt over the vest and around my hips. I pulled the vest up a bit, so it didn't seem so long and big. Turning to Sam, I asked, "How do I look?"

Sam bit her lip the way she does when she's trying to be seriously not serious and replied, "Like Virginia Woolf trying to be an Abyssinian prince." She smiled. "Too bad we won't be trying to fool the British Navy."

I smiled back. "Yeah, yeah. How about you, smart aleck? Which costume d'ya want?"

Sam picked one with a fake metal bib and skirt. She put it on. "Yup, genuine Virginia. This'll do." She moved on to the boxes of dress-up props beside the costumes. "Weapons next. And, oh, look at these helmets!" Sam held up a foam helmet that looked like it was from the time of the Renaissance. The tag on it claimed it was an "Italian Barbute Helmet." Sam put it on. It had a T-shaped facial covering. But for her eyes, nose, and chin, it covered her head completely.

I took another out of the box and put it on. We stood next to each other, looked in the mirror, and giggled. "You know, Sam, these helmets together with our costumes—I think the boys are gonna crap themselves."

Sam added, "Yup, either for real or with laughter!"

Just then Bob suddenly appeared behind us. We saw him in the mirror and jumped and yelped, then fell over each other with laughter. "Now, who do you we have here today?" he said.

We were laughing so hard we could hardly speak. I pulled Sam's helmet off. "Don't be fooled, it's Virginia!"

Sam's face had turned scarlet, and she was trying hard, but unsuccessfully, to compose herself for Bob. "Oh my gosh, I've been struck by giggle lightning!" she exclaimed and then doubled over with laughter again.

Bob eyed us with curious amusement, scratched his chin, considered how to react, opened his mouth, then closed it again. He seemed to conclude that it would be best to give the giggly girls their space. He went to wait for us behind his counter.

When we had managed to contain our laughter to random fits of giggles, we took the costumes off, gathered our props, and put them all on Bob's counter. We bought two helmets, along with six foam swords, cobwebs, the costumes, and fake blood and bones. We still needed paper, some old cloth, some reflective material, thread, and some Christmassy extras. Most of these we could get from home and make ourselves.

That weekend we spent together, writing the naughty stories we had promised to thirty-four horny boys and preparing an awesome gag for our four favourite boys.

,

We played our prank the following Thursday. It was the last day before the Christmas vacation. It would be our "Christmas-gag gift" to the boys. We arrived early that morning to set everything up, entering from the school's less conspicuous side door to avoid running into early bird teachers with our big bag of props. The door led directly into the stairwell. We descended the half-floor flight of stairs that led to the basement and opened the door to the hallway just enough to peek through to ensure we were alone. When we were satisfied the hallway was empty, we proceeded toward the pool room in silence. To get there, we had to walk past the gym and along another narrow hallway that ran behind the gym, and then into the short dead-end hallway that lead to the Drama room, which was across from the spooky shower entrance to the pool room. We were just turning the corner into the Drama room hallway when we had a full-on collision with our gym teacher. We really should've been ready for it. The gym room storage locker was at the end of this hallway, and Ms. Jones was both early for everything and a really fast walker. And now we stood, facing her, stunned, with our mouths hanging open and our bag of props, along with the beanbags she had had in her arms, all over the floor by her feet.

"Whoa, girls! Where did you come from? So early this morning!" she exclaimed with a surprised laugh. We looked at her silently, trying to think our way through our response. Then we decided silence was best and bent to pick up the beanbags Ms. Jones had dropped.

That's when she looked down at the melange of bones and costume bits on the floor.

"What's all this?" She asked. I looked up at her, and my brain froze as curiosity entered her expression. She was still smiling, but her gaze had now entered its inquisitive "I'm a living lie detector" state.

Sam and I were the worst liars in the history of lying. We'd have to make this extremely short and sweet. Without looking at Sam, I said simply, "Drama."

Sam added, "Yup. Drama. We're doing a play." Luckily we were also two of the most trusted kids in our class, as our grades were great and we weren't trouble—or, rather, we hadn't yet been caught making trouble.

Ms. Jones replied, "Oh, OK, looks like it will be an interesting play!" And miraculously, that was it. We helped her pick up the beanbags, put our props back in the bag, and, with a huge (silent) sigh of relief, we were on our way again.

9

We entered the spooky shower room. Sam took a big flashlight out of her backpack, turned it on, and we walked down the short corridor to the pool room door. She pointed the light at the door while I picked the lock. Once inside, we fell back against the door together and collapsed in nervous fits of laughter.

We had an hour before classes started. Our plan was to create a medieval battle ring in the pool. We hung grey paper chains along the edges of the pool on top of old brown tattered cloth that we had found in the "paint rags" box at a thrift store near Sam's place. To create a more eerie atmosphere, we put fake cobwebs over the desks and big fat candles on top of the filing cabinets. And for special effect, we stuck some bones and dry leaves in the cobwebs. We left the weapons and costumes in the bag as we'd need those later.

Then, for a bit of extra fun, we booby-trapped the spooky shower room. I smeared fake blood all over my hands and made bloody prints on the door and its lock to make it look like someone had been trying to claw their way up to the lock. Then we taped reflective eyes that we had made with pieces of a road worker's reflective vest (another great thrift store find) to the walls in the shower. When we were done strategically placing the spooky eyes, I gave Sam a boost on my shoulders so she could reach the ceiling, where she strung a cloth filled with Christmas tinsel, curled ribbons, and glittery confetti to the broken light fixture. The thin thread that kept the cloth closed had an extra-long tail. At the end of thread, we carefully attached a rolled-up homemade weathered scroll. We placed the scroll on the floor to the left of the door. We hoped that the boys would see it after they saw the blood on the door and the glowing eyes. When the scroll was picked up, it would release the cloth, and its contents on top of them. We felt like MacGyver geniuses.

The scroll read, *"MUAHAHAhahahahahahhahahahaha-hahahahahhahahahhaha! GOTCHA', SUCKERS!"* Which was followed by, *"ENTER AT YOUR OWN RISK AND CHALLENGE US IN COMBAT! Yours truly, the Girls xoxoxo"*

The plan was for the boys to enter and be faced by us, fully costumed, swords in hand and ready for battle. At which time we'd throw them their swords and demand them to challenge us in the battle ring, and the party would begin.

When we were finished setting everything up, Sam looked at me and said matter-of-factly, "Frankie, we *so* rule. Where were you all those years before we met?"

"Great minds *do* think alike." I smiled mischievously at her.

And, except for one hugely unfortunate glitch, all went exactly as planned.

❡

We arrived in the pool room with lots of time. The boys had headed up to the cafeteria to pick up some food. We had at least fifteen minutes to get costumed, light the candles, and be ready for battle. It took us only five minutes, at which point we sat in front of the door inside the pool room and listened for them. Five more minutes passed, and then we heard movement. But no talking. We thought that strange. The boys were usually louder. Then, *"Merde!"* Pause. *"Quel genre de blague?"* Pause. "Aye." Pause. "Heh? *Ah!* What the...? What?" Pause. "Who the...? *Colisse.*"

Shit! We froze. That wasn't the boys. We heard the lock latch click open. We suddenly found our brains again and jumped up from the door. We had launched into an instinctual sprint toward our hiding spots when the door swung open. We dove behind the filing cabinets. The room now had a beautiful glow from the lit candles sitting on top of the same cabinets. I wished we had not lit the candles.

"Hey! Who's in here?" It was the janitor, Sylvain, speaking.

The light went on.

Silence.

Then footsteps. Sylvain was approaching the pool.

"What's all this?"

Silence.

"Well, you are creative. I'll give you that. Scared the bejesus out of me out there."

Silence.

"Ok, then. We can play this two ways. Either you come out and do some explaining, or I find you and drag your asses straight up to Mr. Baldo's office and tell him how uncooperative you were. And you still do some explaining. So-o-o-o, what's it gonna be?"

I could hardly breathe. This was so, so bad. We were in so much trouble. I looked at Sam. She looked terrified. She had her hands over her mouth. She was looking at me with big scared eyes as if trying to prompt me into coming up with a solution. I had no solution. We were going to have to reveal ourselves and face the music. There was no way around this. I took her hand in mine. We nodded to each other, then stood up and stepped into the light.

Sylvain nodded. "Uh-huh. Well then. I have to admit. I thought you'd be boys." There was a slightly amused look on his face, mixed in with an undertone of annoyance. "This'll have to be cleaned up. Mr. Baldo's going to want to see it first. Nothing I can do about that. If I don't tell him, sure as hell your drama teacher will."

So that was it. Our teachers must've talked. Our lie had come out.

We were sure in a pickle. Little did we know at that moment that getting caught with our prank in the pool room would disastrously turn out to be a tremor that would trigger a tsunami of problems to come.

CHAPTER EIGHT
[OFFBEAT]

My Christmas vacation fell flat. We'd lost the pool room. The boys were angry at us. Sam was grounded. Seb gave me a stern lecture, which was a first from him. Pete was up north for most of the holiday. Sam wasn't even allowed to talk on the phone. My dad wasn't with me. My happy beat had faltered and then metamorphosed into a melancholy ballad of lonely self-pity. For the first time ever, I was glad that my vacation was approaching its end.

It was New Year's Eve, and I sat alone, wrapped in a blanket, on Ani's front step under the stars. Ani was throwing her annual New Year's Eve bash, and besides a few smokers, most of the neighbours were inside. Someone had put the ABBA record on, and a posse of dancers had claimed the living room. The music blared and the house thump-thumped with drunken glee. There were three other kids at the party: two sugar-pumped little kids and one angry looking teenager with a spiked mohawk, black lipstick, and ripped clothing. It was a mild night, only minus three degrees, and the sky was clear and beautiful, the moon waning slightly. Outside on the step was exactly where I wanted to be, given my options.

Then I was interrupted.

She sat down beside me and pulled out a cigarette. I glanced at her from the corner of my eye. It was the angry teen I'd seen inside. She paused. I felt her studying me and I tried to keep my eyes on the stars. She said, "You want one?"

"Uh, no, no, thanks. I don't smoke," I stuttered, now trying to look at her but not too closely, my eyes fluttering between her and the sky. Now that I could see her better, it struck me that her mohawk was very well done. The sides of her head were shaved. She had eight well defined four-inch spikes that ran from the top of her forehead over the centre and down the back. Her hair was naturally dark, and the ends of each spike had been dyed purple. There wasn't a hair out of place.

"Hmmm. Well, whatever floats yer boat. You live with Seb and Pete?" she continued.

"Uh, yeah. I'm Frankie. Uh, you? Where d'you...?"

She interrupted me, "Sunny. Ani's my aunt. Well, my dad's sister. Didn't really get to know her till a coupl'a years ago. I live across the bridge with my mum." She motioned toward the train bridge that lead to the West Island suburb of Montreal.

We sat in silence for a few minutes, looking at the stars, next to each other on the step.

"Nice sky." Sunny flicked her cigarette into the snow. "Catch you 'round." She smiled, stood up, and returned to join the discoers inside.

I followed her with my eyes. As Sunny entered the house, Seb and Pete came out.

"Hey, Frankie, there you are! We were looking everywhere," Seb said.

Then Pete bowed and added, "Will you please honour us with the next dance, me lady o' the step?" He straightened, and they both looked at me with big expectant smiles. How could I say no? I stood. They looped their arms in mine, Seb on my right and Pete on my left, and escorted me into the party. Ani was in the living room, standing on a coffee table, giving ABBA dancing lessons to her drunken neighbourhood gang. Despite myself, I laughed and allowed Seb and Pete to pull me into the fun. Quite unexpectedly, New Year's Eve turned out to be OK.

,

1986 began with two huge dumps. The first consisted of a shitload of snow, and the second consisted of mostly just shit.

I arrived at school late on the first day back after our vacation. The tracks were a snowy mess and the early trains had been delayed by half an hour. I walked into biology class twenty minutes late. It wasn't the worst class to be late to as Mr. Kabira was our friendliest teacher. He was a silver-haired Kenyan with a deep rumbling laugh that he wasn't afraid to use. He filled his lectures with humour and we loved him for it. Learning about biology could not have been more fun with any other teacher. His easygoing sense of humour encouraged kids to ask questions, no matter how awkward they felt. So when Mr. Baldo decided to assign Mr. Kabira with teaching us sexual ethics, as an added section in our biology course, everyone in our class looked forward to it. Not because of the content, exactly, but because we all wanted to experience how he would handle the awkwardness of the subject. He was almost as giggly as we were when it came to awkward subjects. On this particular morning, he was teaching the class about consent and responsibility.

As I walked in, he was holding a banana with a condom rolled onto it, demonstrating how to apply a condom correctly. Startled by my interruption, he started laughing, and to everyone's sheer amusement, the condom he was holding on to rolled up and off the banana. As the banana fell, he tried to catch it with his leg and then with his foot, but it hit the floor and he stepped on it instead. The banana burst and he did a classic Charlie Chaplin banana peel slip but then grabbed the desk and managed to save himself from landing flat on his back. I stood still looking at him, not knowing how I should react. Mr. Kabira stood up, collected himself, gave us a grave gaze, and said, "Now, children, that's what can happen when you don't protect yourselves." He was trying hard to keep a straight face, but his eyes gave him away. His dark cheeks had turned plum red and he was trying hard not to laugh. The rest of us could contain ourselves no longer and the classroom suddenly burst with laughter. Mr. Kabira laughed so hard that he had to wipe tears from his eyes. I took my seat next to Sam and she high-fived me. I thought the school year was getting off to an OK start after all.

At recess we met up with the boys, unintentionally, on the 4½ floor landing. We were sitting up there, catching up. Sam had also had an awful vacation. She had been grounded the whole time and not allowed contact with anyone outside her family. Her parents had even considered enrolling her in a private boarding school. They were no longer sure whether Beats High was the right place for their daughter. Sam was now on probation so had to be extra careful to stay out of trouble. We decided that it would be best to abandon our little business venture. As we were discussing the pre-Christmas events, we heard the boys in the stairwell. Dave was talking about the pool room.

"It has a new lock. I checked. And it's different. New. I dunno. I don't think it's pickable." Dave sounded concerned.

"We gotta get in there. What are we gonna do?" Raph said.

"Maybe Sylvain would let us in. You know, he's kinda OK." That was Matt. Wishful thinking that the janitor would let them in though.

"We could just *try* to pick it. I mean, we haven't tried." Raph again.

"My mom is going to kill us all. You do know that, right? She ain't gonna stop at me," said Amir.

"Why didn't you just bring those magazines home, Dave?" Raph sounded annoyed.

"Like you didn't enjoy them. Loser." Dave responded defensively.

"Anyway. Even if they find them, how're they gonna know whose they are?" Matt said.

Matt's comment was followed by a head-slap sound. "From the fucking sex letters sitting on top of them, ya douche!" That was Amir.

Damn. Amir sure had a point. Sam looked at me with those terrified big eyes I'd seen before. Then the boys appeared in front of us on the landing.

They abruptly stopped talking and glared at us.

"Well. Look who it is," Dave managed.

Raph turned to leave. "Let's get outta here." The rest of them followed suit.

"Wait!" I blurted and they turned back. "Maybe I can pick the lock. I can try."

"No way. If we get caught, we'll never see each other again," Sam said very seriously.

"I say they try. It's 'cause of them that we lost the pool room. They can at least help save us from going to Baldi-office-hell." Dave said, also seriously.

"Fine. I'll go check out the lock during lunchtime and do some research," I said to Sam's chagrin.

"Agreed. Do it," Dave answered. The boys turned and started down the stairs, leaving us alone on the landing. Matt gave us a concerned glance but then followed the others.

When we were alone again, Sam looked at me with dread. "I can't go back there, Frankie. I'm in enough trouble as it is."

I tried to calm Sam's nerves. "Hey, don't worry. I'll do it. You don't have to come. Probably better anyway that we're not so many people at the door. I'll just take a quick look at it and then you can help find some info on picking modern locks. Then it's up to the boys. They can get the magazines and stories. They don't know we wrote them. As long as they get them, we'll be fine."

,

I arrived in the shower room a few minutes into our lunch hour, with my pad and paper. My plan was to draw the lock, so we knew what to look for during our research. Asking Pete wasn't an option this time. We'd have to hit the public library. I took my flashlight out of my pocket as I entered the short hallway and shone it at the door. To my surprise, the lock was open. This could only mean one of two things. Either someone was in there or someone forgot to lock the door. Hoping it was the latter, I opened the door just a crack, really slowly to keep it from creaking, and listened. When I was sure there was no one in there, I opened it a bit more and slipped through the crack. There were packing boxes on the floor. It looked like someone had been organizing stuff into boxes. My heart sank a bit. The room was dark, but I stood still a moment longer anyway, listening. Nope, definitely no one in there. I decided not to turn on the light and instead used my flashlight to find the desk that held the magazines and erotic stories. I opened the desk, and to my relief, they were still there. I couldn't contain myself. I thought out loud, "Wow! Yes yes yes! Day saved!" I hadn't thought I'd be collecting the goods, though, so I hadn't brought my backpack with me. The pile of magazines and stories together was about 2 centimetres thick. I breathed in and stuffed the pile into my pants. Then I thanked god I had worn a baggy hoody that day. I covered the pile with my sweater. Then I remembered the D&D figurines. I found those in the next desk over and stuffed them, along with the dice and a few character cards, into the big pocket on the front of my sweater. If I met anyone, my plan was to put my hands in my pocket and bend over a bit as if I was feeling unwell, so it wouldn't look too bulky and suspicious. I gathered my nerves and made my way toward escape.

I put my ear to the pool door and listened. Completely quiet. This was going to be a squeaky clean getaway. So easy. I opened the door, again slowly, without any creaks, and entered the shower room. Dark, quiet as usual, perfectly lonely, and utterly spooky. I listened again, this time for people in the hallway outside the shower room. I didn't have to worry too much as most people would be up in the cafeteria eating lunch. Still, I listened just in case. Nothing.

Just quiet. Feeling thoroughly confident now, I left the shower room at a faster pace, turned down the hallway, with my eyes plastered to the end of it. Once I reached the end of the hallway, I'd be free. And I was sure I'd reach it. WHAM! I was struck head on by the door to the drama room. Someone had suddenly swung it open from the inside.

My senses were thrown out of whack and my arms flew forward, trying to grasp something, anything. My hands came up empty and I crumpled to the floor, landing on the figurines that had just spilled out of my pocket. As I fell, my bending legs shoved the magazines and letters upward out of my pants and farther up into my sweater. Then, as if things couldn't get worse, Mr. Lopez instinctively came to my rescue. As he grabbed my arm to pull me into a standing position, the magazines and erotic stories fell from my sweater and scattered across the hallway floor in all directions, each one seeming to come to a stop in its own glowing spotlit circle on the floor. The students who had materialized out of the classroom alongside Mr. Lopez immediately moved into helping mode, gathering up the evidence, their eyes growing bigger the more they helped. The only thought that came to me was *Oh, merde*. I should've considered the possibility of lunchtime drama rehearsals.

9

Baldi stood behind his desk, pretentiously towering over me. He had spread the magazines across his desk. The erotic stories lay open on top of the magazines. I sat, feeling very alone, in the chair opposite him. I felt a lot like Alice in *Alice's Adventures in Wonderland*, in her super small state, so small that she couldn't reach the key to the beautiful garden that surely led to a blissfully free world—a world without tall, mean, balding ogres that only speak in dry riddles for hours on end. The only thing worse than this was to imagine Sam having to go through the same horrible ordeal with her parents sitting beside her.

"What is this trash?" That was his first question, and it spiralled downward from there. By the time he was finished with me, my pride, honour, and self-esteem had been ground down to microscopic proportions. The worst part of it was that no matter how much I thought I could resist him when I first walked into his office, he had easily managed to get me to turn in my friends. He told me that he would punish our whole class if I didn't reveal the names of all pool club members. He had already guessed them correctly, but he wanted my confirmation. He had also figured out that Sam and I were the ones behind the erotic stories. And teachers had brought him more copies of the stories they had confiscated during class. He had *everything*.

My eyes and cheeks were wet and red when Baldi finally dismissed me. I had been suspended for three days. I was ordered to wait for Seb in the waiting room outside Baldi's office. Sam was sitting in the waiting room when I entered. Her eyes were already red and puffy. Baldi entered and motioned for her to follow him into his office. She complied, with her eyes on the floor, and I sat alone. A few minutes later, all four boys walked in and sat down. I didn't bother trying to talk to them. The harm was done. I was the reason we got caught. Seb arrived and spoke briefly with the vice principal. Then he collected me from the waiting room and we headed home in silence.

CHAPTER NINE
Message in a Bottle

April 1, 1986

Dear Frankie,

Happy April Fools' Day! I am thinking of you today especially. I miss you so much! I hope you like the Abyssinian prince teddy I left with this letter—I saw it in a store and thought of all the fun we had pranking the boys.

My parents won't let me see or even call any of my friends from Beats. I'm so lonely without you. My new school isn't much fun. The kids are not the same. They only care about winning. And it's all girls—no boys here. My parents say it's the best school in town. I'm not sure what they mean by best.

How's it going at Beats? How are the boys? Have you played any cool April Fools' pranks?

My mom works in the McGill admin building, behind the chapel. I'll meet her at work again on Friday at lunch. It's too risky to meet you—she would kill me—but I'll check our secret spot for your reply.

Your forever bf,

Sam

I sat in the upper balcony of the McGill Chapel reading Sam's letter, with the Abyssinian prince teddy in my lap. The balcony was small and isolated from the rest of the chapel. Standing in it, you could see most of the main floor below, but the few visitors who ventured in through the chapel's main entrance rarely looked up. This gave a person sitting in the balcony a sense of peaceful privacy. The day before, one of the third grade kids had run up to me in the Beats courtyard and handed me a note from Sam. The scrap of paper that her message had been written on was folded about a hundred times until it was the size of a quarter. Her note read, "I'm leaving you a letter in the McGill Chapel, corner University & Milton, tomorrow. Go to the chapel balcony on the third floor. Under a cushion, second row pew on right. —S." So here I was, at church for the third time in my life. The first two occasions had been for funerals, so this was an exceptionally positive third experience.

I held her letter to my heart and smiled. Finally. Sam was back. I hadn't heard from her since before we were suspended. She never returned to Beats, and her parents wouldn't permit us to communicate. I had tried calling once, but her mum answered, briefly lectured me on my morals, and then told me that Sam wasn't interested in my friendship. As Sam had not tried to reach me previously, I had, quite depressingly, thought that her mum could be right. I felt ecstatically happy to have her back. The last few months had been horrible. I was back to being the shy nerdy alien in class, either completely ignored or incessantly bullied. The word went around that Sam and I had written the erotic stories, and then I really discovered just how mean kids could be. I went home that evening fully intending to spill my guts to Sam on paper.

That evening went something like this:

April 2, 1986

~~Dearest Sam,~~

~~My life has been so, so horrible without you. The boys won't talk to me. They ignore me as if I'm invisible. When I try to talk to them, they behave as if there's an annoying mosquito in the air and move out of reach. I'm so miserable without you.~~

~~Hi Sam!~~

~~It's so great to hear from you. I miss you too! The boys are fine and they say hi. The past few months have been horrible without you. Remember Terrible Tammy and her side kick Dreadful Deirdre? The ones who always sat behind Helen and bugged her? Well, now they're sitting behind me. They call me "wannabe-slut." In front of everyone, all the time. They even shout it at me when~~

~~I'm sitting alone on the steps eating lunch.~~

~~Hey Sam,~~

~~I miss you so much. I've nick named your mum the Evil Queen.~~

~~Hi Sam,~~

~~I don't know how I have survived without you. Mr. Lopez is sick and Baldi is substituting as our drama teacher. He's so boring. The last three classes he has just gone on and on about lighting. And he hates me. Every time I pause during my lines, he tells me that I'm useless and am not trying hard enough. Yesterday I was late for class by 1 minute and he shouted at me that I was a troublemaker in front of the whole class and told me to get out.~~

~~Hey you,~~

~~I miss you too! Things haven't been going well for me. Everyone knows we wrote those stories. On April Fools' Day, I was sitting on the Beats steps outside when Tammy and her friends walked up to me. Deirdre squirted ketchup all over my crotch, and Tammy told me that at least now I could pretend I had hit puberty and was old enough to be a genuine slut. Then they all laughed. I got angry and shouted at them and threw my muffin~~

~~at Tammy. Then Baldi was suddenly there and practically dragged me to his office by my arm. He told me I was good for nothing and gave me lunch detentions for the rest of the week. Tammy and Deirdre never get punished for anything they do! I hate this school!~~

Hi Sam,

I miss you too! I'm so glad to hear from you! I was worried that I'd never see you again. It's too bad that your new school isn't much fun. My life has been holy moly horrible without you. I want to see you. I have a plan.

Remember Sandy, the girl who works at the McGill Metro cinema? She tutors some Beats kids in flute, clarinet, and sax. She's cool, and I think she'd help us. Do you think you could convince your mum that you need tutoring in flute? Sandy's dad is the manager at the cinema and she uses a back room for her tutoring. We could both take lessons on Saturdays and grab a movie after. I think Seb would go for it.

Will this work for you? Write your answer on the back of this note and put it back under the cushion. I'll pick it up after school on Friday. I'll leave another note for you at lunchtime next Tuesday.

Can't wait to see you!

Your BF,

Frankie

I was so anxious for Sam's reply that I couldn't concentrate during our last class on Friday. Mr. Grayson, our choir teacher, kept reminding me that I should be singing soprano, not alto. When the bell rang, I sprang for the door a little too enthusiastically, and tripped over Tammy's strategically placed outstretched leg. Somehow my fast forward motion came to my rescue, and rather than hitting the ground hard, I flew forward a few feet, right into Deirdre, who broke my fall as I pushed her over with my velocity and landed on top of her, spread-eagle on the floor. For the briefest of moments a smile itched my lips, and I thought about how revenge really did taste sweet. Then she opened her mouth. What came out of her was a whispered hiss, "Get the fuck off me, you lesbian whore!" Then, as she shoved me away from her, she started crying about how her leg hurt. Mr. Grayson suddenly noticed the commotion and pulled me to my feet, demanding I answer for myself. And there it was. I was off to visit Baldi once again.

To my relief, Baldi was busy and I was sent to the vice principal, Mr. Rossi, instead. If Mr. Baldo was the bad cop, Mr. Rossi was the good cop. When I entered his office, he smiled warmly and motioned for me to sit in one of the two chairs in front of his desk. Then he said, "Frankie, Frankie, Frankie. What is going on with you? You keep ending up in the office. What happened in choir just now?" I told him what had happened. He nodded and looked at me quietly. So then I told him about the bullying I was being subjected to by Tammy and Deirdre. I couldn't contain my emotions and started crying as I told him. He offered me a tissue and nodded some more. When I was finished blubbering my sorrows to him, he said, "Do you like Fridays?" I replied that I did. He said, "Me too. Let's just let this one slide and go home for the weekend. How does that sound?" I looked at him through blurry eyes. I felt confused, unheard. But leaving school without a detention sounded great, so I nodded, thanked him, gathered myself up, and left his office.

9

I walked up University Street with my eyes stuck to the sidewalk. I crossed the street at Milton and entered the old stone building that contained McGill's Chapel. The foyer was empty of people and the antique doors to the chapel's main floor were propped open. A man and woman were talking to the reverend. Other than them, the chapel looked quiet. I stood in the foyer for a moment, gathering my thoughts, and then walked up the stairs on my right and entered the chapel balcony from the third floor. The heavy door closed softly behind me. The chapel was completely quiet. The people who had been talking to the reverend must have left. I took my coat off and lay down on a middle bench. The benches had long soft cushions and were quite comfortable. Today, I welcomed loneliness. I closed my eyes and cried silently.

I must've fallen asleep, because when I opened my eyes again the lights had been turned off. I felt a slight panic in my gut as it crossed my mind that everyone may have gone home for the weekend and locked the doors as they left. I jumped up from the bench and pushed the door. This one wasn't locked. I crossed my fingers that the main door to the building was also unlocked. I grabbed my jacket from the bench and checked under the cushion for Sam's reply. It was right where it was supposed to be. I put it in my backpack, left the balcony, and headed down the stairs to the main doors. The janitor was mopping the floor in the foyer. He stopped mopping and looked up when he heard me. He must've noticed my panicked expression, because he chortled as he said, "Let me guess...sleeping in the chapel? Don't worry, my dear, front door ain't locked."

When I got outside, I checked my watch. 6:04 p.m. Good, not too late. Seb usually took the 7:20 p.m. train home on Fridays. He'd never know I had stayed so late in town. I took off in a sprint and caught the 6:20 train with no more than a minute to spare.

❦

The train looked like a series of sardine cans with windows. Homebound travellers were squished in so tightly I was sure that the bigger ones must be holding their breath. Being a scrawny kid wasn't so bad at that moment in time. I squeezed my way down the aisle, past briefcase-wielding men and perfumed women, toward a less crowded space in the middle of the carriage, stopping next to an ear-phoned boy with a skateboard. His music thumped and screamed so loudly from his earphones that I could hear each beat and word clearly. I wondered if this was a strategic play on his part—it sure worked as a great repellent. The crowd had given him lots of space. I recognized his music as Metallica. Pete played it at home sometimes.

Most of the passengers had emptied off the train by the time we reached my halfway-home point. The seat I was standing beside became available at Val Royal station, so I slipped my bag off my shoulder, sat down, and slid myself over to the window. I took Sam's reply out of my bag. As I read it, I felt a joy well up within me that I hadn't felt for months.

Friday, April 4, 1986

Hi Frankie,

I'm in a rush. The music lesson idea won't work cuz my mom has like a million sixth senses. She'd be on to me like an ant on jam. But I think I can meet you at the cinema next Saturday. My parents are going away for the weekend and my uncle's staying with me. He's super cool. He'll let me go.

I'll leave a note for you next Friday to tell you if I can for sure meet.

See you soon!

Sam

The next week inched by incredibly slowly. My school hours consisted mainly of burying my nose in books and avoiding the Terrible Tammy gang. I spent my lunch hours in the music room, impressing my teacher with my sudden dedication to sax practice. My interest in playing instruments had waned since my dad died... as if he'd been the passion in my music and that passion had died along with him. But I needed a hiding spot and band room during lunch hour was by far the safest place to be. And it worked. Besides a little whispered name-calling in class, I managed to stay out of Tammy's and Deirdre's target range for the whole week.

Sam's note on Friday confirmed that she had secured several hours on Saturday to meet with me. After reading her note, my joy hit maximum velocity and kept me up all night.

9

On Saturday, April 12, I met Sam in the food court at McGill metro station. She had changed her appearance a bit. Her hair was cut into a bob, like Molly Ringwald in *Pretty in Pink*, and she was wearing lipstick, but she had the same huge warm signature smile. She had a big winter coat on, which was a bit odd in April, and I wrapped my arms around it as I gave her the biggest hug ever.

After stopping in at the arcade to play a game of *Pole Position*, we headed downstairs to the Cineplex Centre Ville cinema and bought tickets to *Lucas*. It was a comedy about a smart underdog kid who is relentlessly bullied just for being him but overcomes his challenges also through just being him. The theme fit us perfectly. After buying extra-large bags of overflowing popcorn, we headed into the theatre. We had first dibs on seats as we were the only customers, and we sat in the highest row at the back. Sam talked almost nonstop until the movie started. She told me about how it was to attend a girls-only private school. Competitive sports were really big at her new school. She was no longer the fastest girl in her class and she wasn't very good at team sports, she said. But she was still the top of her class in the more academic subjects, like math, science, and history.

Sam then did something that I had never heard her do before. She started criticizing the other kids in her class. In an exasperated voice, she said, "The girls in my class are such idiots. Even the ones who aren't blonde are 'dumb blondes.' I wouldn't waste my time with them if they begged me." I thought her comment was oddly negative as I had always known her to be very positive and happy. The movie started and she stopped talking.

Sam's mood was more positive after the movie. The next movie that was scheduled to play was *Violets are Blue*. It would start in twenty minutes in the same theatre room. Retreating into our old conspiratorial selves, we hid in the bathroom while Cindy checked the theatre room, and giggling nervously, we snuck back in to watch the next movie.

The movie turned out to be a dull romance about something I can't remember. We talked most of the way through it. Then Sam got up to go to the bathroom. After a few minutes of being all alone in my boredom, I decided to join her in the bathroom. I glanced out into the hallway from the theatre to be sure Cindy wasn't around and then quickly made my way over to the bathroom. I pushed the door open quietly and entered.

Sam's jacket was lying on the counter next to the sinks and she was in one of the stalls. I opened my mouth to say something to her and then stopped myself as I heard her start to retch. I stood still and quiet. She was throwing up. She had seemed fine in the theatre. I thought about this for a moment and then asked her if she was OK.

Sam replied, "Oh. Uh, Frankie. Yeah, I'm fine. I think I ate something wrong." Then she opened the door and walked to the sink.

That's when I noticed some other changes. She had always been thin, but now I could see her bones. She was wearing a thin white baggy T-shirt with a wide neck. Her collarbone protruded across her upper breastbone, and I could see much too clearly how it linked to her shoulder bones. Although her T-shirt was baggy, it failed to add bulk to her, as I assumed she had hoped it would do. Sam looked a like a Halloween ghost prop, as if there was nothing under her flimsy white T-shirt but a pole linking her shoulders to her hips. I didn't know what to say. My expression was likely giving away my stunned thoughts, but I'd never come across this situation before. She was either really sick or starving herself.

She finished washing her hands and saw me staring. She said a bit aggressively, "What?" then grabbed her coat and covered herself up again.

I found my voice and replied, "Are you OK, Sam?" When she didn't reply, I continued, "You were just throwing up, and you're...uh, quite skinny. Are you sick or something?"

That got her attention. Her face flushed angrily and she replied, "What are you talking about? I told you I'm fine! Stop looking at me!"

"You don't look fine," I replied, tentatively.

Then she screamed at me. ""Just... just... FUCK OFF!" She stormed out of the bathroom. I had never heard her use real swear words before, and with such rage, directed at me. I felt as if she'd slapped me across the face with something hard and emotionally devastating. I stood in the bathroom for a few seconds, surprised and hurt. When I resurfaced from my emotional confusion, I couldn't find her anywhere. She'd left the cinema without saying goodbye.

It was months before I heard from Sam again.

PART 3

Let's Talk About Love

CHAPTER TEN
It's Only Love

September 1986

I won't bore you with the details of my lonely summer. Summer sucked. And that's about the gist of it. Seb worked. Pete worked. Ani was away for most of the summer. Sam remained silent. Our reclusive neighbours remained reclusive (apparently they only came out of hiding once a year—I suppose to celebrate a new year of reclusiveness). Although I did get a babysitting gig going with the Langley family a few doors down. So far, I had made eighty dollars and saved seventy-six. Yup, my summer was nail-bitingly boring. At least for the most part.

The only mentionable highlight was the little mink I rescued in August. I found them as I was walking along the train tracks one lonely afternoon. They were chirping like baby birds and circling their more unfortunately quite squished mother. Seb and Pete let me keep them, for a while anyway. Possibly out of pity for me and my loneliness. I collected construction scraps, an old deep bathtub (the kind with the funny feet), wire netting, and wooden picture frames from neighbours around the island and built them a cage. Then I made a whole habitat inside it. They had branches to climb, rocks to hide between, sand to dig in, leaves to jump in, a tiny pond, and an Abyssinian prince teddy to play with. Initially, I fed them milk from a comically big syringe and pureed perch that I'd caught in the river. By the end of August they had moved on to whole fish. The littlest one I named Pinky. She was the friendliest of them all. Then there was Minky. Ani named the third one Flinky, because "flink" means "clever" in Norwegian and this particular mink quickly proved to be a relentless escape artist. The last one I named Stinky, because it was, well, the most fitting name I could think of. Pinky, Minky, Flinky, and Stinky kept me going that summer.

,

Labour Day weekend came and went, and grade nine started uneventfully, which was a good thing I suppose. As of lunch hour on the first day back in school, Tammy, Deirdre, and co. hadn't paid me much attention. That was positive. I had to count my blessings I guess. We also had a new kid in our class, one person who didn't see me through history's eyes. Hope tickled my senses, and I wished silently for a new beginning. I sat on the Beats concrete front steps under a blue and white breezy sky, holding my sandwich in one hand and twirling my hair with the other. I had grown it long again. Twirling my hair helped me relax. My dad told me once that when I was little I would twirl my hair so much that my fingers would get all knotted up in it, and on three occasions he had to cut them loose. Twirling my hair was my comfort crutch, *my thumb*.

Ms. Bean, my music teacher, walked stiffly across the courtyard toward me. Kids nicknamed her "Beanpole" because of her very erect, tall, skinny stature. She also had these thin down-turned lips that gave her an unfortunate, overly serious grumpy look when she wasn't smiling. Ms. Bean was actually one of our most fair teachers, but you had to get to know her in order to understand that. Most kids were too afraid to approach her. As I had spent several lunch hours in the music room during grade eight, avoiding Tammy's and Deirdre's target practice, I had had the opportunity to get to know Ms. Bean on a deeper level than what her appearance suggested. She wasn't someone who I'd share my intimate feelings with, but she was someone who I knew would treat me with respect.

I watched her as she walked up the steps toward me. She looked at me and smiled. Her thin lips curved upward and pushed the corners of her eyes up along with them. In an instant, her face had transformed from stern to warm and welcoming, and her golden-brown eyes shone with interest. Her appearance completely changed when she smiled. She paused for a moment in front of me and then said, "Hello, Frankie! It's so nice to see you again. Tell me, how was your summer?"

"Hi, Ms. Bean. It was OK. Pretty quiet. Yours?" I smiled shyly. I hadn't yet adjusted to being back around teachers again.

"Great. It was really great. I spent most of it at my cabin in PEI. You know, I've been thinking of you. You're so wonderful on that sax of yours. Would you like to help me choose some music for our fall concert in November? I'm undecided on what type of music we should focus on. Classical? Maybe Mozart? But we did classical in the spring. I was thinking maybe rock this time? Can you join me for lunch tomorrow in the music room so we can discuss it. You're more tuned into modern music than I am. I'd love your help." She looked at me with hopeful question marks in her eyes.

At her request for my help, my mind lit up just a bit, and I replied gratefully, "Uh, sure. Yeah. I'll be there. Uh, thanks."

Ms. Bean's smile grew again. "Wonderful! I'll bring my suggestions along and you should do the same. Then we can compare notes and talk about possibilities. I look forward to it!" She nodded with satisfied approval. I smiled back at her, a bit less shyly. Then she made her way up the remaining steps and into the building.

9

That evening I sat on my bed, going through all my music, listening for tunes that could be played by an orchestra. Stinky, Minky, and Flinky were chasing each other around my room. Pinky was cuddled up on my shoulders, under my hair. There were so many possibilities. I hadn't been this excited over music since I had played with my dad's band at the Montreal Blues Festival the year before he died. That thought reminded me of the box I had been given by his band members after he died. It contained bits and pieces of his musical life, along with a tape collection. I reached under my bed, pulled out the box, and placed it on the bed in front of me. I rested my hands on top of it for a moment. It was just a plain cardboard box, but this plain box was more valuable to me than anything else in the world. Within it was my link to the person who I had loved more than life itself. Besides my memories, it was all that was left of him.

I opened the box. His old Irish Aran sweater lay on top. I picked it up and put it aside. In the box was his clarinet, a few reeds, his favourite sheet music, some concert photos of him with his band, and his most listened-to tapes. I took the tapes out and spread them across my pillow. The tapes featured music greats, including the Oscar Peterson Trio, Leonard Cohen, Nina Simone, Buffy Sainte-Marie, Miles

Davis, La Bottine Souriants, Albert Burbank, Simon and Garfunkel, the Beatles, Pink Floyd, and Queen. I'd heard each of them played many times over, but I'd only listened to them with my dad. I spent the next couple of hours listening to my favourite songs on my dad's tapes. After a bit of indecision, I managed to choose four songs that I thought would fit a "rock" theme for our school band perfectly. The winners were "Let It Be" (Beatles), "Shine On, You Crazy Diamond" (Pink Floyd), "Killer Queen" (Queen), and "A Hazy Shade of Winter" (Simon and Garfunkel). I presented my suggestions to Ms. Bean the following day. She brought the sheet music in on Thursday and we looked over it together. Ms. Bean was quite a musician. She could pick up any instrument, whether wind, string, or percussion, and could play it without much effort. I could handle the clarinet, alto and soprano sax but was at a loss with the others. After playing a few bits and pieces from each with her, we decided on "A Hazy Shade of Winter."

I arrived home on Thursday evening daydreaming about playing music. It was a strangely invigorating feeling. It had been a while since I'd had music beating in my heart. Lunchtime in the music room would be taking on a whole new feeling. The music room would no longer be my *escape room*; it would now be a room where I could learn to love again. I took my sax home with me on Friday, along with the sheet music for "A Hazy Shade of Winter," and played all Saturday. At one point, Seb and Pete joined in. Seb playing the spoons and Pete playing, well, anything he could find within reach. They always made me laugh. We had quite a gig going. It was a good weekend. And then it got even better.

9

Sam finally called on Sunday. The phone rang as I stood in the living room trying to untangle Pinky from my hair. She'd been on my shoulders playing with my hair when she got her paw all knotted up in it. She was the only mink that I'd let crawl on me. The others were all biters. I hoped she would keep her patience through this minor ordeal. On the third ring I managed to free her paw and she disappeared down into my sweater. I picked the receiver up, expecting it to be for Pete, as he'd just left for his flight up north and I had come to believe strongly in Murphy's Law. I picked up and my "Hello?" was followed by silence. My heart started beating a little faster. I hated Murphy's Law. But then her voice broke the silence.

"Frankie?" Sam sounded... anxious? Nervous?

"Sam?" Silence. "Sam, are you there?"

"Yeah, it's me, Frankie. I... I'm sorry. It's been so long. I... meant to call, but..." She seemed not to know how to continue.

I was so shocked to hear from her. I felt tears start to well up behind my eyes. "Sam..." A lump in my throat suffocated me for a moment. "I was so worried, Sam. Why did you run away like that? Why did you stop writing? Why were you... are you... Why... Are you sick, Sam?"

"No, well, yeah, well, kind of, I guess. I spent the summer in hospital. Well, not all of it... mostly actually in a rehab centre." She paused for a moment, then continued, "My doctor says that I have a sort of obsession with control. So I guess I felt out of control at my new school. And it doesn't help that my school is filled with rich douchebags, and that my mom has been possessed by overactive mom-o-meter aliens. Anyway, I have this eating problem. Or I guess it's more like a starving problem. But I'm working on it. And

I'm back at home now. But school still sucks." Sam's last few words were almost whispered.

"Oh. OK." I really didn't know how to respond. I'd never known anyone with the same type of issue. Sam had been so happy at Beats. This wasn't her as I remembered her. "Sam? I'm happy that you're OK."

I heard Sam breathe out heavily as if relieved. "Hey Frankie? I want to meet, but I won't be allowed out of my house for a while. But my mom is letting me speak to friends by phone. Including you. So you can call me now, you know, if you want."

"Yeah, for sure." I paused. Then continued, "Sam? I'm glad you called."

"OK, well, clock just struck twelve. Gotta go eat lunch. My mom's got my eating schedule under strict guard. No deviating for me. Anyway, bye, Frankie."

"Bye, Sam." I put down the receiver. My mood had changed. I was glad to hear from Sam but sad that she was struggling.

Pinky crawled up the front of my T-shirt inside my sweater and into my sleeve, then attempted to make herself comfortable in the crook of my armpit. Her three brothers were somewhere outside, with Flinky playing guide. It had become impossible to keep Flinky from breaking them all out of their cage. He was just too nifty. But they weren't lost or in danger. On the contrary. They always presented themselves on our doorstep for breakfast and supper. Pinky was special though. She was usually the only one that hung around after her meal. I put my fingers in my sweater and scratched her under her chin. She grabbed my forefinger playfully with her front paws and gave me a gentle love bite, then licked where she had bit as if to say, "Oooops, sharp teeth. Sorry, just playing!"

,

My second week in September whizzed by. I spent all my breaks in the music room, practicing for our November concert. Terrible Tammy and Dreadful Deirdre, and co. had readjusted their focus. Hiding from them had worked. They must've become bored with me. They'd now isolated one of their own to pick on. I have no idea what Ally had done to attract their wrath, likely not much, but she was sure suffering. If she hadn't been so nasty to me I might have cared. But under the circumstances, I was just glad I could walk down the hall in peace.

I sat alone in the music room that Friday, daydreaming, my sax across my lap. Motivation was extra hard on Fridays. If it hadn't been so miserably rainy outside, I would've taken my lunch over to the McGill campus and napped on the grass. I was so sleepy. I moved my sheet music stand to the side and placed another chair in front of me. I put my feet up on it and relaxed my body, sinking down a bit in the chair I was sitting on. Ms. Bean spent most lunch hours and recesses elsewhere, so I usually had the room to myself. There was little chance she'd walk in on me napping. But if she did, she probably wouldn't mind anyway. I stuffed my bag behind my lower back to make the chair a little more comfortable. As my mind drifted off into Neverland, my thoughts wandered through the lyrics for "A Hazy Shade of Winter."

Of all things I could dream of, I found myself dreaming of tobogganing at Mount Royal Park. My dad and I spent many of our winter days playing on that slope. It was the biggest tobogganing slope I knew of. If you wanted to, you could pick up tremendous speed. The bottom was stacked with bales of hay to keep speed devils from flying into traffic on Avenue du Parc. In my dream, I was zipping down the slope on my flying saucer, twirling around and around while playing "A Hazy Shade of Winter" on my sax. My dad was behind me, on his stomach on a flying carpet, trying to catch up to me. In a panicked voice, he yelled at me, "Frankie! Head for the luck dragon! Head for the luck dragon!" I stopped playing and looked ahead of me down the slope. There were two dragons entwined, fighting. The blue one faced me with its absurdly huge mouth open, its long razor sharp fangs glittering like snow does on a really cold day. It fixed its yellow eyes on me and I saw hunger and anticipated satisfaction in them. The other dragon was Falkor, the white luck dragon from *The Never Ending Story*. Falkor attacked the blue dragon's neck, biting and screeching. But the blue dragon threw him off easily. Strangely, Falkor seemed to be shrinking. My dad yelled again, "Play, Frankie! Play your music! Change the beat! Head for the luck dragon!" I was heading straight for the blue dragon's humongous and terrifyingly jagged gaping mouth. I would surely disappear forever in there if circumstances didn't change quickly. Almost frozen with fear, I managed to get my sax back up to my lips and I started to play again. The blue dragon began to shrink immediately and Falkor doubled in size. The luck dragon now had the advantage and pinned the blue dragon down on the ground, but as he did so, the blue dragon swung its tail around toward me and swatted my sax out of my hands. Falkor instantly shrank to the size of a cat. I tried to roll off my flying saucer, but some unseen force wouldn't let me. I was stuck in a trajectory, flying straight for the blue dragon's jaws of death. I felt fangs on my arm and woke up with a start.

"Ah! What? Who? Back... back off!" I was breathing heavily and my hair was stuck to drool on my cheek. There was a blue-eyed blond boy standing over me. He had uniquely well-kept hair, unlike most kids at Beats. Then I recognized him. It was the new kid.

"Oh... Uh, sorry, I didn't mean to scare you." He looked genuinely sorry and partly amused. "That was some dream you were having. You were flailing your arms around and shouting about dragons. Anything you feel like sharing, or is this one of those embarrassing moments best left ignored?" He smiled teasingly.

"Uh... Uh, yeah, I think... I think the latter." I tried desperately to control the blush in my cheeks.

"Frankie, right?" he asked, and when I didn't reply, he added, "Gil," and motioned to himself.

I ran my fingers through my hair in an attempt to tidy up a bit. "Uh... Hi. Yeah, uh, I know. You're the new kid," I said because nothing else came to mind.

He sat in the strings section and opened his violin case. "So, you escaping something in here?"

"What? No... No... Well, you? What's your excuse?" My brain was still trying to shake off my crazy dream. At this moment in time, I felt about as socially inclined as a surprised turtle. If only I had a shell to retreat into.

"Well, band *is* about to start in ten minutes. Yup, that's pretty much why I'm here." He had that teasing smile on his face again. He wasn't a natural "looker," but the charisma in his face when he spoke gave him a spark that made him uniquely interesting. And when he smiled, he was the best-looking kid in our class. Suddenly, I didn't mind his interruption in the least.

I looked at the clock. Yup, I'd almost been caught napping by my whole class. "Oh, shit... Yeah, that's right. Shit. Thanks!" I laughed nervously and began to tidy my lunch away.

Other students arriving for band then interrupted our somewhat awkward first meeting. Ms. Bean walked in as the bell rang for the second time. She had this amazing effect on kids—everyone hushed up as soon as she presented herself.

My mind was all over the place during band. I couldn't concentrate. Dragons were haunting my sheet music. For the first time in a while, I was glad when band class came to an end. After class, I packed my sax into its case, threw my backpack over my shoulder. I looked up in time to see Gil walk by me. He smiled "Hi again" at me. I noticed his beautiful eyes and I was momentarily transfixed. They were the colour of glacier ice. I headed for the door, following him a little too quickly.

As I walked past the flute section, my gaze fixed dreamily on the back of Gil's head, I tripped over a sheet music stand. Flying forward, my hands shot out in front of me, and I grabbed onto the first solid object that could potentially break my fall: Gil's backpack. Gil buckled and fell sideways to the ground and we landed in a tangled heap with the sheet music stand on top of us.

"Oh my god, oh my god, oh my god, I'm so sorry!" I was horrified and thoroughly embarrassed. This was even worse than being woken up by a cute guy during a nightmare while flailing my arms and drooling.

After a moment of initial shock, Gil relaxed and looked up at me. I was now kneeling over him, looking very concerned. His smile began to creep across his face, and his eyes twinkled. A nervous laugh escaped from within me.

He returned a more uncontrolled laugh. With a shy smile, I said, "Can I help you up, Sir Gil?"

When we were both standing again and on our way out of class, Gil smiled a little awkwardly, then said, "Hey, uh, I've seen you on the train. I just go a couple of stops. I live near Mount Royal Station."

"Oh yeah? Cool. I'm much farther. When you hit the boondocks, that's my stop." I smiled back. Then I gathered my nerves together and continued, "You taking the three forty-five today?"

"Uh, yeah, think so. If I can run fast enough. Gotta talk to Mr. Kabira after school 'bout that ethics assignment. But that shouldn't take long." Then he said, half-jokingly, "Want to run together?" Every bit of his face shone with that characteristic "my attention is all yours" smile of his.

I nodded. Yup. Absolutely. "I'll wait on the front steps." With intrigue thumping in my heart, I reflected his smile back at him.

CHAPTER ELEVEN
Eternal Flame

Everything about Gil made my heart thumb a little faster. Unlike my extra shy crush on Amir, being around Gil made me want to talk to him forever about everything. And the coolest part about it was that Gil showed just as much interest in me. Over the month of September we became inseparable.

Gil and I spent our sunny lunch hours on the grass at McGill campus, lying next to each other with our heads together, talking and laughing and talking and talking. Rainy days we spent in the music room, where we jammed together, in between talking and laughing and talking some more. We honestly didn't do much jamming at all, but we always planned to. Gil made me feel invigorated in a way that I had never felt before. At times, when our eyes would meet and hold on to each other, just for a moment, butterflies would flutter in my heart and I'd become speechless, just for a moment. But then he'd smile, and I'd be completely disarmed, my shyness swept out of me just as quickly as it had overcome me. By the beginning of October, I was quite sure I had discovered what true love felt like.

9

On the first Friday in October, Gil came home with me on the train. It was a beautiful fall day. We lay in a pile of leaves in my backyard, looking up at the deep blue sky, through the oranges, yellows, and reds that composed our maple tree canopy. All four mink were playing in the leaves around us.

"I think I love the boondocks," Gil interjected during an odd bout of silence.

"Yeah, until you're stuck here, ten thousand miles away from your friends, every weekend!" I laughed and nudged him jokingly.

"No really. It's so quiet here. Where I live, houses are like a meter apart. My backyard is literally the size of your living room and kitchen put together. The only thing back there is a veggie patch, about the size of your kitchen, and a patio. We don't even have grass back there." He glanced at me and laughed jokingly. "My neighbourhood is like a sci-fi evil urban emperor movie where the Joker reigns and has forbidden any form of wilderness beyond bad hair days." He laughed again but something in his voice told me he was only half joking.

Pinky had jumped into the leaves between our heads. She kept surfacing and then diving back in under them, after some unseen treasure.

"Yeah, I used to live in the city. It is different. But it's also closer to things. We're in serious boonie-land here. To get anywhere, I have to take the tr—" I was abruptly interrupted by Gil's yelp.

Gil jumped up, panicked. He was fiddling desperately with his sweater, shaking himself and dancing around as if he had ants in his pants. "Oh shit, oh shit, ahh, shit, get out, get out, get out!" I'd never heard him panic before. It was so unlike him. I started to laugh and then controlled myself.

"Fran... Ahh! Frankie! Stop laughing. Get it out!" He looked at me pleadingly. Suddenly Pinky poked her nose up out of his collar, sniffed his neck, then pulled herself through with her little paws, ran down his front, and jumped back into the leaf pile, disappearing once again.

I tried hard to hold on to my laugh, but the scene had just been too funny. The friendliest little pet in the world had just caused I'm-not-scared-of-anything Gil to go weak in the knees with fear. My laugh burst out of me, like a cork from a champagne bottle, and I fell backward into the pile of leaves, cracking up, holding my stomach with the hilarity of it all.

Gil stood beside the pile of leaves and looked at me straight-faced. Then amusement started to sink into his expression.

"You are in so much trouble." His smile was growing and there was an "I'll get you" glint in his eye.

I was holding my stomach; laughter was the best pain ever. I'd lost complete control over my giggles. "You... you..." I couldn't stop laughing enough to speak clearly. "You'll never dare get me in this pile of mink I'm lying in!" That didn't quite make literary sense, but my mind was too far gone with the humour in it all to think literately. "Beware! My army of mink are ready to... ready to... ready to take you down!" And with that, I curled up with laughter again.

Gil's sense of fear must have been weaker than his sense of humour, because he shuffled his way back into the leaf pile, scaring the mink away from his spot, then dropped down beside me and started tickling me. I felt like I would die with laughter if he didn't stop. I begged him to stop, but he kept at me. With some hidden stop-tickling-me strength I had within me, I managed to push him over onto his back and roll myself on top of him. I tried to pin his arms down with my own, but he was too strong. We were both laughing and struggling to gain control. He got hold of my hands and held them in front of me, above his chest. I twisted my hands inward and broke free. As I did so, I fell forward, my hands slipping down on either side of his head. Our lips were suddenly only centimeters apart. His hands were now on my waist. We paused for just a second, acknowledging our mutual shift in emotions. I moved my hands closer and touched his head, then drew my fingers through the hair on the back of his neck. His eyes got lost in my own. Our lips touched, touched again, and again.

Calling my first kiss magical would be an unjust misrepresentation. Kissing Gil was beyond such a simple description. When we kissed, we were no longer two people but more like a joined concept of pure joy that was not of this world but rather belonged to a whole new set of meanings beyond anything that could be described with human language. We spent a lot of time kissing after that first kiss.

9

Gil left after supper on the eight o'clock train. When I returned from walking him to the train station, Seb was doing the dishes, singing to himself, and Pete was lying on the couch in the living room reading his book. I walked through the kitchen to the living room on my way to my room. I had almost cleared the living room when Pete looked up from his book.

"Soooo, Frankie. Gil's nice." He smiled inquisitively. It was that kind of smile that said, "Do tell, do tell!"

I froze in the hallway and thought, "Darn! So close! Just another few silent steps and I'd have been on my merry way up to my room, question-free."

"Uh, yeah. He's OK. I mean, yeah, nice guy, I guess." I took another step closer to escape but wasn't aggressive enough.

"C'mon, Frankie. Haven't seen you for a while. Join us for ice cream?" It was more like a friendly order than a question. Pete had arrived home late last night after almost a month up north. Normally, I would have loved to catch up, but today I just wanted to avoid questions that had anything to do with the new flame in my life.

"Sure. I'd love some ice cream. Uh, so, how was the north? Hunting season going well?" I tried to change the subject, but he wasn't having it.

Pete's smile grew. "The north is the north. Same but different. So, Gil in your class? You haven't talked about him before."

Yup, Pete, there was a reason for that. Pete put his book down, got up from the couch, and walked to the kitchen, motioning me to follow.

Seb was drying the dishes and looked over his shoulder at us as we entered the kitchen. He smiled and unknowingly repeated Pete's line. "So, Frankie, Gil seems nice."

Oh my god. These guys shared a brain. I would never escape this conversation.

"Yeah, so, did you say he's in your class?" Pete asked with relentless curiosity.

"Uh, kinda, yeah. And we take the train together sometimes. His stop is Mount Royal. He just wanted to see the boonies firsthand so came home with me today." I gave Pete a crooked grin and then averted my eyes to the side.

"Uh, huh." Pete smiled a little too knowingly, "Well, good to see he got along with the mink. They can be little terrors!"

My face froze in horror. I could feel my cheeks begin to burn. I looked at him intently. He looked back with an utterly clueless expression. I began to breathe again. Thank god. His comment was just lucky. He hadn't seen anything. He opened his mouth, a question mark lurking across his face, and thankfully that was when the phone rang. I turned to it and, without hesitation, picked up the receiver.

"Hello? Sam! Hi! Yup, I'll just move to the phone in my room. Hold on." I turned to Pete and Seb. "Hey, uh, I'll eat ice cream later." I headed quickly down the hall and up the stairs to my room. When I'd picked up the receiver in my room, I yelled down to Pete, asking him to hang up the one in the kitchen. I waited to hear the click on the line, then proceeded to tell Sam all about my first kiss.

9

Later that night, I lay on my bed in the dark, looking up at Corey Hart. Corey's time was up. I'd found true love beyond the poster kind. I reached up and pulled him down off the low slanted ceiling above my bed. I let the big poster fall to the floor. I'd ditch it tomorrow.

I closed my eyes and thought of Gil. I thought of our first kiss. In my mind, I could feel the memory of our kiss, his soft lips on mine. I felt his hands on my hips. I felt his stomach between my legs as I straddled him. Then I felt his hips between my legs as we kissed some more and my own hips glided farther down his body. Then my imagination, along with my magic fingers, took it all to the next step.

9

Monday morning was only slightly awkward. We usually didn't talk much in class anyway. I was continuously worried about drawing Tammy and Deirdre's negative attention, so tried to keep to myself as much as possible when they were in the room. Gil had figured out what was going on and had begun to refer to them and their followers as *the Terrible Twos*. I thought that to be a pretty accurate description as everyone else in Tammy and Deirdre's gang were really just reflections of the main two terrible characters. Currently, the Terrible Twos had moved on from Ally and had now targeted Sandy. Like Ally, Sandy was also part of their inner circle. But Ally had moved right back in there with them and was relentlessly harassing Sandy alongside the rest of them. I tried to see these girls three-dimensionally. I mean, they must have selfless bits hidden somewhere within their hearts. I'd hoped Ally's experience being the target would bring out a previously hidden nice-person side. But nope. I just didn't get it.

Gil slipped me a note during our last class before lunch that morning. It had been folded several times into a small triangle. He shot me a sideways glance with a little smile, then he sat down next to Raph. Gil had begun to hang out with the old *pool club* gang over the last couple of weeks. Initially I was anxious about it, but it turned out to be in my favour. The boys had begun to acknowledge my presence again. And it appeared they were also good at keeping some things secret. The last thing I wanted was to have to explain my brief career as sleazy-sex-story writer to Gil. I doubted he'd understand the comedy in that prank.

I opened Gil's note on my lap, out of sight, below my desk. He was asking whether I'd like to go the arcade at lunch. I wrote my reply below his scrawl, telling him to meet me on the front steps, and then I folded the note back up into a triangle and kicked it across the floor at his feet. He put his foot on it and dragged it under his desk. When the teacher turned to the chalkboard, he picked it up and put it in his pocket. He read it as the bell rang, caught my eye, and smiled.

9

When the bell rang, I gathered my books and stopped at my locker before heading outside. Gil, Raph, Matt, Dave, and Amir were waiting by the steps. My heart started to beat a little faster, and I slowed my pace. I was on talking terms again with the boys, but I hadn't hung out with them since our pool club days. I wished Gil would've told me we'd have company. But then again, why should he have? He knew nothing of our history together, or very little anyway.

My anxiety was relieved a bit when Matt smiled blithely at me and said, "Frankie! *Grouille-toi*, we only have fifty minutes!" His mother tongue wasn't French, but he'd developed a habit of playing with catchy Francophone expressions as he spoke.

I gave him a crooked smile. I wasn't quite ready yet to banter. Gil interjected, "Well, guess we'll have to run then. First one there is a rotten egg!"

Matt took off in a sprint, then stopped when he realized no one else was following. When he turned back to us, we were all looking at him, totally amused. Dave started laughing. "Guess we know who's the rotten egg! Hey, Matt, was that you then who let one loose in English earlier?"

Matt laughed, a little embarrassed, and replied, "Fuck off, Dave."

Then Dave took off in a sprint, and on his way past Matt, he shouted, "Good answer! It was me!" Then continued, "I get first dibs on Space Harrier, suckers!"

Matt shouted back, "The rest of us will be playing Gauntlet, mother f-er! Have fun on your lonely planet!"

Everyone laughed, then Amir said, "Screw that, I'm getting Space Harrier." He took off on his long legs after Dave, racing him for the game. Space Harrier was new to the arcade. It was some kind of space fighter fantasy game, with airborne robots and dragons and other weird creatures. The point, as I understood it, was to kill 'em all. The only games I really enjoyed at the arcade were the ones that involved races. I never paid much attention to the others.

Raph watched them run along the sidewalk toward the Sherbrooke Street junction. They were almost at the lights. "Guess there's a line up for Space Harrier." Then he looked at me. "Hey, Frankie? Wanna be player number four on Gauntlet?"

Normally I would've replied with a flat "uh, no," but something was happening here and I felt it was important. I smiled at him. "Yup, sure thing.

9

Gil came over again that weekend. I had agreed to babysit the Langley kids on Saturday while their parents did kitchen renovations. Lucy was four and Marc was five. They arrived on my doorstep, bright-eyed and fully charged, just past nine in the morning. Their mum, Lynn, waved from the street, then turned and walked back to her place. I returned her wave and looked down at the kids. Marc had his arms wrapped around a huge guinea pig. I was momentarily gobsmacked; that thing had grown since I had last seen it. It was now about the size of a small fat cat. The guinea pig had not been part of the deal, but OK, we'd manage.

Marc looked at me with a huge proud smile on his face and, struggling to keep his grip on the massive ball of fur with-feet in his arms, said, "Look, Frankie! I've brought Twinkles!"

Lucy then interjected, "Dad calls him Roadkill."

Marc shot her an angry glare. "Shut up, Lucy! He does not!"

She looked back at him. "Yes he does."

Then Marc said, "No, he doesn't. Shut up!"

Then Lucy looked at me and whispered her words almost silently, drawing each word out for effect. "He-e-e do-es." Marc shoved her to the side, annoyed, and walked past me into the house. His sister followed him, smiling triumphantly. I closed the door and quietly thanked God that Gil would soon arrive to share in my struggles.

Gil arrived at eleven o'clock, just as Lucy and Marc were lying down for their "nap." Lynn had some strict priorities when it came to her kids' daily schedule and naptime was top of her no-flexibility list. I wondered what planet she must live on, because these kids were like long-lasting energizer batteries. As far as I could tell, every morning Marc and Lucy rose with the sun, fully charged, and lasted without exception, like reverse vampires, until the sun set again. When Gil knocked at the front door, they jumped up from my bed and ran downstairs to greet him. I got up and checked myself out in the mirror. My boobs had begun to show more and, I'd become really uncomfortable in T-shirts. I grabbed the old big lumber jacket that I'd adopted from Pete, threw it on, and buttoned it part way up. Then I picked up the giant lethargic guinea pig and followed the kids downstairs.

Marc had opened the door and was now grilling Gil for his identity and credentials. Gil stood on the step with all four mink by his feet, slightly bewildered by Marc's lightning-speed questions. Pinky was standing on his right foot, with her two front paws up on his leg, looking up at him. I motioned to Pinky and smiled at Gil. "So I see you've grown a backbone."

Gil looked at me sheepishly. "Uh-huh." He shook his leg a bit. Pinky resisted and tightened her grip on his pants. "Just practicing my tolerance." He smiled, paid the imaginary toll that Marc was now requesting, and entered the house with Pinky clinging to his ankle. The other three mink zipped by our feet and into the kitchen, which was unusual as those three normally preferred to stay outside.

Twinkles suddenly became active and clawed his way up onto my shoulder, then pushed his way down through my open collar, almost getting stuck halfway, and into my lumber jacket. He made himself comfortable on my shoulder inside the jacket, then poked his nose out from my collar and sniffed the air. It briefly occurred to me that he may be scared of the mink, but they had never hunted anything. All they cared for was easy food and a bit of people love. Besides, Twinkles was twice the size of the male mink and three times the size of Pinky. He could just roll over on top of them if they tried anything. He had nothing to worry about. I put some cat food in a bowl for the mink and placed it on the porch outside. They all scampered out and I closed the door after them.

Naptime is *way* overrated. We gave up within a few minutes. Screw schedules; super-charged kids belonged outside, and that was that. As Twinkles's nerves itched around the mink, we thought he'd feel more comfortable inside, out of mink-range. Lucy and Marc made a little bed for him in the bathtub and we left him with a bowl of water and a carrot. Marc lowered him into the tub. The fat guinea pig took a couple of sluggish steps toward his "bed," then collapsed in a heap in front of it and went back to sleep. I looked at him and felt pity mixed with sympathy. I was starting to understand his Roadkill nickname.

We took our lunch outside. Gil brought out the cucumber and tomato sandwiches he'd made while the rest of us were struggling with naptime. The mink had disappeared somewhere unseen. Marc headed straight for the leaf pile, with Lucy on his heels. Gil and I sat at the picnic table, stealing kisses when we thought no one was watching. We snuck many kisses that October, but it hadn't yet crossed my mind to take it any further. I was way too insecure about my budding body to share it with someone else. I was more interested in the *idea* of sex than the real thing. Penises grossed me out. But when Gil and I kissed, I felt warm and tingly all over. All I wanted during those moments was to feel his hands on my bare skin... as long as his eyes didn't follow them.

Marc soon realized what was going on in our secret corner at the picnic table, and we were indefinitely interrupted with a series of questions concerning the possible hidden meanings behind *kissing*. "Are you in love? Are you getting married? Kissing is gross. My mom says you're only allowed to kiss when you're married." After a few moments of harassment, we jumped up and chased him around the yard. Then we all collapsed in the pile of leaves together, giggling. Our laughter was followed by a brief moment of silence. The kids had taken off to investigate a moving bush. I assumed it was probably the mink. Gil and I lay there, looking at the clouds roll by through a blue sky above the fall colours.

After a couple of minutes, I turned to Gil and asked him, "Your house next weekend?" He kept his gaze fixed on the sky and didn't respond. I continued, "Gil? I could get off the train with you on Friday. That work?"

Gil continued to look intently at the sky. "Uh... I want you to. But it's not a good idea," he finally stammered.

"What? Why?" I was totally confused. Things were great between us.

Still staring at the sky, he continued, "Uh, it's nothing to do with you. Uh, I mean, with the way we are... uh... you know, I really like you. Anyway, it's my mom." Gil's cheeks were turning a light rosy colour. "We're Jewish and... uh... She wouldn't like it if she found out I was dating anyone yet... and, uh... especially not a girl who isn't Jewish."

"Huh? What? That's... that's... What?" Now my confusion was mixed with a weird feeling of shame. But, shame for what? It was the kind of feeling you get when someone has pointed out that *you*, with your born-into heritage, are just not good enough. It was an irrational sense of self-shame at the thought that Gil's mother would think that I was somehow wrong for him just because I was *me*. *Me* did not have any Jewish ingredients and there was nothing I could do about it.

Gil finally looked at me. He touched my hand with his. "Frankie. It's not how I feel, though. Adults are full of walls and stupid arguments. I just don't want to deal with my mom. She won't understand. Not yet, anyway. She's got these ideas, you know... I think she's already planning for who she wants me to marry!" He laughed painfully. Then he put his hands to his head as if feeling for the headache she'd surely cause him if she knew about us.

Lucy suddenly interrupted us as if she'd been waiting for the worst moment ever. She ran toward us from the house with a wide-eyed expression on her face. She glanced at Marc, who was still playing by the bush. She stopped as she reached the leaf pile, looked at us with a sense of urgency, and said in a careful whisper, "It's Roadk... Uh, Twinkles. I think he's had an accident."

I was the first to reach the scene. The hallway between the bathroom and kitchen was covered in little bloody footprints. I reluctantly followed the footprints into the bathroom. In spite of myself, I yelped when I saw it. It was so bad that it was almost funny. I turned to stop the kids from entering the room. Lucy was in the hallway. She looked at me and said in a low, secretive voice, "Don't worry, Frankie. I'll keep Marc outside." I looked at her, amazed at how matter-of-factly composed this four-year-old was.

I nodded and she turned, paused, and took a deep breath, as if composing herself, and returned to the backyard.

I looked back at the horror scene in the bathroom. There was blood, hair, and little mink footprints all over the bathtub. The only thing left of poor Twinkles was his nose and four paws. I heard Gil choke with surprise as he poked his head in from behind me.

He said conspiratorially, "Guess we have a murder scene to hide." He grinned and winked at me.

I elbowed him in the ribs. "Hey, stop joking! This is horrible! Look at his poor little feet and nose! This is like that shower scene from *Psycho*!" My nerves threatened to get the best of me and I put my hand over my mouth in an attempt to stop the nervous laugh that was bubbling up in me. I controlled myself and continued, "Where do you think the rest of him is?"

"Dunno. Maybe they've hidden him in the attic?" Gil gave a crooked grin. His eyes sparkled with humour. I could tell that he was trying hard to contain his laugh. "Maybe they've stashed him away for winter?"

"You think Pinky was involved too?" I said kind of pointlessly.

"Why? You planning on a trial?" Gil's smile kept growing.

We stood in the bathroom doorway, looking at each other and trying not to look at what was left of poor Twinkles. Then my nerves won the battle, and we both doubled over with laughter. What had happened to Twinkles wasn't funny in the least, but the situation was so absurdly awkward that it was inescapably comical.

I grabbed a sponge, gave Gil a mop, and we set ourselves to eliminating the evidence. The trail of blood led into the kitchen, up onto the counter, and out the open window above the sink. I had no clue what I'd tell Marc. Lucy was bound to spill the beans, likely during their next quarrel. I crossed my fingers and hoped they wouldn't quarrel before we'd finished our crime scene cleanup job.

As it happened, Lucy had spun quite a tale for Marc while she was keeping him outside. We'd barely got the door open before Marc ran up the lawn toward us, shouting, "Did ya find him? Did ya find Twinkles?" When we didn't answer, he continued, "I didn't open the doors. Stayed outside so he couldn't get outta the house, just like you said! He likes to hide under beds. Did ya look under the beds?" Lucy stood on the lawn behind Marc. She looked at me, smiled, and then gave me a hugely exaggerated wink. She would never cease to amaze me. But I'd have to come clean with their mother.

I kissed Gil goodbye at ten past three. Then I took a deep breath and mentally prepared a semi-honest explanation for Marc and Lucy's mum.

CHAPTER TWELVE
Crimson and Clover

November 1986

I got my period for the first time the day after my fourteenth birthday. It came upon me, without any warning, as I sat listening to Mrs. White convince us of the importance of Shakespeare to the history of English literature. Feeling uncommonly wet between my legs, I excused myself to go to the bathroom. Yup, there she was. "Aunt Flo" had finally come to visit and she'd laced my knickers with her red badge of courage. Luckily her courage hadn't seeped through to the outer layer, and the bloody evidence remained concealed. I lined my underwear with toilet paper and took my woes to the school nurse. She provided me with some clean knickers, a couple of pads, and an instructional pamphlet called "Menstruation and You." I asked her for a few more pads, just to get me through until I got the nerve up to discuss my need for menstrual products with my uncle. She smiled and gave me the rest of the pack.

The morning recess bell rang as I was preparing to leave the nurse's office. I stuffed the underwear, pads, and pamphlet into the big front pocket of my hoodie and made my way into the busy hallway. No one knew my secret, yet I couldn't keep the embarrassment from flushing my cheeks. I entered the bathroom a little too quickly and ran head-on into a grade three kid. She dropped what she was holding, *"Tabarnac!"* She swore in French and bent to pick her things up. I stood there watching her, surprised a bit by her swearing. She must've been no more than eight years old. She picked up a big roll of stickers, scowled at me, and handed me one as she said, *"Vive le Quebec libre!"*

I took the sticker, and she disappeared out of the bathroom. It was a white rectangular sticker. "101" was written in big blue letters across the middle of the sticker. Underneath the 101, it said, "Quebec Francais." I thought it a bit strange. As far as I knew, language had never been an issue before at Beats. English and French kids hung out together all the time. The 101 referred to a language law called "Bill 101" that, if passed, would require businesses in Quebec to remove the English language from all their signs. But it was more than that. Fights concerning language laws in Quebec always involved a separatist-fuelled emotional dimension of "let's break up with Anglophones." Coming from a mixed Anglo-Franco family, I was intimately aware of the roller-coaster ride of political tensions between the two communities. I continued on my way into the bathroom and saw that the kid had been busy plastering the walls with her stickers. I thought, "O-o-o-o-o-K," and then continued with my period business.

When I got home that evening, I called Sam to fill her in on my first visit from Auntie Flo. Sam had got her period a month ago and had told me all about what to expect. Sam called for a celebration.

"Oh my god, Frankie!" Sam had recently started to use the Lord's name in vain, which was both surprising (as it was *so* not her) and refreshing (as maybe it *was* actually her, and now she sounded less like her mother). She continued excitedly, "We have to celebrate!"

"Yes, let's do that! *Coming up this weekend, Sam and Frankie will celebrate their official introduction to womanhood. Special guests will include the number-one showgirl band 'Aunt Flo and her Red Courage.'*" I said the latter sentences in the tone of a news broadcaster—seriously serious and don't-miss-it matter-of-factly.

Sam laughed and replied eagerly, "I have *the* perfect idea! My uncle Rick is DJ-ing an event on Saturday. It's gonna be like a dance party. It's not so far from your place—in Deux-Montagnes. My parents trust him. I'm sure they'd let me go if he invited me. He lives near there too. Maybe we could even sleep over."

"Wow, that would be so cool. I've never been to a DJ-ed party. Or a dance party," I said thoughtfully. The idea made me feel curious and excited, and maybe a little scared too. What would I wear? What if I looked like a total geek? Maybe I wouldn't feel comfortable. Maybe everyone would treat me like a little kid.

"OK, I'll talk to Rick and call you back. Bye." Sam then hung up before I could reply.

I lay on my bed, looking at the ceiling, thinking about how this would be my first real party. It would be my first *grown-up* party—the perfect way to celebrate becoming a "grown-up." But something inside me kept screaming, "Danger!" I think that was Seb's voice. I laughed at my nervousness.

The phone rang a few minutes later. A super excited Sam was on the other end of the line.

"He said yes, Frankie! Woohoo!" She was ecstatic. "He told me to just tell my mom that I want to go for a sleepover at his place and not to mention the party bit cuz she won't get it. I told ya he's cool!" I could feel Sam beaming through the phone.

"Wow. OK. Uh, I'll uh... What should I tell Seb? Can I sleep over too?" I replied, slightly in shock at how fast all this was going. Sam and I hadn't seen each other face-to-face for months, and now all of a sudden we were planning on sneaking off to a highly off-limits grown-up party. I was both extremely thrilled and skin-tingling terrified.

"Totally! He said I could bring a friend, so yeah!" Sam was so happy. There wasn't a spot of doubt in her voice.

"But, Sam, what if your mum finds out? I mean, she'll never even let us talk on the phone again if she finds out," I said, genuinely concerned.

"No way. She won't find out. I've gone for sleepovers at Rick's before. He said he wouldn't tell. He thinks she's too strict with me. Our alibi's bombproof. She'll never find out." Sam sounded ultra-confident. Then the volume in her voice dropped a notch. "And I'm so done with her stupid rules. She won't let me do anything. She hates my friends. She needs to know everything about my life. Even when I'm honest, she doesn't believe me. And I'm almost always honest. I can't stand my mom." Sam sounded frustrated. "She's such a control freak. I think I'm beginning to hate her." She almost whispered those last few words. She paused for a moment, then her voice changed again and she was back to her happy-go-lucky self. "We're gonna have such a blast, Frankie! I can't wait!"

❡

Just as I hung up with Sam, Seb knocked on my door. After receiving my permission, he opened the door wide and leaned against the doorframe. He looked at me with that odd expression he has when he's amused and curious and frustrated all at the same time.

"Frankie, I had an interesting visit from Lynn Langley after supper. Do you... Do you know anything more about why Marc's hamst... uh... guinea pig is missing?" Seb paused, then continued, "Because she seems to think you lied to her about it running away."

I had chickened out when trying to tell Lynn the truth about why Twinkles was missing. As I was trying to communicate my semi-truth concoction to Lynn, Lucy had helpfully interrupted with the lie we had told to Marc, and, well, Lucy's story had stuck... until now, anyway.

I looked at Seb with big innocent eyes and began to speak. "What? I'm sure he's arou—" Seb's eyes hardened immediately and I decided to change my tune. "OK, OK. The mink ate him, Seb. I tried to keep him safe. They got him in the bathtub." I looked at my toes.

Seb replied, "Uh-huh. Well, Lynn knows the truth, and she's not pleased in the least. Apparently, Lucy was quite graphic when she finally let it all fly. Lynn wants us to get rid of the mink. I agreed that would be a good idea. We can't risk them slaughtering anyone else's pets."

I looked at Seb incredulously. "What? No way. We can't get rid of them, Seb. They're *our* pets! What about Pinky? No way she was part of it. Please, Seb!"

"Well, I was thinking about Pinky, and I'm willing to give her another chance. But we have to keep it between us, OK?" I nodded, relieved, and he continued, "As for the others, we can boat them over to the little vacant island a short ways down the river. They've proved well enough that they're ready to fend for themselves." I looked at him concerned and he read my mind. "We can make them a den with rocks and hay. They'll be fine for the winter. Mink are survivors."

I asked, "Can we wait until Saturday? I just want some time to say bye and prepare them, you know?"

Seb looked at me and smiled. "Sure, Saturday it is." He turned to leave. I sensed he felt bad about having to get rid of the mink.

I grabbed the opportunity to ask him about the weekend. "Hey, Seb?" He turned back toward me, waiting for my question. "Can I go for a sleepover with Sam at her uncle's place on Saturday? He lives in Deux-Montagnes."

"Sounds OK to me. I'll need his phone number." He smiled again and left my room.

9

I arrived at school on Tuesday morning, my head filled with excitement for the upcoming weekend. Gil met me in the hallway and, noticing my super happy demeanour, asked me what was up. I couldn't explain it to him. What was I supposed to say? How do you talk about period celebrations with your boyfriend? I decided to let him in on half the truth and told him I'd be spending time with Sam this weekend after not seeing her for seemingly endless months.

Band was our first class of the morning. We were early, and the door was locked, so we sat down on the floor in the hallway outside the classroom. The old pool club gang were the next early birds to arrive. They all had Bill 101 stickers plastered to their chests. Except the slogan "Quebec Francais" had been edited on each of them; the word *Français* was crossed out with a marker. Matt's now said, "Quebec Trinidadien." Raph's said, "Quebec Italien." Amir's said, "Quebec Éthiopien." And, in the spirit of unification, Dave's said, "Quebec multilingue et multiculturel, tabarnac!" All four boys had ear-to-ear grins on their faces, proud of their politically expressive creativity.

"Holy shit! Aren't you worried you're gonna make some enemies with those stickers? Take 'em off!" I said with amusement and concern battling it out in my head.

Dave replied first. "No way, man, I've had it with being treated like the bad guy just cuz I'm not French. Screw them."

Raph chirped in next. "What d'ya think their intentions are, wearing these stickers? It's not to make friends, that's for sure."

Amir was next. "Totally. I mean, maybe we're going just *a tad* overboard." He laughed, and then continued, "But seriously? What are they wearing these stickers for? It's such a joke. I've had it with being targeted because I speak English and they have a crappy history with the Brits. Geez, I wasn't even born here. Any of you even have British ancestors?"

We all looked at each other, shaking are heads for "nope."

Then Matt stood up straight, put his hand to his heart, and exclaimed passionately, *"Vive le Quebec multilingues! Vive la liberté multiculturelles!"*

Band was a mixed class, consisting of kids from both the French and English sides of Beats. More and more students were gathering in the hall. One of the kids from the French side who was wearing a Bill 101 sticker noticed the edited stickers and stopped in front of us. He looked thoroughly hurt and angry. I thought, *Oh shit, here we go.* Trying to find his words, he looked at the four boys and finally spat out, "Do you think this is a joke?"

Ms. Bean abruptly appeared as if summoned by the gods of fight-prevention. She opened the door and we all piled into the classroom as quickly as possible, trying to avoid our thoughts surrounding the whole sticker business. When everyone was seated, she looked us over. Then she said, "OK then, I want everyone wearing 101 stickers to take them off. The garbage is over there." She pointed at the corner beside the door. "We will play music in this room, not politics."

Thank goodness, I thought. We got on with our practice session for our upcoming concert. It was less than two weeks away. There may have currently been political tensions outside the classroom, but we remained an excellent team within the classroom. We performed "A Hazy Shade of Winter" like perfectly fitting parts of a beautifully diverse puzzle.

After class, my mind drifted back to my weekend anticipations with Sam.

9

Friday arrived with a bang as a fall thunder storm rolled through the sky above our house and lit the heavens with an animated display of vibrant power. As I lay in bed, I felt each jolt of lightning rumble through my veins. Heavy raindrops hammered against my window as if trying to summon something within me. Mother Nature had awoken me with her *Percussions of Life* orchestra. The energy that radiates from thunderstorms always makes me feel ultra-alive, as if I can do anything and be anything I want to be in that moment. I woke up excited, feeling like a Friday superhero. Today was going to be an excellent day.

The storm continued to roll in and out of the sky throughout the day, interspersed with brief periods of blue breaks in the clouds. The energy in our class was high and positive. Everyone seemed to be affected by the storm. It absolutely poured during our lunch hour. Gil and I made a mad dash for the Milton Street Dépanneur and brought back an order of soggy fries for ourselves as well as one for Matt and Dave. They weren't as keen to get wet as we were. We were absolutely drenched when we got back to school.

Gil looked me over in the doorway, laughed, and commented, "Hey, maybe Baldi won't allow us in drama class this afternoon 'cause we're too wet. We wouldn't have to suffer through his theories on stage prop management. I'd way rather spend that period with you in detention." He shot me a vivacious smile.

I laughed, grabbed his hand, and pulled him back outside. "For that, we're going to have to have a little more fun in the rain!" And we chased each other through the puddles in the courtyard to the side door, re-entered the school, then ran up the stairs to the 4½ floor landing, where we shared our soggy bag of fries. Getting soaked with a lover in this type of storm was somehow exuberantly romantic, even when it was a chilly seven degrees outside.

After school, Gil and I said goodbye to each other just before we reached his train stop. We wouldn't see each other again until Monday. Not comfortable kissing in public, we looked at each other and then squeezed our hands together in a silent *I'll be thinking of you* gesture. Gil got off the train, turned back, looked at me through the window, and waved another goodbye. I was so thoroughly in love at that moment that I thought my heart might just burst with all the joy thumping through it.

❦

Sam came over before the party on Saturday. As far as her mother knew, she was taking the train to Deux-Montagnes, where she would go directly to her uncle's place. What her mother hadn't considered was that I lived on the same train route, just a couple of stops before Sam's intended destination. She arrived at my place shortly after Seb and I had returned from releasing Stinky, Minky, and Flinky into their new pet-less world farther downstream.

As planned, Seb and I had made the mink a little den with rocks and insulated it with hay. They weren't too sure about the whole adventure at first. Although Flinky had jumped overboard and swum for the shore as soon as we'd cleared the strong current, we'd had a difficult time luring Stinky and Minky off the boat. We had to bait them with fresh fish just to get them onto the beach. To lure them into exploring their new den, I tied their well-loved Abyssinian prince teddy to some fishing string and played with them until they chased it right into the den. Then I let the string go, whispered my goodbyes, and we left them playing in the den.

Sam and I spent the latter part of the afternoon listening to music as we prepared ourselves for the big event that evening. Sam had brought over her new Joan Jett and the Blackhearts album. She popped it into the tape player as we sorted through all the other stuff she had arrived with: hair products, makeup, jewellery, and fashion magazines. We spread everything out on my bed and got to work. The magazines were a treasury of all sorts of different hip hairstyles and makeup combinations. We tried a number of eye-makeup colour combinations, laughing hysterically at the results of our attempts, and couldn't come up with anything that we would feel remotely comfortable displaying to the outside world. Finally, we decided on some minimally risqué pink lip-gloss and blue mascara.

Clothes were a whole different matter. We didn't own anything risqué, so didn't have much to debate. We both wore jeans secured tightly high on our waist with belts. Sam wore a pink, baggy, light-cotton, buttoned-up blouse tucked into her jeans and I wore a similar light green blouse. We also kept our jewellery simple. Sam wore small gold hoops in her ears and I wore the silver unicorn earrings that my dad had given me shortly before he died. Then we put on the rainbow-coloured bead bracelets that we'd made for each other way back, when we were in the pool room once with nothing better to do.

Finally, we teased our bangs a bit, hair-sprayed them in place, and then headed downstairs. Seb turned and looked at us as we entered the kitchen.

"Hey, look at you two! You look fresh and ready for a night on the town!" Seb laughed. I glanced at Sam and saw her blush a little. Seb was completely oblivious to how right he actually was.

I tried to smile honestly and replied, "Yup, catching the six-fifty train. Gotta run!" Then Sam and I headed out the front door to freedom.

❡

Rick's place was quite small. He had a one-bedroom apartment in the basement of a suburban house near the Deux-Montagnes train station. It had a combined kitchen and living room. The front door opened into his kitchen area. We entered and Rick greeted us with an enthusiastic "Hello!" and introduced himself to me. Closing the door behind us, I noticed another man and three older teenagers sitting on leather couches in the living room to our left. Rick introduced us to his friend Christien. Both Rick and Christien looked to be in their late twenties. Christien was Rick's co-DJ. In their physical appearances they were opposites. Rick was tall, slim, had a tanned complexion and bleached blond hair. Christien was short, muscular, with pale skin and black hair. The other three were named Luc, Dan, and Cécile. I recognized Luc and Dan from school. They were English side, grade elevens. Dan's sister was in my grade. Everyone sitting in the living room had a cigarette in one hand and a glass in the other. Ozzy was playing on the stereo.

Christien was sitting on a chair next to Cécile with what looked to me like an electronic pen in his hand. She was sitting on the couch with her arm extended and he seemed to be giving her a tattoo. She saw me staring and informed us with a smile that she was his first victim. Christien was training to be a tattoo artist.

I felt a mix of discomfort and curiosity and I glanced at Sam. She shook her shoulders and gave me a little smile, as if to say, "Well, we're here, might as well say hi." We hung our coats up beside the door and I followed Sam over to an empty love seat. Rick said he only had Sprite and orange juice and asked us which one we'd like or whether we'd like them mixed half and half. We both chose the mixed Sprite-orange option. Then he said he had some things to take care of before the dance party started and he left us with Christien and the others.

Sam and I sat on the love seat, side by side, awkwardly in silence, listening to the others chatter away. The conversation sounded typically Quebecois as it was a good mix of English and French. Although they were all speaking to each other, Christien spoke almost entirely in French, Dan spoke English, and the other two switched back and forth between the languages depending on what they were talking about and who they were talking to. Everyone understood each other, and no one cared which language the other chose to respond with.

The conversation went something like this.

Luc said, "Hey, did ya catch Ozzy at the Forum last week? They were so fuckin' amazing, man. *On a eu accès au* mosh pit. It was wicked!"

Christien replied, *"Ouais, c'était cool. Malheureusement, Metallica a dû se retirer..."*

Then Dan added, "Yeah, so crazy what happened to Cliff Burton. That was nuts, man." Dan was referring to the recent death of Metallica's bass guitarist. I'd heard Seb and Pete discussing it. Apparently Metallica had been touring with Ozzy when there'd been some kind of terrible bus crash.

Cécile shook her head in disappointment at her peers and added her two cents. "Whatever, metal sucks. *Ils crient, ils chantent pas.* I can never understand what the hell they're saying. And why does everyone jump around like lunatics at the concerts? *Aw, des* head bangers, *vous êtes fou!* Head bangers make no fuckin' sense, man."

The others laughed at her straightforward sincerity. Christien had just finished her tattoo. He looked at her with a flirting smile and asked, "Schnapps?" She nodded, and he got up to mix some more drinks. He brought back a tray with four shot glasses and two small juice glasses. Each glass had been filled with a substance that smelled strongly of peaches. Christien gave each of the older teens a shot glass. Then he handed Sam and me the juice glasses. We both looked down at the liquid inside them, with suspicious curiosity.

Christien noticed our hesitation and said, *"Ne t'en fais pas. J' suis gentil. Les vôtr' sont mélangés avec du Sprite."* Don't worry. I'm gentle. Yours are mixed with Sprite. He grinned mischievously at us and then added, *"T' es si jolie. J' voudrais pas détruire ton innocence."* You are so pretty. I wouldn't want to destroy your innocence. He let his gaze rest on me for a couple of seconds. I noticed how good-looking he was. I felt both flattered and embarrassed. He then asked us if we'd like a free little something tattooed on our wrist or ankle. After confirming that it would be very small, we looked at each other, feeling a mutual thrill of naughty conspiracy, and nodded yes. We agreed on identical butterflies.

That tiny tattoo hurt like hell. To get through it, I drank the drink he had brought us and then another, which Christien claimed would take care of the pain.

When he was finished with our butterflies, he turned and addressed the others. *"Alors, qui a un bon* drinking game?" So, who has a good drinking game?

Cécile downed another shot, then said, "I'm out. I gotta go get ready for the party. Ciao." She got up, put her sweater and shoes on, and left without saying another word.

Dan said, "I got one." He took a quarter out of his pants pocket and proceeded to tell us novices how to play. While Dan spoke, Christien put a cup on the floor, a few feet from where we were sitting. "So it's pretty simple. You get the quarter in the cup and you can tell someone to drink. Get it?" We nodded in silence.

I thought to myself, *Wow, this is it, my first time playing a drinking game.* I was curious, excited, a little scared, and another feeling that I couldn't quite make out.

Sam said, "Can I start?"

Christien looked at Dan and Luc and laughed. While motioning to Sam, he said, *"Ouais, elle a l'esprit d'équipe que j'aime!"* Yeah, she's got the team spirit I like!

Dan threw the quarter over to Sam. She aimed at the cup, threw it, and missed. Dan said, "Ooops, ya miss, ya drink! Did I forget to explain that part?" He smiled at her expectantly.

Sam took a sip and immediately started choking as her taste buds rebelled. "Oh my god! This is too strong!"

The boys started laughing. Christien switched to English and said with a very strong accent, "OK, I make you deal. I put more Sprite wit de schnapps and you drink all glass when you miss de cup." We looked at him incredulously, so he continued, "No, no, mostly Sprite, OK? Jus teaspoon schnapps. Promise. Dis jus fun." He flashed us a James Bond *you can trust me* grin.

I looked at Sam and shrugged. Seemed OK to me. A teaspoon wasn't much. She agreed and Christien took our glasses back to the kitchen and changed the measurements.

❦

Half an hour later, Sam and I were giggling like nine-year-olds and had lost all sense of how much we drank and what we were drinking. Our aim at the quarters cup kept getting worse and Christien just kept filling our glasses. Then the dares started. Christien dared us to drink a shot of pure schnapps. If we drank the whole thing, then he'd dedicate a song to us at the dance party. At the time, that deal sounded like a no-brainer. Well, of course we'd at least try, we told him through teary-eyed giggles.

After the second straight shot, I started to feel a bit strange. My head was full of fuzz and my eyes were playing tricks on me. I got up to go to the bathroom and discovered that my legs were no longer synchronizing with my brain. I was wobbly and had to steady myself on various pieces of furniture until I finally made it into the bathroom. I closed the door after me and held on to the sink. I immediately felt seasick as my stomach started to give in to my dizzied vision. The room was rolling around me, like ocean waves, and I couldn't stop it. I closed my eyes, but then the waves just got bigger and stormier. Holding on to the sink, I lowered myself to the floor. Then crawled closer to the toilet, pushed up the lid, and lost my supper.

Throwing up made me feel only slightly better. I was no longer nauseous, but I was still fuzzy and unbalanced. And I had also become extremely exhausted. All I wanted was to lie down. I opened the door and found myself in a bedroom. Initially confused, I shook my head and then realized that there were two doors into the bathroom. I closed the bedroom door again and opened the other door. I fumbled my way back into the living-room, tried to lean on the back of the couch, but instead fell over it and slid sideways down onto its front cushions and then continued onto the floor. I laughed at myself along with everyone else, then I sat up on the floor and said to Sam, who was now lying on the love seat as if she'd melted into it, "I can-t-evn walk. Gotta go t' bed. Where we sleepin'?"

Sam looked at me with hazy eyes and replied, "Think on'a floor 'ere."

I looked around at the others in the room. "Ah. No. T' many peopl'."

Then Christien entered the conversation. "You can sleep on Rick's bed. He'll be home late." In my confused state, I wasn't sure if he'd said that in English or French. I just nodded, pulled myself to my feet, and wobbled through the bedroom door that Christien was now holding open for me. I let myself fall down onto the bed. At that moment in time, I thought that it was the most comfortable bed that I had ever lain upon. I went to sleep instantly.

9

I woke up to someone taking my pants off. Still extremely fuzzy in my brain, I had trouble comprehending what was going on. I was lying on my stomach and my pants were around my knees. I tried to pull them up again, thinking, in my irrational state, that they had somehow fallen down. Then I felt hands on my legs. I turned my head and tried to roll over, but I was so tired and my body just wouldn't respond to my wishes. I saw Christien kneeling over me. He was the one pulling at my pants. I asked him what he was doing.

Christien looked at me with that signature James Bond grin of his and said in English, "You look not comfortable. I jus undress you. Help you be comfortable. Is OK."

I responded, "No. Nope. I'm 'kay. Comf'terbl'." Naively, and in my inebriated state, I still thought his intentions were good.

But he didn't stop.

He pulled my pants completely off. I said, "Stop. What'r doin'? Stop it. Hey. I don' need help." I was getting scared, but I was also confused. My brain was having trouble connecting the dots and my muscles were like jelly. I tried to roll over onto my back, but he was kneeling on my legs and I couldn't move below my waist. Now that I was slightly more conscious, I could feel that he didn't have his pants on either.

He forced my arms up and pushed my blouse up over my head. For a few moments, my arms and head were pinned inside my blouse above my head. I couldn't breathe properly and I made a more assertive attempt to roll over. Panic started to well up deep inside my gut. This was all wrong. I thought, *Why is he doing this? I need to make him understand he must stop. I don't want this.*

Christien then freed my head and arms from my blouse, rendering me completely naked, and said, "Dat's it. Relax. I be gentle. You know you want dis. Tha's my little butterfly, my little angel. Relax."

This was all exceptionally strange. I pleaded in French, "*Laisse-moi. S'il te plait. Laisse-moi.*" *Leave me be. Please. Leave me be.*

I felt his hands on my bare back, moving lower and lower. Then he shoved his knee in between my legs, separating them. I felt frozen in place. I didn't know what to do or what to say. So I exclaimed, as if it would change his mind, "*J'ai un* boyfriend!" *I have a boyfriend!*

He replied, "Not such an angel, eh? A liddle dirty girl, eh? *Et bien*, my liddle dirty Engleesh girl, stay still and I be gentle, OK? Move, and not so gentle, OK?"

And then my life changed forever.

On that evening, two things were stolen from me. The first was my virginity, and the second was even more sacred. It was my love for myself.

CHAPTER THIRTEEN
Close My Eyes Forever

I lay on the bed, naked and crying, after Christien exited the bedroom through the bathroom. I heard him put his shoes on and leave the apartment. Then there was silence. The music had stopped long ago. Everyone must've left for the dance party. I managed to sit up. I paused for a moment before attempting to stand. I was still dizzy. I fumbled around, looking for my clothes on the floor. I found everything but my underwear. After I had dressed myself, I tried to wake Sam, who was sound asleep on the couch, fully clothed. She didn't budge. I put my shoes on and walked home along the train tracks in a trance.

Seb was out when I arrived home. I looked at the clock. It read 10:50 p.m. Then I remembered that he had gone for dinner with friends in Montreal. Pinky was curled up just below my pillow when I entered my room. I collapsed on my bed next to her and cried myself to sleep.

,

The next morning, waking up in my own bed, dazed with sleepiness, I initially thought the whole thing had been a horrible dream. I inhaled deeply, relieved, got up, and headed for the bathroom. Then I caught sight of reality in the mirror. Residue from my blue mascara was smeared across my cheeks, my eyes were puffy and red, and the collar on my blouse was ripped. I looked like a zombie from Michael Jackson's *Thriller* video. Then the pain hit me. My back and legs were sore. I took off my clothes, turned around, and looked in the mirror. Bruises were scattered down my body, from my shoulder blades down to the backs of my knees. I was also sore between my legs and inside. The horror of the night before shocked me for the second time. My whole body began to tremble. The room was warm, but I suddenly felt really cold. All sorts of thoughts were erupting in my head. *How had I let this happen to me? What was I thinking? Why did I drink? Where was my self-control? Why did I wear makeup? How could I betray Gil like this?* I whispered to no one in particular, "What's wrong with me?" My eyes filled up with tears. I went back to bed and didn't get up again until Sam called around midday.

I heard the phone ring, once, twice, three times, and then Seb answered it. I heard him say, "Hi, Sam... What?... No... She's supposed to be with you."

I jumped out of bed, opened my bedroom door, and yelled down to Seb, "Seb! I'm here. I'll take it in my room."

He replied, "What? Why are you here? When did you get home?" When I didn't reply, he said, "Frankie?"

I paused, trying to control the emotions that churned inside me as I listened to his concern. Then I said, "I'm talking to Sam. I'll be down soon." Then I shut my door. There was no way in hell that I was going to discuss what had happened to me with my uncle. That would be so embarrassing. I had to keep control over my emotions.

When I finished describing to Sam what had happened the night before, she replied with silence.

I said, "Hey, are you there?"

After a moment, she replied, "Uh, yeah. Uh, that's, uh, bad." Then she whispered, "I mean, I guess you no longer have to worry about your first time, eh?" Her attempt at a joke fell flat.

Sensing her unwillingness to talk, I asked, "Is Christien there at Rick's place with you?"

"Uh, yeah, he's here. Rick's sleeping. Christien's in the kitchen cooking breakfast." Then she continued in a very low voice, "He's a nice guy, Frankie. And he's, like, really popular, and he's Rick's best friend. Maybe he just likes you and misunderstood what you wanted or something. I mean, are you sure of what happened? You couldn't even stand when you went into the bedroom."

Her response stunned me. "I know I was drunk. And I wasn't really with it. And my memory's kinda fuzzy. But he... he... I couldn't move. He wouldn't let go. I remember that. I asked him to leave me alone, and he didn't."

Sam replied, "Yeah, well, listen, OK. Let's talk later. I gotta eat breakfast." I responded with silence. Christien started to sing in the background. Then Sam said, "Uh, bye." And she hung up.

❦

After my shower, I joined Seb for lunch in the kitchen. I had prepared myself for his questions. When he asked about why I had come home last night, I told him I'd been feeling sick and just wanted to be in my own bed. Then he said something I was unprepared for.

"So how'd you get home? I mean, with the trains being out of service, with that technical difficulty and all?" Seb looked at me inquisitively.

I hadn't known the trains hadn't been running. I glanced down at my sandwich. "Uh, I walked."

"You walked all the way home feeling sick?" His expression said, *Really?*

I glanced at him, then took a bite of my sandwich while I gathered my story together in my head. When I finished chewing, I replied, "Well, it was more of a headache thing. I thought the fresh air might help."

"Uh, huh... OK. Anything else you feel like sharing?" He prompted me with his eyes.

"Nope," I said definitively.

"Well, then. Can you explain to me why your jacket smells like alcohol mixed with something even more sour? And, while you're at it, what's the bandage on your arm covering? Are you hurt?" This time he looked directly into my eyes, as if he were trying to reach inside my brain for the correct answer.

"What? Uh... What?" I instinctively put my hand over the bandage on my arm and wracked my mind for how my jacket could possibly contain evidence of the night before. Then I remembered that I had spilled my guts all over the tracks halfway home. Shit. Caught. I could feel my cheeks turning colour.

I could only stare back at him. I had no more words to contribute to this conversation.

"Frankie. Please. Let's not do this. I need honesty. I'm on your side. But I need you to be honest with me. Were you drinking last night?" Seb looked at me with sincere question marks in his eyes.

"OK. Yes. I drank a bit. It was my first time. I got sick and I wanted to come home, OK?" My emotions had started to escalate. I could feel tears welling up within me again.

"OK, thank you for telling me, Frankie. We obviously need to have a talk about alcohol. Don't get all flustered. I've been a teen too, you know. I just want honesty between us. I can't help you if I don't know what's going on. I know I'm just your weird uncle, but I do care about what's going on with you. I want the best for you, Frankie. You're just such a great kid. You mean a lot to me." That was the closest Seb had ever come to telling me he loved me. My eyes filled with tears and they just started pouring out of me, down my face and off my chin. I had turned into a blubbering two-year-old.

Seb's expression switched to surprise. Then, just as fast, he softened his expression, rose from his seat at the table, then gave me the warmest hug I'd received in a very long time. I let myself sink into his arms and cried my sorrows out into his shoulder.

When my sobs had somewhat subsided, Seb let go of me and said, "Hey, Frankie, you know I'm here for you, right? If there's anything you want to talk about, I'm here for you. Was it just drinking last night? Anything else going on? Did you hurt your arm?"

At that moment, I really did want to tell him everything. But it was just too weird. What would I say? I was so ashamed. Seb was a guy. It was just too weird. Instead I said, "No. It was just drinking. I just had too much. And it was my first time trying it. Yeah, I hurt my arm, but it's fine. I'm such an idiot!" Then I actually managed a convincing laugh.

Seb laughed with me. He replied, "We've all been there."

9

A horrible dream shook me back to life on Monday morning. In my dream, I was pinned down, unable to move or even scream. Something was on top of me. It was like an all-encompassing and terrifying invisible force that had rendered every muscle in my body immobile. I woke up and opened my eyes, but the force persisted. I tried to scream again, to call for Seb, but could only manage a hoarse desperate whisper. Then suddenly the force released me. I was breathing heavily and tears began to roll down my cheeks. What if I was attacked again and this is the way I responded? What if I got so scared that I couldn't fight back, couldn't even yell? I curled up in my bed and sobbed until my alarm went off an hour later.

Monday morning continued along the horrible path it had begun on. The last place I wanted to be was anywhere near Gil. I wasn't looking forward to bumping into Luc and Dan in the hallway either. I wore my armband that morning to cover up the bandaged tattoo on my arm.

As the morning train approached Mount Royal station, I sank down in my seat to avoid being seen by Gil. I switched on my Walkman and Lita Ford's voice filled my ears. She was singing the duo "Close Your Eyes Forever" with Ozzy. The song spoke to something deep inside me. I was about to start crying again. I quickly switched off the tape. When we pulled into Central Station, I exited the station through a lesser-used back stairwell, past McDonald's, and into the Via Rail taxi terminal. Rather than take our common route to school through Place-Ville Marie and McGill metro station, I took the longer route along Rue de la Gauchetière, then up Boulevard Robert-Bourassa. I entered Beats through a side door and went right to the bathroom where I sat on the floor, doodling in my English exercise book, waiting for the bell to ring.

English was our first class of the morning. I sat in my usual spot in the middle of the aisle next to the window. To avoid eye contact with others, and in particular with Gil, I opened my exercise book immediately and continued my doodles. I'd been drawing a luck dragon, but I was having trouble keeping it gentle-looking. My current drawing looked like it wanted to eat me up and spit out my bones. I normally enjoyed English class. I loved to read and write. But on this Monday, I wasn't mentally present. I couldn't focus for the life of me. I was so worried about what I would say to Gil. I had betrayed his trust. I felt awful. My heart was in pieces.

Toward the end of the period, a note hit the side of my foot. It was one of Gil's, typically tightly folded and triangular. I waited for the teacher to turn to the chalkboard and then picked it up. It read, "Everything OK?" As I read it, I bit my lip. No, everything was far from OK. I stuffed the note into my textbook without responding.

9

The morning inched on slower than a three-toed sloth, but finally lunchtime arrived. My plan had been to hide in the bathroom again, but Gil caught me at my locker.

A note fell out of my locker as I opened it. It wasn't triangular like Gil's typical notes, but rather it was in a small, rectangular red envelope. I picked it up and opened it. There was a homemade card inside. On the outside of the card, someone had stuck a clipping from a magazine that depicted a flowering cherry tree. I opened the card. Scrawled inside was "Welcome to the de-flowered club."

I subconsciously caught my jaw as it dropped. My cheeks had instantly become as hot as Venus. This reeked of Terrible Twos crap. Dan, the older Beats kid who had been at the party on the weekend, must have known what happened between Christien and I, and he must've told his sister. Lucy was a suck up and was in most of my classes. Although she didn't spend a lot of time with Tammy and Deirdre, she enjoyed the attention of the popular kids when she could get it. As I stood there, stuck to the floor in front of my locker, my brain began to throb inside my skull as the reality of my situation sank in. By the end of the day, everyone would know about my betrayal to Gil. I had to remind myself to breathe.

Gil suddenly turned up behind me. I jumped as he touched my shoulder, and then instinctively turned to him while simultaneously shoving the little card into my back pocket. This was it; I'd have to talk to him. Gil must've noticed the anxiety tightly wound up within me, because his eyebrows furrowed into a *What is going on?* look in response to my reaction. I stood there in silence, willing myself onto another planet, and then he spoke.

"What's up, Frankie? You haven't said a word to me all morning. And now you look like you'd rather be anywhere else than standing here with me. Did I do something wrong?" I detected a mixture of concern and annoyance in his voice.

I thought a little too long about how I would respond, so he added, "And don't say 'nothing.'" Then he relaxed and smiled. "As Mr. Kabira said in chemistry today, 'There are many right answers, but *saying nothing* isn't one of them.'"

Gil was trying to lighten up the situation with some humour, but I was having trouble relating.

I finally managed a few obvious words. "Gil, we need to talk."

Gil responded, "OK. So, music room?" The concern had returned to his eyes.

❦

Gil and I sat beside each other in the empty music room. It had begun to storm again outside, just like on Friday. The light outside had dimmed to a dark angry grey and rain was hammering against the big windows. It looked more like evening outside, rather than midday on a Monday. Now and then, lightning would flash and it would be daytime again for a split second. I normally liked storms, but this one seemed fitting in a more dismal sense, as if it was reflecting the tempestuous path that my life had surely embarked upon.

I looked down at my knees and said to Gil, "We have to break up, Gil." I bit my lip to keep myself from crying.

I could feel his gaze on me, as if it was about to bore through me. He seemed to be speechless for a few moments. Then he replied, "What? What? Why?" His voice was full of confusion.

I just had to get it over with and tell him. I forced the words out. "On the weekend... You know, I went to that thing with Sam?" Gil nodded in response. "Well. I'm not a virgin anymore." Then I lost control of my tears and they began to escape down my cheeks.

"What? Huh, what? That doesn't make sense. What? You? What?" Gil was obviously trying to get his head around my deviation of character but just couldn't manage it. Then he added very bluntly, "Were you raped?"

My reaction was instinctive and strong. "No!" Then, just to drill my answer in, I added, "Rape? What? No! How could you..." I got angry for reasons I couldn't comprehend and stormed out of the room.

I ran to the bathroom and locked myself in a stall. I couldn't breathe properly. My hands were all clammy and cold, and my brain felt as if it were being squeezed with a vise grip. My thoughts were all over the place. Rape victims were... Well, they were victims of terrible acts of violence that only happened to people in movies or at least to people I didn't know. I'd never met a rape victim. As far as I knew, *they* all ended up in hospital with broken bones and bloody noses, and most of them were from horrible neighbourhoods and were in bad relationships. I wasn't hurt. Well, not really, I just had a few little bruises. And if I hadn't had so much alcohol, I would've been able to tell Christien clearly that I didn't want it. I would've been able to make him understand. He didn't understand me. If only I could've been sober enough to make him understand. It was just like Sam said; he probably didn't understand. It wasn't rape. It was something else.

Gil found me at my locker before math class that afternoon. He walked up and stood beside me, but I wouldn't look at him. So he said simply, "Frankie, if you didn't want it, it was rape. If you did want it, then look at me and tell me to go away." I didn't respond, so he continued, "You need to tell someone. The counsellor or someone." I still didn't respond, so he added, "My mom works at a women's shelter, OK. I know a lot about stuff like that. I just want to help."

Then I turned to him. My legs had started to tremble. I looked him in the eyes and said in an ashamed whisper, "Gil, you need to leave me alone."

9

Gil didn't show up for math class, and when I returned to my locker after class, the counsellor was waiting for me. She asked me to follow her to her office. My irrational anger at Gil immediately doubled. I followed Mrs. Tanner to her office.

The counselling office was set up differently from the other staff offices. It was more like a living room. There was a couch, a reclining chair, and a couple of big house plants. She also had photos of her travels on the wall. I recognized Italy, as my neighbour Ani had similar photos of the same Italian hotspots. Mrs. Tanner motioned for me to choose between the chair and the couch. I chose the chair.

When I sat down, Mrs. Tanner smiled warmly at me and said, "You can call me June."

I nodded, then waited, silently annoyed, for her to proceed.

"One of your friends came to speak with me after lunch. He was concerned about you. How are you doing, Frankie?" She sounded overly concerned as if we'd known each other since I was born. In actuality we had only just been properly introduced about a minute ago.

Fiddling with my armband, I responded with a curt, "I'm fine."

She looked at me expectantly, waiting for more.

I pulled my hands up into the sleeves of my sweater and tightened my grasp around the cuffs, while I gave her a hard look. "I don't know what Gil told you, but I'm just fine." I paused and then added, "I broke up with Gil. He's just mad at me. He doesn't understand. Can I go now?"

Mrs. Tanner nodded and smiled sympathetically. "OK, Frankie. I can't force you to talk to me. I just wanted to check in with you. I want you to know that I'm here for you. So if something is happening in your life that you would like to discuss, you can talk to me. Everything we discuss in this office is confidential. I won't tell anybody what we talk about unless you give me permission or unless I think you might harm yourself or someone else. OK?"

I stood up abruptly as I replied sarcastically, "Strange that we've never met properly before." I left her office before waiting for an answer.

It wasn't like me to be cheeky with school staff, but her fake concern for my well-being was making me nauseous. Over the last year, I'd been left to suffer alone through my bullies' bad behaviour as they'd terrorized me and isolated me. I was forced to hide during my lunch breaks and cower every time they looked my way. And when I finally started to react to them and stand up for myself, I was punished with public scolding and detentions. Where was *June* when I needed her then?

9

Sam called after supper that Monday evening. She sounded happy, almost elated, as if something really great had happened. I needed some good news so asked her what was up.

She answered before I'd had time to finish my sentence. "Christien wants to see you again!"

Her statement stunned me. Why would she say something like this? And she even sounded happy about it. I replied with a bewildered, "What?"

Sam said, "Frankie. He is so hot. And he's a DJ. He's like the most popular boyfriend a girl could have! Get with it!"

"Sam, I don't want anything to do with him. He... He... I didn't..." I was having trouble stringing my thoughts together. "I never want to see him again, Sam."

Sam paused for a moment, then said, "Nothing bad happened, Frankie. I mean, you were both drunk and things happened, you know. He likes you. He told me so. He says he's gonna visit you at school. He wants to see you again. He's super cool, Frankie. He's like Rick's best friend. Give him a chance."

Panic immediately rushed through me. The concept of Christien searching for me at school was horrifying. I whispered, "He's gonna what?" Sam didn't answer. Perhaps she didn't hear me. I couldn't think of anything else to say, so I continued in a louder voice, "I already have a boyfriend. You know that."

Sam responded offhandedly, "Oh, come on. Gil? He's just a kid. Christien is, like, in a totally different league."

Sam had never met Gil. She hadn't seen for herself how deeply we cared for each other. But I was surprised by her easy dismissal of both Gil and of my experience with Christien. Sam had changed. She was no longer the soul mate I had once thought her to be. Something between the time she left Beats and now had changed her heart. At this point in time, talking to Sam made me feel thoroughly alone.

Feeling sad and unsure of how to continue our conversation, I replied, "Seb's calling me, Sam. I gotta go."

The thought of Christien hanging around outside my school, waiting for me, searching for me, terrified me. On Tuesday,

I used some of my saved babysitting money to buy two more hoodies. Over the next month, I wore hoodies on weekdays, with the hood drawn up every time I stepped outside at school.

CHAPTER FOURTEEN
A Hazy Shade of Winter

Our fall concert was coming up quickly. It was scheduled for Monday, November 17. I decided to focus my attention entirely on practicing for it. I didn't want to think about the other things happening in my life. I wanted to change the tune and erase the negative notes that had forced themselves into my *Self* melody.

My emotions were chaotically offbeat, but my sax didn't have to be. In fact, I had never played my sax so passionately than I did that week. Ms. Bean allowed me to practice in the small tutoring room next to her class, so I would have complete privacy. I locked myself in that room during every recess and lunch hour throughout that week. And to avoid meeting Gil on the train, I also stayed after school for an hour each day, practicing as if my life depended on it. Then I continued practicing in the same manner in my bedroom after supper on each night and throughout the weekend before the concert. When I had mastered my soprano sax part for "A Hazy Shade of Winter," I put my old clarinet together and got to work on the sheet music for the clarinet part. Then, on my soprano sax, I played the alto sax and flute parts too. When I wasn't playing music, my emotions sabotaged my thoughts. Playing my sax kept the confusion in my life outside on the doorstep rather than inside my mind.

❡

Just in case I hadn't figured it out, a few days before the concert the Terrible Twos claimed responsibility for the "Welcome to the de-flowered club" note I had found in my locker earlier that week. Tammy and Deirdre and co. cornered me during recess on Wednesday in the first floor bathroom next to the office. I'd begun using this bathroom specifically to avoid them, as the first floor was used almost entirely by the elementary school kids. The first floor bathroom was only rarely used by high school students.

I was washing my hands when they came in behind me. If they had come in just a few moments earlier, I may have heard them and could've stayed in the stall with my feet up until the bell rang. But they caught me, out in the open, by the sinks. These girls made class time seem like a holiday compared to the breaks between classes. During breaks, the Terrible Twos roamed the hallways like overcaffeinated rednecks, as if *nerd* hunting season were in full swing throughout the entire school year.

As usual, Tammy spoke first. *"¿Qué pasó, chiquita?"* From the moment I had met her, Tammy had assumed that I was Mexican because of my slightly tanned complexion. I'd never had the guts to correct her. Her wrath just wasn't worth it. Besides, I tended to keep my ethnicity to myself. You could never tell what kind of prejudices people held within them. It was safest to just be Irish-French-agnostic-Montrealer, and most people identified me as such. Tammy was just an ignorant idiot who assumed all people with my colouring were Mexican.

Registering her voice, I initially froze for a second, then I turned off the tap and mentally prepared myself for the crap that was about to be spewed at me.

I didn't respond, so she added, "Hey, so, I hear you had some fun last weekend." She paused and grinned slyly, "Not such a good girl after all, eh? Thought you were just a poser for a while there. Ya know, just *pretending* to be a slut. Turns out yer the real deal!" Tammy looked at Deirdre when she said this and Deirdre sniggered.

I looked blankly back at them, waiting them out. Two of their following stood in support at either side of them. They resembled a posse from an old Western movie, except rather than fight with guns, they armed themselves with venomous insults.

Then Deirdre stoked the fire. She added, "God, Tammy, let's get outta here. This one smells like she's goin' off. Pew! Smell that cheese!" It was Tammy's turn to snigger.

Tammy looked at me, still sniggering, and said, "You may wanna get checked out. I hear Dan and his buddies get around. And so do their crabs."

Tammy's comment brought a roar of laughter from the three others. Then, thankfully, a teacher walked in looking for some first grade kid. The Terrible Twos fell quiet.

Wondering about the sudden silence, the teacher asked, "Everything OK in here?"

Deirdre recognized her and said, "Hi, Ms. Turner! Yeah, alls just great! We're just on our way to math class." Then Deirdre smiled extra sweetly and continued, "I wish you were still teaching us math. I loved being in your class! You were the best!"

Ms. Turner beamed, enjoying the compliment. "Oh Deirdre, you're so sweet. See you around!" She turned to leave the bathroom.

As they were speaking, I had been inching my way around the girls, closer to Ms. Turner, who was standing near the exit. As Ms. Turner left, I followed her out. I made my way quickly to the stairwell and ran up the stairs to the 4½ floor landing, where I was almost sure not to be found. I still had eight minutes before math class would start.

Tammy and Deirdre's horrible comments got me thinking. What if I *had* caught something? Or worse, what if I was pregnant? There was no way I wanted Seb to find out what had happened to me, so the school nurse was out of the question. A doctor would likely tell Seb too, so I couldn't go to the clinic. I didn't trust the school counsellor either.

As I sat alone, with my back against the wall, on the 4½ floor landing, thinking about my predicament, a spark of panic began to grow within me. My hands turned cold and clammy, and I was having trouble breathing. It felt as though my chest muscles had constricted around my lungs and there was no longer enough room for air. Then my ears started to ring and something went very wrong with my vision. My sight was narrowing into a circle, as if I were looking through one of those flutes in my dad's old pub again, but this time the circle just kept getting smaller and smaller until I could barely see any light at all. As my sight left me, I started to shake and I became physically disoriented. I thought, *Oh my god, is this it? Am I dying? Is this the day I die? What's wrong with me?* I tried to say something, to call for help, but all that I could produce was a hoarse, terrified whisper. Then I got really dizzy and could no longer remain sitting. The floor seemed to be magnetically pulling my upper body down on top of it.

I lay on the floor, curled myself up in a ball with my eyes closed, and I started to cry.

After a few minutes, I regained my senses. My vision cleared; my hearing returned to normal. I was no longer cold and clammy, nor was I dizzy. I was just a bit shaky and had been left with a killer headache. I sat up carefully and looked at my watch. The whole episode had lasted only ten minutes, but it had made me late for math class. My eyes felt damp and itchy. They were likely red and puffy. The last place I wanted to be was in class with Tammy and Deirdre.

On unsteady legs, I made my way down to the nurse's office and told her I had a bad headache. She allowed me to lie down and I went right to sleep.

I woke to find myself alone in the nurse's office. I looked at the clock. Math class was long over and it was already halfway through lunch hour. My headache had subsided and I was excruciatingly hungry. Tammy and co. would likely eat lunch at the food court in McGill metro station, as they normally did on cold days, so I could probably make it to my locker and then to the music tutoring room without bumping into them. As I got up to leave, I noticed some piles of pamphlets concerning sex education on the nurse's desk. Two of them, in particular, caught my attention. Written in bold capital letters across the first one was **CONTRACEPTION** and the other one said **All You Need To Know About SEXUALLY TRANSMITTED DISEASES**. I grabbed one of each, stuffed them up the sleeve of my sweater, and left the nurse's office unnoticed.

9

That Wednesday, after school, I stood in front of Ville Marie Pharmacy in Central Station, willing myself to enter. My feet were glued to the floor. The only part of me that wanted to continue with the task at hand was my common sense. My common sense could've done with a little more grit, because my feet seemed to be winning this battle. The pamphlet on contraception had noted that there was no need for a doctor's visit to get a pregnancy test, because you could get that done at any pharmacy for five dollars. And, luckily, thanks to Seb, five dollars just happened to be the amount I kept in my school bag at all times for emergencies.

After a few moments of standing there in the busy train station in front of the pharmacy, still as a gopher on its two hind legs, with people shuffling past me in all directions, I finally convinced the rest of my body to move on with my intentions. I entered the pharmacy, and walked down the aisle to the back of the shop where the pharmacist and his assistants worked. There was one person ahead of me in line and I waited nervously behind him, using all my willpower to keep my legs from making a run for it. Then it was my turn.

The pharmacist's assistant who called for me to be "next" was middle-aged with permed blonde hair. She did everything quickly and seemed impatient with how slowly her day was going. I looked at her and tried to speak, but my words got caught in my throat. That had been happening a lot lately. I looked around to be sure no one would hear me, and I tried again.

I whispered awkwardly, "Uh, Hi. Uh… do you do pregnancy tests?" As the last two words left my mouth, I blushed profusely.

She looked at me impatiently. She didn't have time for kids who mumbled. She replied, "*Quoi?* What? *Répéter.* Speak up, kid. I don't have all day."

I glanced around nervously again. Other than the pharmacist, we were still alone. I said a little more loudly, "Do you do pregnancy tests?"

From the shocked expression on her face, I knew she had understood me this time. I was unsure whether there was concern mixed in with her shock. I suspected it was more likely the kind of shock someone displayed when they were sure to tell their family and friends all about the incident as soon as they sat down for supper that evening.

After a couple of excruciatingly quiet seconds, the pharmacist's assistant replied, "For you?" I bit my lip and nodded. My cheeks felt as hot as bubbling lava. She continued, "Uh, well, yes, we do provide that service." She passed me a small lidded plastic container. She said, "You'll need to pee in this container three weeks after the day of possible conception. Then bring the container in to us that same day, and we'll test it for you. Got that?" I nodded, unable to speak again. I paid her, then took the container and put it in my bag.

As I was turning to leave, she stopped me and said, "Hey, kid, if you need to go to a clinic, the NDG Community Clinic is a good one. It's drop-in, so no need for an appointment. You can just go after school sometime. And they don't need to speak with your parents. Unless, of course, you need any medical procedures beyond blood and fluid tests." Her tone had changed from impatience to concerned empathy. She wrote the name, metro station, and address of the clinic on a piece of paper and handed it to me.

In that instant, I felt cared for. I took the piece of paper and responded with a sincere "Thanks." Then I left the pharmacy and caught my train home.

That evening I removed the bandage from my arm and sat on my bed staring at the little black butterfly that would forever mark that day. His mark. Tears filled my eyes yet again. Pinky climbed my bedpost, then crawled up my sweater and sniffed my face. She licked what was likely spaghetti sauce off my chin, then descended into my lap and curled up. If she had been a cat, she would've been purring.

9

The rest of the week inched by with a painful slowness. The Terrible Twos kept trying to get a rise out of me and I kept trying to avoid them. Gil left me notes in my locker and kept trying to corner me, and I managed to avoid him too. Like a gecko on a stone wall, I quickly learned to master my invisibility cloak. All I wanted that week was to become invisible. I didn't want to have to deal with anything, especially not the type of crap that Tammy and Deidre thrived on.

As for Gil... I didn't deserve Gil. I wished he'd just leave me be. Why did he keep bothering with me? I was nothing. I was just some stupid girl who'd fallen into a typically obvious trap of my own making. If I hadn't been so stupid, if I hadn't worn makeup, if I hadn't said yes to alcohol, if I hadn't gone to sleep on some stranger's bed, if I hadn't been so naive as to think I was old enough to go to a dance party, if, if, if, if. I could reduce it all down to one common denominator: my own poor judgment. *I* put myself in that situation. *I* was responsible. Now I'd have to live with the consequences.

That's what I thought at the time anyway. And that's why I let go of Gil. Although our friendship was short, he had been a true friend. He was there for me, but I could no longer be there for him.

Thankfully, Saturday arrived as usual. Living on an isolated island in the boondocks had its advantages. There was no way I'd run into anyone from school. People only came to Ile des Voyageurs if they intended to visit someone. No one ever wandered onto the island just because. It was my safe place. It was my little weekly vacation from the hard world of peer scrutiny. And this week, I needed that vacation more than ever.

Sam called again on Sunday. Her call interrupted my attempt at playing the flute part of "A Hazy Shade of Winter" on my sax. Seb knocked on my bedroom door, poked his head in, and let me know that she was on the phone. I honestly wasn't sure whether I wanted to talk to her, but I put my sax down on my bed anyway and picked up the receiver.

I paused for a moment before saying tentatively, "Hey, Sam, what's up?"

Now it was her turn to pause, then she replied, "Uh, nothing, well, not much. Uh… I uh… I think you're right about Christien, Frankie." She paused again, then continued, "Yeah, uh, I was at Rick's place again yesterday. He, uh, tried something. You know that girl who was there last weekend? Cécile? Well, she kind of saved me. She walked in and just started screaming at him. I think she's like his girlfriend or something. Anyway. He's a creep. And, Frankie? I'm really sorry. I didn't want to believe you. I was such a jerk."

Emotion flooded into my every pore and tears filled my eyes. Hearing Sam tell me that she believed me and supported me made me feel instantly *not alone* anymore. I had been so alone in my experience over the last few days. Sam had turned her back on me and I'd had no one to talk to. She was the best friend I'd ever had. Her lack of support had hurt me deeply. The return of her support filled me with hope.

I reined in my emotions and replied, "Thanks, Sam. He *is* a creep. Did he hurt you?"

She answered me in a slightly shaky voice, "No. Well, not really. I was really scared, though. But he didn't, you know, put it in me. He tried, but then Cécile walked in." Then Sam laughed. "She was like a she-devil hurricane! You should've seen her, Frankie. She grabbed him and pulled him off me and just started hitting him and hitting him and screaming at him in French until he left the apartment. Then she sat on the couch for a few minutes, just like catching her breath or something, and then she left too."

I laughed, in relief at Sam's escape and in surprise at Cécile's intense reaction. "Wow! That's nuts. So where was Rick?"

Sam replied, "DJ-ing. Uh, and I didn't tell him. I just won't go there anymore. If I tell him, he'll tell my mom for sure. If she knows... Geez, who knows what she'll do. But it'll likely ruin my life. And she would get so angry at Rick. It would be horrible."

I thought about Sam's reply for a moment. I didn't really want to tell anyone else either. The whole thing was just too embarrassing and painful. I still blamed myself for letting it happen. Christian had been a creep, but I'd been an idiot. I just wanted it all to go away. I wanted not to have to think about it anymore. I'd already lost Gil because of it. And the Terrible Twos would likely never let me live it down. I'd already be referred to as "the slut" at school forevermore. I didn't want it to affect other parts of my life. If Seb knew, then I'd also have to deal with it at home. Who knew how he'd react? And he'd probably tell Pete too. He told Pete everything.

I said, "Yeah. Maybe... let's just keep it between us?"

Sam replied, "Yeah, just me and you. Thanks, Frankie."

My emotions rumbled around inside me again. I said, "Uh, Sam?"

She said, "Yeah, Frankie?"

I stuttered my reply, "I—I have to... uh... I have to get a pregnancy test. The—the... uh, pharmacist told me to come back in two weeks. It's kinda weird going there, you know. Can you come with me?"

Sam answered quickly, "Yes, for sure, Frankie. I'll think of an excuse for my mom. I'll go with you. Maybe we should, like, wear our hoodies though. You know, my mom has friends everywhere."

9

Monday morning felt brighter. The sun was shining, I was wide-awake, and there was a happy spark inside me that made me feel less destructible. Sam was back on my side and my life felt a little easier to handle. The fall concert was that evening. The beat to "A Hazy Shade of Winter" thumped in my head throughout the day. I was thoroughly ready for the concert.

The concert was scheduled for seven that evening. After school, I met Seb and Pete for supper, then returned to school for six o'clock. Seb and Pete hung out in the auditorium, chatting with teachers and parents, while I prepared myself for the concert. My first stop was the bathroom where I brushed my teeth. The last thing I needed was to be spitting pizza goo into my sax as I played. While I was there, I also got dressed. We were all to wear black bottoms and white blouses. When I was presentable, I joined the rest of the band in the music room. I carefully took my sax out of its case and cleaned the inside its trunk and mouthpiece. Then I removed a new reed from my reed box, sucked on it until it was thoroughly soaked, and fit it into the mouthpiece. When I was satisfied with the reed's position, I assembled my instrument, fitting the mouthpiece onto the trunk of my sax. Deirdre, who purposefully bumped me as she walked past on her way to the trumpet section, briefly interrupted my ritual. I summoned my tolerance and ignored her. When I'd assembled my sax, I played a few chords to test my new reed and to align my mind with my instrument. The other students chatted excitedly between themselves as they completed similar habitual tasks with their own instruments.

As I played chords, my eyes wandered inadvertently over to the strings section and met with Gil's. We both paused for a moment, looking at each other. A pang of pain pricked at my heart. Then he looked away, and the moment passed. I felt tears bubbling up on the doorstep of my mind. I shut the door on them quickly and re-focused on my music.

At six-fifty, we followed Ms. Bean to the auditorium. The grade sevens and eights opened the concert with the Beatles's "Yesterday." We were next in line, and then the high school seniors were to finish with Pink Floyd's "Shine On, You Crazy Diamond."

When the grade sevens and eights finished their bit, the curtain came down, and we took our places on stage in a semi-circle, facing the audience. From the moment the curtain rose again, the concert proceeded beautifully. Ms. Bean stood facing us. She smiled confidently and raised her baton, ready to start. Everyone sat at attention, hanging on her every move, waiting for her direction. I imagined her baton as a magic wand and her the wizard, directing life's beats. She pointed her wand at the percussion section to start, and then the magic began. All the band parts played together as if they were part of an intricate biosphere, each part relying on the other to keep the wheel of life turning. No matter what differences or disagreements students may have had between them, as we played as members of our band we became one perfectly tuned organism. After our last note, the room fell momentarily silent before erupting into applause. Seb and Pete were the first to their feet, leading a standing ovation.

Every one of us was unreservedly thrilled with our performance. I turned to Eva, who stood beside me, and we hugged. I'd seen her often hanging out with the Terrible Twos, but on that night I didn't care.

CHAPTER FIFTEEN
You Give Love a Bad Name

At times my life felt like a roller-coaster ride. If Monday ascended toward high and happy, Tuesday had more of that scary face-freeze-speed falling feel to it. The worst part was that I seemed to be blindfolded on this crazy ride. I had a hard time predicting what might befall me around the next corner. And hiding didn't always work.

My horrendous day started on the morning train. Gil must've scoured the train looking for me because I had hidden myself deliberately in the last carriage. I was sitting low in a window seat with my hoodie up when I heard him say my name. Hearing his voice, I reflexively glanced up, and there he was, standing next to my seat, squashed in between stone-faced men in suits with briefcases. I was both secretly glad and thoroughly perturbed to see him. My heart ached to have back the love we had shared not so long ago, while I was simultaneously terrified of having to enter into another conversation with him about what had torn us apart. I was also still angry with him for betraying my secret to the school counsellor. But there he stood with my name on his lips, drawing me in with those hypnotic, glacier-blue eyes of his. I looked up at him, silently wondering how to respond. My emotions flowed through me in contradicting waves. I was beginning to feel seasick.

Gil stood silently looking at me for another moment and then mouthed the words, "We have to talk." My mind panicked, and I thought: *no, no way, not happening.* But my head nodded in agreement. I felt so confused.

The train pulled into Central Station and we disembarked together. I followed Gil out with the crowd and we all moved forward like a tightly knit migrating school of herring. We were heading to the closest set of stairs that led up to the main floor in Central Station. It briefly occurred to me that I could make a run for it in the other direction, escape up another set of stairs, and Gil would likely not notice until he emerged with the crowd on the main floor. But something in me kept my feet on track, and I continued to follow behind him. We walked silently together through Place Ville Marie. Gil finally spoke when we surfaced onto McGill College Street.

Without looking at me, he said, "Hey, uh, Frankie?" I looked at him, and he kept looking ahead. Then he looked down and continued, "I get that you don't want me around, you know. I mean, I get that you're going through something. I'm sorry if I made you angry. I just told the counsellor because I wanted to help." He paused, then looked at me and said, "I think you're right, you know. I'm gonna go my own way. And, uh, if you want to talk, you know, just come get me." Gil looked away again and said, "Anyway, see you in class." Then he took off in a sprint toward school. I stopped walking and watched him disappear up the street and through the rush-hour crowd. There was a lump growing in my throat pressing on my windpipe, threatening to suffocate me. I couldn't proceed. I was about to break out in tears again. I tried hard to block them. Cold sweat tingled on the palms of my hands. My vision blurred and my ears began to ring. I reminded myself to breathe, but some remote part of my brain just wouldn't listen. I turned back toward Place Ville Marie and walked unsteadily over to the steps beside the main entrance, where I sat down, closed my eyes, and held my head in my hands.

That morning would be the first time I skipped a class without having an excuse, beyond the fact that I just didn't want to be there.

9

I arrived at school in time for the second period. To avoid having to socialize with anyone, I timed my arrival at school perfectly and walked through the classroom door with only a minute to spare. Mr. Kabira, who was teaching us chemistry that year, was busy writing on the chalkboard. Gil, Amir, Dave, Raph, and Matt were sitting in their usual spots, next to the window. Tammy and Deirdre sat beside each other, surrounded by their posse, in the back rows. I noticed Eva sitting apart from them. This was unusual. It probably meant that the Terrible Twos had chosen her as their *target of the week*. Eva and I had forged somewhat of a bond, hugging at the end of the concert the day before. I sat down next to Eva and Tammy sniggered in our direction, then whispered something to Deirdre. Eva looked down at her desk, her cheeks flushed. My temples tightened, but I ignored them and took out my books. There was something brewing and I wasn't looking forward to being confronted with it.

As Mr. Kabira was giving his lecture, a folded note hit the back of my head and fell to the floor behind my chair. Then another hit Eva's shoulder and landed on the floor beside her chair. I thought that was quite bold of Tammy, Deirdre, or whoever threw them. Mr. Kabira's great sense of humour and laid-back aura stopped at note-throwing in class. If he'd caught them, they'd have spent their lunch period in the office writing lines. I left the note on the floor until class was dismissed, then shoved it, unread, into my bag along with my books.

Continuing my quest to avoid people, I spent my recess in the shower room that led to the now securely locked pool room. Gym class followed recess, and the gymnasium was close by. My plan was to resurface just in time for class and therefore limit the risk of bumping into unwanted company. To my misfortune, I turned the corner into the hall that lead to the shower room and walked right into a confrontation between the Terrible Twos and a crying Eva. They didn't initially notice me, as they were too absorbed in their terror tactics, and I instinctively turned to leave before detection. But as I was turning, their words registered and something inside me shook with anger.

Eva was standing with her back against the wall, frozen and silent. Her face was red from crying. Tammy, Deirdre, and two other girls were standing in a semi-circle around Eva, blocking her in. Tammy had her finger on Eva's shoulder and was spitting "humorous" vileness at her while the others laughed. This tactic was common among the Terrible Twos. And the especially spicy meanness was Tammy's signature. Hurling "funny" vileness at people was Tammy in a nutshell. However, on this particular occasion she was really outdoing herself.

As Tammy's posse blocked Eva in against the wall, Tammy put her face right up to Eva's, with their noses only two inches apart, and shouted at her, "Admit it, you fuckin' lesbo, you like cheesy pussies! I can smell it on yer breath!"

Eva flinched and shook her head for no but didn't speak.

Deirdre sneered and added her own noxious two cents. "I saw you checkin' me out in the bathroom last week. Didya like what ya saw? And that hug last night? With *Trampy Frankie*? You two hooked up now? She'd like that, ya know. She's a real slut, into all kinds of kinky shit. I'm sure she'd do you too, maybe for a coupla bucks?" Deirdre laughed again and the others followed suit.

That's when I broke. I'd had it with the way these girls persistently controlled the fear in people and held our weaknesses hostage. I'd had it with having to hide from these nit-witted witches every time I walked into school. I'd had it with the fact that they kept getting away with their crap, through sucking up to teachers with their *I'm-so-sweet* act. I stood behind them in the hallway, stiff as a post. My eyes felt like daggers, my fists were clenched, and my anger had made its way up from my gut and into my throat. My lips trembled. Then I erupted.

"Get the fuck away from her!" I shouted with such fierceness that it almost felt as if the shout had come from someone else. I couldn't remember ever being so angry. I was not a natural at this kind of fierce anger.

They all turned and looked at me in shock. Then the smug and satisfied "oh, lookee what we have here" faces returned on each of them. Tammy curved her scarlet-lipsticked mouth into a sneer and began to speak. "Looks like your lesbo hero came to save you, Ev—"

That's when I let out my war cry, which sounded something like "*AHHRGGGH!*" and charged her. I wasn't going to let her turn this around. We had learned football charges in gym the week before and now I put it into practice. I rammed her with all my body weight.

And then bounced right back off and landed on the floor.

That girl was made of pure steel. Tammy's unfit clumsy appearance was evidently deceiving. She stood above me with a mix of surprise and sheer pleasure on her face.

But I refused to back off. I stood up and started yelling at her. Everything I thought about her and her gang came out. Eva took advantage of her sudden invisibility and slipped away. I kept yelling until I was interrupted by our drama teacher and ordered into the drama room.

Mr. Lopez shut the door behind us and stood facing me with a look of confused frustration. He had just returned from sabbatical and this kind of crap between students was not what he had signed up for. The last time Mr. Lopez had scolded me was when he caught me with the sexy letters and magazines the year before, just before he had gone on sabbatical. We stood alone in his classroom while he thought of how to proceed. He'd identified me as the main instigator and had let the others go on with their business. Tammy and co. were probably hunting for more innocent victims on their way to gym class. Predators. That's what they were. Predators that prayed on people's happiness. Just as vampires gain strength from drinking human blood, Tammy and Deirdre gained strength from sucking happiness out of their victim until the person shrivelled up and suffocated in their own insecurities. And yet I was the one facing the consequences, while the Terrible Twos blamelessly moseyed off to gym class, free to hunt again. I was beginning to hate authority figures. Mr. Lopez must've noticed the stony resistance in my eyes because handed me off to Principal Baldo immediately, rather than deal with me himself.

Once again, I stood in front of Mr. Baldo's desk, listening to him rant about how much of a misfit I was. Apparently I had caused him so much trouble that he had been forced to miss an important meeting in order to deal with me personally. He had also received word from my French teacher that I had missed class that morning. He demanded to know why. I told him I'd been feeling unwell, so he demanded I bring in a note from Seb the next day. I nodded. He continued his arrogant rant for another few minutes, listening to himself, like a cock crowing, then ordered me to lunch detention and sent me on my way. He hadn't bothered to ask me what had triggered my anger in the hallway. The expression of anger, apparently, was simply inexcusable.

On my way home on the train, I finally read the note Tammy had thrown at me in class. It said, "Cheesy lesbo slut!" I thought, *Wow. How creative.* I scrunched up the note and pitched it out the window. On that day, I grew a new type of armour. I called it *I don't give a fuck.*

9

On Wednesday morning, I brought in a note for my absence from French class the previous day. I'd spent all evening practicing Seb's handwriting and signature. After throwing out several attempts, I finally produced a note that I considered a good enough imitation of the real thing. I submitted my forged note to Baldi's secretary and wasn't called back to the office, so it must've been convincing enough.

English class was first on the agenda for today. I arrived just as the bell rang. With the exception of Eva, everyone was sitting in the usual spots. Eva sat strategically apart from the Terrible Twos. I sat down next to her and passed her a note, folded into a tight triangle. On it I had written, "Hey, we don't need those jerks. Want to meet for lunch?" She read it, glanced at me, smiled a little timidly, and nodded. I smiled back. Behind me, I heard a loud teeth-sucking noise. Tammy had disapproved of our smile-language.

Eva wore tight stretchy acid-washed jeans with a hole in each knee and a baggy Bon Jovi T-shirt. She had long, straight ginger hair, freckled cheeks, and golden eyes that complimented her hair and freckles. She knew a lot about music, especially hard rock, and we spent most of our lunch hour talking about what music we could suggest to Ms. Bean for our next concert. We had never talked much before, as Tammy and Deirdre kept a tight rein on their *in* crowd, and until recently Eva had been "in." I, on the other hand, had never been in. By the end of lunch hour, we'd bonded like long lost sisters. We both had something to offer that the other needed—unfettered friendship. Eva had been growing tired of the Terrible Twos for quite some time but had been afraid to break free. She considered this her chance to be done with them for good. I was more than happy to help her with this quest.

Besides several ill-intentioned pokes and prods from Tammy and Deirdre, the rest of the week was relatively painless. Everything seemed easier with an ally. As long as Eva and I stayed unified, we remained (somewhat) mentally untouchable.

9

December crept up all too quickly. It was three weeks after *the incident* in Deux-Montagnes. Sam and I had planned to meet at McGill metro station after school on Monday and walk to the pharmacy in the train station together. I hadn't let Eva in on my secret. Only Sam knew the whole truth. I didn't want anyone else to ever know. Before leaving home that morning, I peed in the little container that the pharmacist had given me and screwed the lid on extra tight. I wrapped the container first in a plastic bag, and then, to make it look less conspicuous, I put the little package into a paper lunch bag. If anyone happened to see into my bag, it would just look like my lunch.

My Monday classes seemed to inch by with a feeling of jittery foreboding. I couldn't focus, I wasn't listening, and I didn't want to be there. We had a test in English and another in chemistry. I was sure I'd failed both. Until recently, I'd been a good student. My grades had remained mostly steady, even through all the bullying and loneliness I'd suffered with because of the *sexy letters affair*. Things had changed after that weekend in Deux-Montagnes. My mind had been hijacked, my thoughts kept hostage by the emotional roller-coaster ride I was stuck on. I tried to block that weekend from my mind, but the surrounding reminders just kept hammering it in. This pregnancy test was one of those frustrating reminders.

The bell finally rang. As I left through the school's main doors, I pulled up the hood on my sweater, as I had done every day for the last three weeks. I still feared that Christien would make good on his word to Sam and search for me at school. I glanced around the courtyard anxiously, checking for him, then quickly left the school grounds and made my way down University Street toward McGill metro.

I waited for Sam for over an hour at our planned meeting spot in the metro station food court. I was on my third soda when I finally gave up and came to terms with the fact that I was going to have to deal with the pregnancy test issue alone. I felt let down by Sam. I wasn't angry, just sad and disappointed and all alone. I walked slowly, disheartened, exiting the metro station onto McGill College Street, then across Sainte-Catherine's Street, through Place Ville Marie and into the train station.

This time I didn't pause in front of the pharmacy. I walked directly to the pharmacist's counter at the back. There was no lineup. The same pharmacist's assistant who'd helped me the first time stood behind the counter. She seemed to remember me and welcomed me with a sympathetic smile. I put the paper bag on the counter and pushed it toward her. She opened it and lifted out the plastic bag containing my urine sample. She started to open the plastic bag and I reflexively scanned the area behind me for possible witnesses. The pharmacy was still quiet. The assistant took the container out of the plastic bag and was about to stick a label on it, but then something occurred to her and she paused.

The pharmacist's assistant asked me, "Did you have this in your bag all day?" I nodded. A look of concern entered her eyes. She said regretfully, "Oh my. I'm afraid that the sample is no longer good. For the results to be correct, the sample must either be fresh or kept refrigerated. I wish I could just give you another container so you could get it done with now, but the sample must also be from your first pee of the day."

I looked at her with disbelief. I couldn't speak. I had been mentally preparing myself for entering the pharmacy all day and now I was being told that I must do it all again on another day.

The assistant saw the distress in my face. Trying to help, she said, "Have you gone to the clinic yet?" I shook my head for no. She began to speak again, but I was no longer listening. I tried to smile and I said, "Thank you," then I turned and left to catch my train.

9

Sam called the following evening. Before I had finished saying hi, she frantically interrupted me with, "Frankie, I have no time. Not allowed on the phone. Check the chapel for a letter. I hate my mother. Gotta go." And she hung up.

I spent Wednesday thinking about what possible predicament Sam could have gotten herself into. I had planned to go to the clinic after school, but I'd make a quick detour to the chapel first. Seb would be working late again, so I wouldn't be missed at home before half past nine. Although he'd likely be on the eight-forty-five train. I'd need to catch the seven-forty-five. That gave me over four hours in town—more than enough time. If he called home to check on me earlier in the evening and wondered why I didn't pick up, I'd tell him I was outside playing with Pinky or something. I'd left my bedroom light on that morning so nosy neighbours would think I was home in the evening. I had covered all possible pitfalls. There was no way Seb would find out I'd stayed in town, and therefore no way I'd have to explain why either. My evasion tactics had improved tenfold over the last few weeks.

Sam had left her note under the usual cushion, on the third floor balcony in McGill's Chapel. I had originally intended to grab the note and read it on the metro en route to the clinic, but the warm, quiet, and peaceful atmosphere in the chapel made me pause and sit for a while. I didn't consider myself to be religious, but there was something very comforting about the silent ambience in the upper balcony of this chapel. I opened Sam's letter and read.

Dec. 1, 1986

Hi Frankie,

I'm sorry I didn't meet you today. I wanted to, but my mother grounded me on the weekend. I'm not even allowed to use the phone. She even picked me up after school and dropped me at home to make sure I didn't do anything else on the way. And she asked our neighbour to babysit me! The neighbour's actually sitting in our kitchen as I write this. My mom's the Evil Queen from the East. I HATE her so so SO much! I'm seriously considering running away. And my dad just does whatever she says. He's not home most of the time anyways. I don't even know why he stays with her. She's so bossy and such a control freak. My dad's like a puppet. I don't want to be her fucking puppet. I hate her!

She grounded me because I lost a bit of weight. She says I'm looking scrawny and she thinks I'm throwing up again. She doesn't believe anything I say. It's true that I lost some weight. I mean, I don't really have an appetite lately. Everything makes me feel sick. I told her that I thought I was just sick with a tummy bug or something, but she didn't believe me. It looks like I'll be stuck in my room for eternity. Whenever I leave my room, she's there. She just follows me around, watching me. And if she can't do it herself, she gets the neighbour to.

I really have to get out of here. I'm going crazy. I'm going to ask Rick if I can move in with him. Hey, then we'd almost be neighbours! But I don't think he'll let me. Besides, then I'd have to deal with that creep Christien too. I gotta figure something out.

I usually go to my mom's work with her on Tuesdays after school. I hope I can drop this in the chapel for you. I'm going to try to sneak a call to you.

Anyway, if you read this on Wednesday, then I'll be able to check for your reply, hopefully, on Friday.

How did the pregnancy test go?

Big hug,

Sam xxx

I felt for Sam. I didn't have the experience of having an overbearing parent, but it sounded horrible. I hoped she wasn't starving herself again. I folded the note back up and put it in my bag. Then I headed to the clinic.

The NDG Community Clinic was in a small redbrick building just off Sherbrooke Street. I'd decided beforehand that I would not stop in front of the building before entering; if I did I might not go in. I would walk directly from the metro station to the clinic and enter immediately. And that's what I did. I opened the heavy metal door to the building, walked up creaky wooden stairs to the first floor, and entered through the door that had a sign on it stating "NDG Community Clinic. No appointment needed. Please take a seat inside to the left."

I had been waiting for five minutes when someone came into the waiting room and greeted me with registration papers. As I read the first page, one sentence in particular stuck out as if it were a blinking neon sign warning me to run. It said, "Patient records are confidential. However, if the doctor suspects criminal activity, s/he is required to report the suspicion to the authorities and a police investigation may ensue." Upon reading this sentence my forehead tightened and my hands began to sweat. What if they were to assume I'd been raped, like Gil had? Would they call the police? I felt sick. I was alone in the waiting room. No one noticed me leave. And I never returned.

,

Sam called me again on Thursday evening, as I was writing my response to her note. She said she was calling from a pay phone. She wanted me to know that she had finally done it. She had run away and broken free. She wanted me to know that she was safe. She was staying at a friend's place out of town. Sam wouldn't tell me where, as she thought her mother might try to contact me. She didn't want me to have to lie for her. I tried to convince Sam to come to my place so we could talk it through. I thought Seb might let her stay for the weekend. But she wouldn't do it. She thought Seb would just call her mum. Sam said she never wanted to go home again. Her plan was to get a job and save up for college. How she would get into college without graduating high school was unclear, but she said she had a plan. Sam sounded overly excited, like she had it all figured out. I was so worried for her, but she kept telling me that everything was fine, even better than fine; everything was better than it had ever been. Sam didn't sound like herself. Usually she was more realistic. I couldn't convince her to tell me where she was. I heard someone interrupt her on the other end of the line, then she ended the conversation with a simple "I'll be in touch, Frankie. Gotta go!" And she hung up.

I didn't hear from Sam again for months. Her mother did call, as Sam had predicted. Seb and I promised to let her know if Sam called back. I checked the chapel for a note from Sam that Friday, just in case, but there wasn't one. I left a note there for Sam anyway, just in case. I checked once a week for a long time to see if my note had been picked up or if Sam had left one for me in return. My note was never picked up. Sam had said she was fine. She had said she was safe. I hoped that was so.

,

I arrived at school the following Monday morning to find Eva being cornered in the bathroom by Tammy. Tammy was up in Eva's face, spitting out typically nasty Tammy crap. But this time Eva fought back. Tammy didn't have her entourage of protective support around her. Eva looked at her, stone-faced, and then spat right at her nose and landed her target with perfect accuracy. Tammy stood there for a moment, stunned, with spittle dripping from her nose. It was quite comical, and despite myself, I laughed. So much anxiety had gathered up inside me over the past few weeks and I just couldn't take another moment of it. Everything suddenly felt extremely funny, especially the sight of Terrible Tammy with someone else's big gooey gob of phlegm dripping from her nose. My laughter grew and grew until I was doubled over. Tammy shouted at me. I wasn't listening. Then Eva broke out in laughter along with me. We were soon doubled over each other, laughing hysterically and completely ignoring Tammy's fuming rant. She was now screaming something about reporting us to the principal. I stopped laughing for just a moment, looked directly into her exorbitantly eye-shadowed eyes, and said, "While you're at it, please tell him I don't give a fuck!" Tammy looked at me, curled her ruby-red painted lips inward, and let out a vengeful hiss. Then she stormed out of the bathroom, leaving Eva and me alone in our side-splitting hysterics.

That evening, my second period arrived.

For the first time in a month, I slept well.

PART 4
Liminal Me

neither here nor there
betwix and between
i am somewhere
not child nor adult
i fumble toward my rebirth
tormented by society's mirth
i struggle to see
in this fucked up world of
liminality

CHAPTER SIXTEEN
Invincible

July 1987

Ani stood in front of the canvas she had been working on over the last two weeks. She had just finished the needle-felting process. Her work was now clipped to an easel and she began making some final minor adjustments. I was sitting on the antique wooden chair next to her, watching her piece of art enter its final transformation stage. It was a picture of me, from the shoulders up. I was lying on the ground in our backyard, on top of flame-coloured maple leaves, my hair spread out in a halo around my head. Ani photographed me last fall and had used the photo as a reference point. Her masterpiece had evolved from its photo stage into layer upon layer of coloured felt, which, with much nurturing, became an autonomous masterpiece.

Ani stopped trimming her canvas and stepped back from it. With a satisfied smile, she said, "Got it. That's it. *You*, in a nutshell." Then she turned to me and smiled warmly. She continued, "You're so beautiful, Frankie. And not that different from a masterpiece in the workings, you know. Creating a piece of art is like nurturing a child into adulthood. The more love you put into your child, the more beautiful the masterpiece will be. You, Frankie, are turning into a beautiful masterpiece. Just be patient. You'll get there." Ani was not only a talented artist, but she was also excellent at reading people. She must've sensed my inner struggles. I hoped she was right, that I'd eventually become something great. Because during the last year, I'd mostly felt frightened and confused, as if I was wandering around in a dark cave, searching for an exit that wasn't there.

Without Seb, Pete, and Ani's love, I would've felt completely lost. Particularly I felt lucky to have Eva by my side, fighting the same battles. She made dark caves that much more survivable.

9

Later that day, I sat just below the tracks on the ledge that was moulded into the top of one of the enormous concrete posts that held the train bridge up. The bridge had three huge iron arches that stretched above it from one end to the other. Iron beams crisscrossed from the tops of the arches down to the mainframe, linking the magnificent structure together. From a distance, at dusk, the train bridge looked like a fantastic beast, like a dragon bounding over the river with its back and tail arching in waves of playful excitement. It reminded me of Falkor, the white luck dragon. I sat on the ledge with my headphones on listening to music, with my back against an iron beam. The river rushed under the bridge, far beneath me. Earlier in the summer, Eva and I had picked this to be our regular meeting spot. It was our secret place, our "club house," where we could be alone, uninterrupted.

Eva lived in Roxboro, the next train stop over toward Montreal. The train bridge was about a half hour walk from her house. She'd only taken the train a handful of times, though, as she said her mum didn't trust any vehicle that she wasn't driving herself. Eva and I had planned to meet at two o'clock. I checked my watch. She was a few minutes late, which was typical of Eva. If I was a *five-minute early bird*, she was a *10-minute late bird*.

I ejected the U2 tape from my Walkman, popped in Pat Benatar, and pressed play. As I was fiddling with my Walkman, Pinky crawled out of my bag, up the front of my T-shirt, sniffed the air, and then made herself comfortable on my shoulder under my hair. I wasn't worried about her disappearing on me. She regularly followed me around the island. She knew her way home. I found a marker in my bag and began to doodle.

A few minutes later, I put down my marker and studied the drawing I'd just completed on my arm. My butterfly tattoo had been transformed into a magical flying luck dragon. I smiled, satisfied with my work. Much better. The dragon was the one from the dream I'd had in the music room, just before I'd fallen madly in love with Gil. Thinking of this luck dragon made me feel happy and safe, and a little sad too. If only my luck hadn't been so delicate, so volatile. If only. I put my leather armband back on, over my luck dragon doodle. It was still technically that damn butterfly tattoo. I preferred it stayed hidden. It wasn't a topic I wanted to discuss with anyone.

Eva showed up a few minutes later. She jumped down from the tracks onto the ledge, surprising me out of my musical daydream. She was dressed in jean shorts and a baggy Metallica T-shirt. Her older brother, Joe, was into heavy metal and it had been rubbing off on us both. I wore my newly purchased albeit secondhand Alice Cooper T-shirt. Clothes were way cooler when worn in. The Army Surplus and Salvation Army had become our favourite shopping spots by far. We couldn't understand why anyone would buy new—new clothes were so passé. Why look like a spoiled-brat *prep* when you could be a more worldly *rebel*? When we did buy new clothes, we had several innovative techniques that we used to make them look old. Our new T-shirts would be put through a million washes and left out in the sun for days. We'd scrub our new Levi's with sandpaper and rip holes in the knees. New sweaters would also be strategically ripped, usually around the collar. We only bought new if the old version wasn't available. Old was definitely in and the more genuine the better.

Eva plopped herself down beside me and reached out to Pinky, tickling her under the chin. She looked at me and smiled mischievously. "I got it."

I returned her sly smile. "Guess we're partying tonight."

Eva rummaged in her bag and produced a mickey of Jack Daniel's. We'd been experimenting with alcohol for the past few months—when we could get our hands it anyway. Eva's brother, Joe, was seventeen and had friends who were of age. If she played her cards right, he'd do our shopping for us. This time she'd traded gardening chores for his services. She'd been weeding and still had dirt under her fingernails.

Eva smiled excitedly. "And I can sleep over too!" I laughed and high-fived her. Seb had travelled up north to visit Pete for the weekend. Our neighbour Ani had been asked to check in on me, but she was busy with her art and could be easily manoeuvred around. I'd received permission from Seb to have Eva stay over, so there would be no trouble there. Seb and Ani thoroughly trusted me. Seb would've lost his marbles if he'd discovered Eva and I had got drunk in his house while he was away and he's trusted us. But I felt only slightly guilty for my betrayal. It was the kind of guilt that flicks on for the briefest of moments, causing you to momentarily think twice, but then switches off again just as quickly and stays off. Unless, of course, you get caught; in which case, the guilt-switch may flick back on indefinitely. But that was a risk worth taking. This was my life, not Seb's. And being the *oh, so innocent* girl hadn't paid off for me. It was time to have some *carefree* fun in my life.

I handed Eva my half of the payment for the mickey and she pushed it back at me. She smiled and responded, "No way, man. It's fine. You bought the snacks. Even Steven." I returned her smile and stuffed the money back in my pocket. We sat on the ledge under the tracks for the next couple of hours, shooting the shit. Eva's brother was dating a real drama queen. There was lots to laugh about. Every now and then a train would interrupt us. Pinky would dive back into my bag and we'd block our ears with our hands as it roared past above our heads. Then we'd continue where we left off, with only the sound of the river and birds as a backdrop, until the next train thundered on by.

9

Seb had left us a frozen lasagna for supper that evening. Which was really sweet, as cooking didn't come naturally to him and it must've taken him some effort and time to put it together. We normally had much simpler suppers, made mostly with stuff you could fry quickly in a pan without much fuss. We'd followed the instructions for re-heating it and now we sat at the table with it on plates in front of us. I studied the lasagne and gave Eva a semi-worried look. It was more like soup than lasagna. And there was a hell of a lot of green in it. Seb meant well, but... We agreed to try it together on the count of three. I stabbed a noodle with my fork and cut a piece off. As I scooped it from my plate, the sauce fell free (as soup would), leaving slimy green something stuck on the piece of pasta on my fork. I wondered where the cheese was. He must've not had any to put in. I gave Eva a crooked *here goes!* smile and bravely popped it into my mouth. She waited, with her fork loaded and ready, for my reaction.

I tried, I really did try hard, to swallow it. That green stuff had to be a mix of parsley and way too much Italian seasoning. He must've dumped the whole jar in there. My tastebuds felt as if they were going to explode with bittersweet agony. My eyes started to water and my tongue curled up in resistance. I just couldn't swallow it. I put my hand over my mouth and headed for the garbage bin. Eva watched me in joyous hilarity, unable to contain her laughter. I spat it out and said, "Holy fuck! I think he's trying to starve us!"

She laughed harder and replied, "Seb should like totally be banned from trying to cook!"

I glanced at Eva through my tears and said, "I know. This is almost worse than last time's frozen gooey brown avocado risotto." I cracked up even more, then held my stomach and took a breath, calming myself, then said through intermittent giggles, "I've gotta start doing the cooking. Poor Seb! He really tries!" Eva headed out of the kitchen, toward the living room, still cracking up, and replied, "Oh my god, I'm dying! Get the snacks!"

I brought glasses and Doritos into the living-room and sat next to Eva on the couch. The bottle of Jack was on the coffee table in front of us. Neither of us had tasted this particular liquor before. We'd mostly stuck to Baby Duck. We'd tried beer once, and thought it absolutely horrendous. White wine was OK if mixed with Sprite. The last time I'd had hard liquor like this, though, was the first time I'd drank in Deux-Montagnes. A queasy feeling struck my gut for a moment. I pushed those thoughts out of my mind. That was never going to happen again. I was alone with Eva and I was safe.

I looked at Eva and smiled. "So, what do we drink this with? I have orange juice or 7UP."

Eva studied the bottle on the table. She replied, "Dunno. Joe said apple juice. Was gonna bring some but forgot. Maybe try both?"

I retrieved the orange juice and 7UP from the fridge and set them on the table beside the Jack. I asked Eva, "OK then, you want them all mixed together? Or, like, just 7UP with it? Or just orange?"

Eva shrugged. "Uh, want to try 7UP first and then orange?"

I returned her shrug, "Sure." I opened the bottles, poured about a teaspoon of Jack in each glass, and filled them with 7UP.

Eva lifted her glass, faced me, and said, "Cheers!"

I clinked her glass and we each took the tiniest sip in the world of tiny sips. I exhaled after my sip, "Well, that was just fine. Didn't taste like hardly anything!"

Eva laughed. "Yeah, this is fine. It's actually sort of just as good as Baby Duck." We clinked our glasses together again and downed the rest of our glass. Then we sampled Jack with orange juice. We clinked our glasses and this time took a big gulp. I screwed up my face in disgust and grabbed for the Doritos. Jack and orange was absolutely horrible! Eva choked on it, ran to the sink, and spat it out. "Holy mother of god!" she sputtered. "Never again!" She started laughing. I was already doubled over in laughter on the couch. I'd have to remember that mix for my enemies.

By eight o'clock, the bottle of Jack was half empty, we'd almost finished the bottle of 7UP, and we'd run out of Doritos. Giggling like the school girls, we practiced our *completely sober* act for when Ani checked in. We were eating peanut butter to get rid of our boozy-breath (one of Joe's tips) when there was a brief knock at the door before someone entered. I grabbed the bottle of Jack and stuffed it between the couch cushions. I gave Eva a hard *this is it, act normal* look. She was trying hard not to laugh. I worried that this whole thing was about to blow up in our faces. Ani wasn't an idiot.

But it wasn't Ani.

❦

Ani's niece, Sunny, walked through the kitchen and stood before us in the entrance to the living-room. The last time I'd seen her was over a year ago at Ani's New Year's Eve party. In fact, that was the only time I'd met her. She'd had a purple mohawk. Now she wore her hair down, and it was dark brown, without the purple, but the sides of her head were still shaved. Her clothes were different too. She looked less punk, more hippie. Or maybe it was a mix of the two. She was wearing a short, well-worn Pink Floyd T-shirt and beige army pants with a leather belt. I mainly recognized her because Ani had a picture of her hanging in her entrance.

Sunny looked at us, taking in our expressions, and smiled knowingly. Sunny was sixteen and far from an angel herself. "Well, then. What have we here? Grown up, have you, Frankie? And Eva. I know your bro. Joe's cool. Can't say the same for that chic he's with, though. What a self-righteous ho...ly mirror fucker!" She laughed and Eva laughed in agreement along with her. Sunny continued, "Lucky for you, my aunt's busy with a project and asked me to keep you guys company for a bit instead." She glanced at the ruffled space between the cushions. "Any left for me? I won't tell if you don't."

Eva and I looked at each other and then back at Sunny. I stuttered, "Uh, yeah, I guess, uh, not much to mix it with, though." I dug the bottle out from between the cushions. Sunny thought for a moment, then replied, "I think my aunt has something in the fridge. I'll be back." She disappeared, then returned a few minutes later with a bottle of Coke and some homemade cookies, with compliments from Ani. Jack turned out to taste great with Coke and cookies too.

Sunny was smart, darkly philosophical, and wildly funny all at the same time. She had an incredibly contradicting personality, which made her all the more intriguing. She was the epitome of *rebel*. From where Eva and I stood, Sunny was the coolest girl ever. By the time the booze was finished, we wanted to be just like her. And the booze sure dissolved quickly. When we were on our last sips, Sunny reached into her pants pocket and pulled out a tiny baggy. She glanced at us, smiled playfully, opened the baggy, and pulled out what looked like a big dried raisin. Sunny saw the confused look on my face and said, "Oh, that's right, the goody-goody non-smoker. Well, then we'll have to break you in a bit." Her smile grew as she threw us each a cigarette. "Those ones are just for you." Then she produced another and said, "This one's for the hash." She threw it over to Eva. "I've seen you roll for Joe." She winked. "You roll a mean J."

I looked at Eva, surprised. She caught my eye, smiled a little guiltily, and explained that she'd been competing with her brother's friends at rolling the perfect joint, but she hadn't actually ever smoked one. When I didn't respond, she flushed a little and then admitted, "OK, OK. Stop looking at me. I smoked once, just a little puff, you know, to try."

Eva tore the cigarette open and emptied the tobacco onto a rolling paper. Sunny passed her the hash. Eva crumbled the piece into tiny bits onto the tobacco, then rolled a somewhat symmetrical joint, twisting the paper at the end of the joint to keep things in place. I watched intently, with naughty curiosity. We were both past the tipsy point by this time, and I was amazed that Eva could accomplish such an intricate task. Then Sunny broke the silence. "Hey, uh, seriously, I'm not wasting my stash. You guys gotta practice inhaling with those smokes first." She laughed, but I think she really meant it. Sunny put a cigarette up to her own lips and lit a match. I woke suddenly from my dazed curiosity and blurted, "Oh no, stop! Not in here! Seb will kill me!"

We walked up the path to the top of the hill in the centre of the island. There were plenty of stars but no moon. It was a dark, warm night. Perfect for the exciting naughty behaviour we had planned. A thrill passed through me. We sat on the rocks on the far side of the hill, to be as far as possible from Ani's sixth sense magical radar. If her senses picked up activity outside, she'd be on to us like a cat on a fishy smell. We wouldn't have a chance. We paused for a moment and listened.

When we were sure no one else was around, Sunny lit a match and asked, "OK, who's first?"

I held the cigarette clumsily between my fingers, like I saw done in the movies, and lifted it to my lips. Sunny tried to light it, but it wouldn't light.

Sunny looked at me, amused, and said, "Hey, are you inhaling?"

I shook my head and she gave me a *well?* look. I inhaled, sucking on the cigarette. It lit and I got a mouth full of the most disgusting taste I'd ever been subjected to. I immediately started to cough and sputter. When I finally managed to articulate my experience, I exclaimed, "Aghh! Who the hell came up with the idea to suck smoke into their lungs! That was so fucking gross!" I spat on the ground in an attempt to rid my taste buds of the recent assault upon them. Eva burst into a fit of laughter and slipped sideways off her sitting rock, then laughed even harder as she tried to right herself but lost her balance and landed on her ass at our feet.

Sunny looked down at Eva and chortled, "Holy shit, girl. I think we need to cut you off. You're already flying!" She slid down off her own rock and leaned her back against it, then lit the joint. She took a long drag, held her breath, and then blew rings as she exhaled slowly. She passed the joint to Eva. Eva took it and tried to imitate Sunny but coughed almost immediately.

Then it was my turn. I held the joint, looked at it, contemplating whether the awful taste would really be worth it. It smelled different from the cigarette, kind of skunky. I involuntarily scrunched up my nose.

Sunny said, "C'mon, man, pass it on if you don' wan' it."

I decided to give it a go, thinking to myself, *You only live once, right?*

With that first joint, my perspective on life changed in an instant. Suddenly I understood my worries to be menial. The only thing that mattered was this place, this time, these people I was sitting with, and the harmony between us. The world around me became bright and happy and peaceful. Life was grand. Life was perfect. Life was made for laughing at. No more worries. No concerns. No bullies. No rules. No social boundaries. Just happiness. Just happiness.

Sunny talked a lot when she was high. I only heard half of it. Eva and I giggled through a lot of what she was saying. We were all lying on the ground, looking up at the stars. Eva lay in the middle.

I squeezed Eva's hand and exclaimed, "I think I'm floating in space, through the galaxy, around the stars." I reached up toward the sky and pretended to pluck a star from it, and then I passed it to Eva. She pretended to take it, study it, and then she gave it a kiss and blew it off her fingertip, back up into its galaxy.

I giggled. "I think I want a star for my birthday. D'ya think that's too much to ask for?"

Eva giggled in response. "No, man, that's perfect. Ask Pete, though. He's a softy. And closer to the stars too, ya know, when he's up north. He can just, like, reach out and grab one as he's flying home." We both laughed.

Sunny was silent for a bit, thinking. Then she began philosophizing about life and what the world could be like without institutions. She speculated, "Imagine. We could build a community on 'nother planet. Ya know, start the world over. No churches. No armies. No politicians. No lawyers. Just believ'n peace. We could, like, take 'way people's war gene, ya know? Make it so they'll have, like, peaceful babies. We could call the new race the *Peacelings*." Sunny laughed, then continued, "Seriously, though, the problem with earth is its dominating race: us. We're the problem! How do we fix that? I'm so lost. I don' know how to fix it." She went silent, thinking.

Eva interrupted the silence with, "I know what to do!" We both looked at her expectantly. She paused and then said, "Shit. Lost it."

Studying the stars, I asked no one in particular, "What's the magic ingredient in this stuff? I mean, like, is there a name for it, like, besides hash n' weed?"

Eva then blurted, "That's it! Put it in the water supply!"

Sunny laughed. "Nice one, genius. How're we gonna get it into the whole world's water?"

I thought on this. "We'd have to dump it in the lakes and rivers." I paused, thinking, then continued, "Then all the fish would get high too. That might be bad."

Eva giggled. "Ha! High fish! What'd that be like? The sharks would get all hippie-like and friendly. Their reign of terror would turn into an ocean-wide peace orgy. No more discrimination 'gainst the littler guys. What a world it'd be."

Sunny interrupted, "Yeah, and the big guy sharks'd starve to death."

Eva replied, "I guess there'd be some wrinkles to work out."

I added, "I like the planet idea. We could—"

Something in the bush farther down Ani's side of the hill rustled. We all instinctively jumped to our feet and began run-wobbling down the path on the far side, away from the noise.

I whispered, "Holy fuck! What was that? Was it Ani?"

Sunny replied, "I dunno, Sherlock, I'm here with you!"

We were almost down at the street when Eva fell behind. I stopped and looked back. Eva was holding her stomach and looked really pale. She said, "Oh... I feel... I feel..." And then she bent over and threw up in the bush.

9

I was startled out of sleep early the next morning. I'd had that dream again. Where I was under attack and unable to fight or scream for help. This time, rather than being pinned down by some powerful invisible force, I was being pushed toward the edge of a cliff and I couldn't do anything about it. I was frozen with fear. I told myself to fight, but my muscles were like jelly, I had no strength. I tried to shout for help but could only manage a panicked, wretched whisper. I cried and begged, but the force just kept pushing me toward the edge. I had woken up just as I'd slipped off the cliff. I was sweating profusely, fully clothed, and on the couch. Safe at home. Not falling off a cliff. I breathed out slowly and relaxed back into the soft couch cushions. Eva was curled up on the love seat with her head resting on its cushioned arm. She was fast asleep.

The place was a mess. Our bottles and glasses were spread across the coffee table, there were Dorito and cookie crumbs all over the place, and the dirty dishes in the kitchen smelled bad. I got up and went to the bathroom. As I was there, I realised that it must not be the dishes that smelled bad, as the smell had followed me in. I sniffed my T-shirt and recoiled. I thought aloud, "Yikes! That's me. I smell like a friggin' skunk's rear!" Then it occurred to me that other things might smell too, like the couch, for example. A wave of panic started in my forehead and tingled its way down my arms toward my fingertips. I ran back into the living room and sniffed the couch. Yup. It smelled. Shit.

I shook Eva awake, asserting urgently, "Get up, get up, we have to clean the couches! Everything smells! Seb'll be home later. He'll kill me!"

Eva looked at me through squinted eyes, then peered groggily around the room until she found the clock on the wall. She grumbled matter-of-factly, "Frankie. It's six o'clock. The sun just got up. Seb's getting home at suppertime. That's like...hours. My head hurts. Shutting my eyes. Going back to sleep." Then she turned over and did just that.

I let Eva sleep while I tidied up the mess. Ani was an early riser. Who knew when she'd pop on by. Pinky followed me around as I cleaned, sniffing the air, evidently wondering who'd surprised the skunk last night. Eva got frustrated with the noise I was making and dragged herself up to my room to crash in peace. I grabbed the cushions from the couches and aired them in the sun outside. Then I jumped in the shower and renewed myself. When Eva got up, I'd throw all other smelly items into the laundry machine. Eva was right about one thing: there were still hours upon hours before Seb would be home.

When I finished in the shower, I looked at my watch. Only nine o'clock. I fell asleep in the hammock outside, sheltered by a huge hovering maple, with Pinky curled up in the crook of my armpit.

9

I woke to the feeling of someone stroking my arm. Eva sat on the ground beside me, studying the tattoo on my wrist. I pulled it away quickly and buried my arm under myself. I'd forgotten to put my wristband on again after my shower.

Eva commented, "Hey, when did you get a tatt? I didn't know. It's pretty. Uh, why did you draw on it?" The marker had evidently not been completely washed off in the shower.

I didn't know what to say. I wasn't ready for this. I paused, kind of dumbly, for a moment, then replied, "Um, yeah, got it a while ago, with Sam. A friendship thing. You know, *BFFs blah-blah-blah*. Then she disappeared. I don't really like talking about it." Lies had become easier to tell since that night in Deux-Montagnes. Although I was emotionally frustrated with Sam's disappearing act, the aversion I had for my tattoo had nothing to do with her.

She looked a bit puzzled. "Oh, OK. Well, anyway, it's pretty. You shouldn't hide it."

I brought out my wrist again and looked at the tattoo. Remnants of my luck dragon drawing made it look like a butterfly trying to escape its shadow. A pain stabbed at me just behind my eyes. "Yeah, it's pretty. And I wish it were gone."

Before Eva could continue the conversation, we heard a *pssst!* coming from Ani's backyard. We looked over and Sunny was standing behind the hedge, smiling at us. She said, "Hey, girls! I gotta skedaddle, got work and all, but... wanna come to a train bridge party next Friday? It's on the other side. Starting at dusk. See you there?"

Eva and I glanced at each other, then back at Sunny, and nodded. I replied, "Yeah, sure, probably! See you!" Sunny winked at us, turned, and went on her way.

CHAPTER SEVENTEEN
Let There Be Rock

Sam showed herself again on Friday morning. I was lying in the hammock reading my book when she materialized, quite out of the blue, beside me. Shocked by the sight of her, I sat up too quickly, causing the hammock to flip and indiscriminately face-plant me into the grass below. I bit my lip, trying not to laugh at myself. I should be angry. How could she do this? No contact at all, then suddenly show up? She'd been gone for months. I was glad to see her, but it was definitely a shock.

Sam immediately jumped to my rescue, laughing, and attempted to help me to my feet. I motioned for her to back off and I stood up. I didn't have any words. I just looked at her, waiting for her to speak.

Sam's smile faltered for just a second, then she said, "Frankie! I've missed you!" and she pulled me into a hug.

I wasn't sure how to respond. I didn't feel like hugging her quite yet. I returned her hug half-heartedly, pushed her away from me, and replied, "Hey, Sam, uh… where have you been?"

Sam glanced down at the ground, then back up at me. She said, "Yeah, sorry for not getting in touch. It's kinda a long story. I got in a bit of trouble. Is Seb at work?" I nodded. She continued, "I'm living in a group home. I can't go home. My mom's nuts. Can't stand her. Can't live with her. Anyway, I was living with some friends of my uncle's. In Rawdon. Ya know that town near the ski resort, coupla hours from here? It's where Christien lives. I didn't know he lived there until I moved out there. Yeah, so he's a real asswipe. And so are his friends. I didn't really get it at first. Things just kinda got bad. I kinda got buried in it all. I didn't call 'cause, I dunno, guess I didn't know what to say. Anyway, I ended up getting arrested for stealing some girl's scooter. That day I just wanted to get out of there. And she just fuckin' left the keys in it, ya know, while she was buying smokes or something, so I took it." Then Sam smiled thoughtfully as she remembered the incident. "There was a cop sitting at the lights. He saw me take it. How fuckin' stupid is that?" Sam laughed, and I laughed half-heartedly along with her.

I looked at her with an attempted smile and said, "You're a jerk, Sam. I was so worried. And your mum was insanely worried. She called us like a hundred times to see if we'd heard from you. She definitely loves you, you know?" Sam nodded but stayed silent. I continued, "How long have you been at the group home?"

Sam glanced down again, considering her response. She replied, "Dunno. Three months. And it's kinda more than a group home. It's sorta like teen jail. They think I'm a flight risk. Maybe 'cause I keep running." Sam smiled mischievously. "I'm actually kinda on AWOL now, so we gotta make the best of the time we've got." Sam winked at me.

My eyes grew wide. "Really? Like, you're on the run? From jail?"

Sam laughed and interrupted my line of thought. "No! Well, yeah. But it's not like real jail. Just kids' jail. There won't be any dogs looking for me." She laughed harder at that thought.

I wasn't sure what to think of it all. "OK. So you can't stay here. Seb's a lawyer. He's like a human lie detector. I can get little lies past him, but this one? No way. He'll call your mum within minutes."

Sam looked a bit disappointed. But she replied, "Yeah, yeah. I know. I just wanna say hi. And maybe we could do something tonight? You could meet me somewhere or something?"

My face brightened. "Yes! You can come to the train bridge party! It starts at dusk. Seb gets home 'round six o'clock tonight. You can stay here until just past five, then meet me on the bridge at six thirty. Below the tracks, on top of the second post. I'll bring food."

Sam looked ecstatic. "Fuckin' A! It's a date!" She laughed, then said more matter-of-factly, "Now, do you have some breakfast I can bum? Been walking for hours. I'm hungrier than a fuckin' werewolf under a full moon." She howled at the treetops, then laughed at herself. Even with all the challenging crap in her life, Sam had still held on to her quirky carefree sense of humour.

9

Sam was already on the train bridge, under the tracks, when I arrived at six thirty. As far as Seb knew, I was on my way over to Eva's for a sleepover. Which was mostly true. I would be sleeping over at Eva's. But I'd be going over much later. I'd learned quite some time ago that half-truths were easier to sneak by Seb than complete untruths. I dropped down onto the ledge and sat down beside her. Reaching into my bag, I pulled out a baggy filled with leftover potato omelette and handed it to her with a spoon. She thanked me and dug in.

I observed Sam, curiously, while she ate. We'd spent the day together. It was good to catch up, but things felt different between us. She'd changed. She swore a lot. But it was more than the swearing. Her sense of humour had developed a bite. She'd become... bitchy. And her style was different. She looked more like a Madonna fan now. She was dressed all in black. She wore a short, tummy-revealing net tank top over a small lace bustier, above tight false-leather shorts. Her bangs were teased and her hair pulled back into a ponytail. She still didn't wear much makeup, but she'd got multiple ear piercings and wore more jewellery. She was far from the Sam I'd met on my first day at Beats. That Sam seemed like a distant, almost surreal, memory from a way more innocent world.

"Got glue in your eye or something? They seem to be stuck in one spot." She smiled jokingly, then continued, "Thanks for the omelette. Way better than the last thing I ate that Seb cooked. Remember the Ba Wan he tried to make? It was so rubbery! I really tried to swallow it, I really did. But I was like chewing it forever, ya know, trying not to insult him!" We both burst out laughing at the memory. Trying to control her laughter, Sam continued, "Poor guy. He was really trying, ya know. Cooking something Taiwanese 'cause of me." She cracked up again. "Seb's such a good guy!"

When our laughter died down, I asked Sam, "So what's the group home like?"

Sam was sitting with her legs crossed, like you do when you're a kid. She looked at her knees and started picking at some invisible scab on the left one. "It's...fine, I guess.

It's just a fuckin' building with windows and locks on the doors. Can't really trust the kids, though. Have to watch my stuff. Others there have way bigger problems than me. From really crap homes. There's a kid there who's been in the system since he was six. He calls it his home. Weird. It *does not* feel like a home at all. I mean, a lot of the staff tries to be friendly, but they're so fuckin' haggard. Like they have their own problems, ya know? Anyway, I just fight with my mom when I'm home. At least I'm left alone at the group home. There are rules, but no one there is trying to change the real *me*. I mean, living with my mom is like…it's like…as if she's always trying to push me through a meat processor that'll grind me up and spit me out as her mini me. Like that Pink Floyd song. I don't wanna be just another brick in her fuckin' wall. I want to be *me!*"

I looked at her, amazed. Sam had really hit the nail on the head with her description of her relationship with her mum. That was exactly it. Her mom was a total control freak, and she had tried to control Sam's social life as if she was a puppeteer and Sam the puppet. I was glad for Sam that she'd broken free. But her current predicament also had clear challenges. I said, "Wow, Sam. That's messed up. But what are you gonna do now? I mean, you're on the run. Are you going back? Where are you gonna go?"

Sam shrugged. "I dunno. I just needed a break. Needed to get out, have some fun, catch up with you, ya know? When I get hungry I'll go back. Or that's what *they're* counting on anyway." She winked at me. "Maybe I'll go back in time for school." She laughed at that notion, then continued more thoughtfully, "No, I actually have missed school. I'm serious. I'm a rebel nerd. Our secret. *The real fuckin' me.*" And she laughed again.

Eva turned up just then, interrupting our conversation. She looked down at us from the tracks. "Hey, girls! Ready to party? I brought the goods!" She passed down a bag containing two bottles of Baby Duck and a mickey of tequila. I grabbed the bag from her and then she climbed down, joining us on the ledge.

Sam smiled and said, "Hey, Eva. Wow, been a while."

Obviously taken aback by Sam's new look and trying not to goggle, Eva replied, "Hey, Sam! Yeah, wow. Great to see you. Last time was at Beats, like in grade eight! I like your style. Different. Kinda rebel Madonna. Nice."

I looked in the bag and said to Eva, "So, what did ya have to do for it?"

Eva laughed. "Nothing actually. Joe's coming to the party. I guess he felt obliged or something. You know, 'cause this time we're both in on keeping the secret from my parents. Maybe that's it. Anyway, it's seven dollars split three ways." I motioned to Sam not to worry, and I handed Eva fourteen dollars. I'd dipped into my babysitting savings, but it'd be worth it.

9

The shoreline on the other side of the train bridge was a perfect place for a party. There was a rocky beach along the edge of the river, bordered by wild grasses that had been trampled down by numerous summer parties. Beyond the grassy zone, forest extended all the way to the residential area called Roxboro. The closest houses on that side were about a twenty-minute walk from the river. There were no houses directly across the river on Ile Des Voyageurs either. And the only ways in or out were the train tracks and a dirt bike path. There was no road access. The place was a teenager's adult-free dream. Isolated, soundproof, and wild.

People began to gather on the other side of the bridge around eight-thirty. Some guys had pulled in on dirt bikes with backpacks full of firewood. They dumped their loads and whizzed off again, presumably to pick up more. A couple of girls stayed behind, gathering brushwood and preparing the fire. Feeling timid, we observed them from the safety of our train bridge perch. We'd make our appearance when the party got rolling.

About a half hour later, the guys on the dirt bikes returned with beer and more wood. Shortly after that, small groups of teens dribbled in. By nine-thirty, there must've been around thirty people gathered, and more kept arriving. We made our way over as dusk dimmed and night fell.

Sunny sat next to the fire on a rock, poking the burning wood with a stick and talking to Joe. She saw us arrive and jumped up to greet us.

"Hey, look who it is! Your little sis, Joe!" Sunny exclaimed.

Joe rolled his eyes and replied to Sunny, "I'm going to get a beer. Want one?"

"Nope. Still have one here," she answered before moving her attention over to us. "Grab a rock, or log, or piece of grass. Make yourselves at home." Sunny lit a cigarette, then smiled and said, "Nice to see you girls. Who's the new one?"

Sam smiled broadly, as if she knew Sunny from way back. "Hey, I'm Sam. Frankie's told me a bit about you. Last weekend sounded fun." She gave Sunny an exaggerated wink. Sam seriously didn't have a shy bone in her body.

Sunny laughed. "Yup. Hoping for an even better sequel tonight." Then she turned toward a guy who was sitting next to a giant boom box and shouted, "Hey, Jack? Crank it up!" She turned back to us. "This song fuckin' rocks!" The song playing was AC/DC's "Let There Be Rock." Sunny jumped up on a rock and shouted to the crowd, "Let the fuckin' party begin!" Then she took on Bon Scott's demeanour and started to sing along to the song. Soon she had a following chorus of about twenty people. And Sam was right in there with them. Everyone was dancing like Angus Young with his guitar and singing like Bon Scott. And it was barely ten o'clock.

Eva and I looked at each other, smiling timidly. We wanted desperately to join in, but the innocent little girls inside us hadn't quite broken free yet. The other teens there seemed so much more...experienced, wild, and free. We had only recently broken through our shell and dared to explore beyond the sheltered safety of our nest. The whole thing was both intimidating and so enormously exciting. I squeezed Eva's hand and said, "Fuck the Baby Duck." She smiled. She was already holding the tequila bottle. She opened it, took a swig, coughed, laughed, and passed it to me. Our brains were connected telepathically.

By eleven o'clock Eva and I were dancing along with the rest of the crowd, as the boom box rolled through cassette after cassette of '80s hard rock and metal classics. I couldn't yet grasp the metal rhythm, but hard rock had found a new and special place in my heart. The beat thumped in rhythm with my life and the lyrics spoke my thoughts.

Sam had become infatuated with one of the older boys. He wore a baseball cap backward over long, straight blond hair. He was a head taller than Sam and had a slim, well-built body. His jeans and T-shirt were ripped in just the right places. He was quite attractive, in a rough and naughty way. They sat together on the beach, in their own world, drinking beer and sharing a cigarette.

Eva and I, on the other hand, remained stuck to each other all night. We were each other's comfort-zone. As Guns n' Roses's "Sweet Child O' Mine" dwindled off, we sat down on a log not far from the fire pit. Sunny followed us over.

"Heya, dancing queens! How's it? Smoke?" Sunny held out her pack of cigarettes, offering us one.

I shook my head. "Not for me. Those things'll kill ya," I said half-jokingly. Then continued, laughing, "I only smoke the hard stuff." I was definitely more than tipsy. In fact, that's exactly why I had had to sit down. My world had begun to get dizzy.

Eva laughed along with me and then added to the joke, "Get it t'ya in a jiff! Just gotta go pickpocket my bro!" She pretended to get up and head toward him.

"Eva! Hold on, you'll need a distraction! I'll trip and spill Baby Duck all over him. You grab the loot while his evil girlfriend bobs me to death with her double Ds!" The reason for Joe's interest in this girl, Eva and I had decided, had everything to do with the huge melons under her chin. Picturing her trying to beat us up with her boobs bouncing all over the place was just too much. Now we were both holding our sides laughing.

Sunny stood in front of us, sporting her typical look of amusement. She was either too old or not drunk enough for our silly humour. But we amused her nonetheless. She waited for our laughing fit to simmer down, then she said, "Scoot over. I come prepared. No need for titty fights."

Laughing, she pulled out a bag with weed in it and sat down beside us.

Sunny rolled a joint, lit it, and was about to pass it around but then paused and said, "Hmm, maybe you should take it easy with the pot. Not always the best thing to mix with booze."

Eva and I glanced at each other, smiling. I giggled teasingly, "Yeah, Eva, don't want a repeat of last time. No wasting the stash, ya hear!" I shook my finger like a schoolmarm at Eva. We both laughed, and I took the joint from Sunny.

Half an hour later, Eva and I were stumbling down the dirt bike trail toward her house, promising each other that we would never, ever, ever mix alcohol and marijuana again. By the time we'd finally reached Eva's place, we'd lost our supper more than once.

,

I woke up on Eva's bed the next morning dreaming of Sam. Eva was fast asleep beside me. We hadn't said bye to Sam the night before. We were all so wasted. She'd been with that guy all night. I wondered where she had got to. I hoped she was OK. Maybe she'd gone home with that guy. I had no way of reaching her. I'd just have to wait until she called me. Knowing her, it might be months before I heard from her again. Guilt, worry, and anger stirred in my gut. Why hadn't she just hung out with *us* at the party?

I glanced at my watch. It was only six-thirty. There were voices in the kitchen. I was wide-awake. And Eva was normally a late sleeper. Rather than waiting around making small talk with her parents, I scribbled her a note and headed home.

It was a beautiful cool morning. By cool, I mean not blistering hot. Summers in Montreal can be real scorchers. Mornings are really the only time of day that a person can walk outside comfortably without swimming in sweat. I followed the dirt bike path back down to the river's edge. Our party place was a mess. The grass and beach were littered with beer cans, bottles, and chip bags. I picked up an empty plastic bag and stuffed as many cans as I could fit in it. Then I found a beer bottle box and filled its twelve slots with bottles. That little bit of cleanup would also bring me a few cents. I thought of what I'd tell Seb and then reckoned on the truth: I'd found the bottles on the way home from Eva's.

I started toward the train bridge and checked my watch again. It was only twenty past seven. There'd be questions if I arrived home this early. As I thought about this dilemma, something on the beach, just under the bridge, caught my eye. It was someone's shoe. But it looked like the someone was still wearing it. I took a few steps closer. Then I recognized the shoe. My heart started to pound as I ran toward it.

Sam was lying on the sand, on her tummy, with her arms at her sides. Her hair was covered in sand and she had bruises across her cheek. She looked like a victim in a crime movie. I fell to my knees beside her. I called her name feebly, unable to find my voice. I felt like I did in those bad dreams I had, where my muscles didn't work and I couldn't call for help. Where I was weak and drained and unable to fight back. Where fear always won the battle. I forced myself to touch her, to shake her awake. Then her back moved. She was breathing. She was alive. My nerves immediately calmed again. I took a deep breath and sat quietly next to her for a moment, gathering my thoughts. Then I put my hand on her shoulder and gently shook her while calling her name.

Sam woke suddenly, with a shocked, "What the fuck?" shout. I withdrew my hand with instinctive quick speed.

I said, "Oh shit! Sorry!" Then a mix of emotions flooded through me. Both relief and anger were at the top of the list. "Oh my god, I thought you were dead! What the fuck? Holy fuck, Sam! What are you doing here? Fuck, fuck, fuck! And what happened to your face?"

Sam looked at me, a little confused, trying to make sense of the emotion I'd just hurled at her. She said, "Uhhh..." Then looked around at the beach, as if trying to remember where she was and how she got there. "I dunno. Uhh, I mean. I had a fight with some chic. I think that guy was her boyfriend or something? I dunno. But she was like, raging. I don't remember much after that. I think I just got tired and crashed." I stared at her incredulously. In an attempt to break my awkward, silent stare, Sam added, "The sand's actually quite comfortable." She smiled. "You should try it sometime."

I didn't laugh. "You have that girl's handprint imprinted on your face." I paused and gave her a hard look. "Holy shit, Sam. You looked fuckin' dead!"

Sam replied, "Sorry, but you fuckin' left last night, man. You just left me!"

That's when I really got mad. "What? I fuckin' left? Where the fuck were you?? I left? Does it hurt, Sam? Did I hurt your *feelings*? Were you worried? Did you wonder if I'd ever fuckin' return? Hey? Did you? Did you think I was fuckin' dead?? Do you even fuckin' care?"

Sam got up and shouted, "What the fuck is up your ass?? You fuckin' left!" She pointed at me aggressively when she said this.

Something inside me was snapping. I pushed her and she tripped backward, falling back down onto to the sand. She glared at me. I shouted, "No, Sam! You fucking left! You always leave! Everything is not fucking just about fucking you!"

Sam seemed to be searching her hung-over brain for a reply, but, failing to find a good one, she just continued to glare at me. Then, as if grasping at straws, she blurted, "You have it all, ya know! Boohoo, poor little angel Frankie got herself raped. You fuckin' spoiled twat!" Then she gave me an extra bitchy crooked smile and said, "No pun intended."

The volcano of emotions inside me erupted. A *spoiled twat?* I yelled at her, "What the fuck is that supposed to mean? You're the one who ran back to the fucker! Followed him to Rawdon? What the fuck was that? You left me and followed that mother-fucking fuckwad of a human being! Why d'ya do it, Sam? Did he give you a fuckin' a peace tattoo?" I had never sworn so much in my life, but at that moment swearing seemed like the most appropriate way to express myself. My emotions were the volcano, and my anger its hot lava. I wanted to fling lava at Sam. I wanted her to feel the burn, just as I'd felt it all those times she'd abandoned me, all those times she'd not cared enough to even call to let me know she was alive.

Sam jumped to her feet and ran at me. She took a swing at my face, but I flinched backward and she missed. I pushed her again. But this time she stood her ground. She grabbed my hair with one hand, pulling my head down, and started hitting me on the side of the head with her other hand. I rammed her in the ribs with my head and she lost her grip on my hair. I rammed her again with my shoulder and took her down like a football player. She was lying on the ground on her back and I was sitting on top of her chest. I held her arms down above her head, my hands on her wrists and my knees pinning down her upper arms, and I glared at her.

"I'm going to get up now, Sam, and I'm going home. I don't want to fight anymore. OK?" I was hurt, angry, and didn't want to deal with her any longer.

Sam looked to the side and didn't answer. I repeated, "OK?"

Then she did look at me. She said, "Fuck you, Frankie."

I replied, "Whatever." I let go of her arms and got off her. I'd had it with her. I would leave and that would be the end of it. I stood up and turned away from her. I heard her scramble to her feet. I decided I would not look back, I was just going to keep walking along the beach, then up to the bridge toward home. If Sam wanted my friendship, she was going to have to work much harder for it. Until then, I was done with her.

As I reached the tracks, Sam yelled, "That's right, run on home to your gay wannabe parents! Fuckin' bitch! You're never gonna see me again! Fuck you, Frankie!" She stopped yelling when she realized she wasn't going to get a reply. I just kept walking. She couldn't see it, but my anger had turned to sadness. Tears filled my eyes until I could barely see in front of me. I walked until I reached the hill in the middle of the island. I sat on my favourite rock on top of the hill. Sam was gone for good, out of my life, and I never wanted to see her again. *How could Sam be so horrible?*

I tore off my wristband and glared at that stupid tattoo. I just wanted it gone. *How could I have let that fuckwad have his way with me? Why didn't I fight him off? What was wrong with me? I was drunk, but I could've bit him or done something!* I found a sharp stone and started scratching at my arm, trying to scratch the tattoo out of existence. The scratches got deeper as my anger grew again. My arm began to bleed. The pain was a relief, and it etched me on. The more pain I caused the tattoo, the less power it seemed to have over me. It had been a constant symbol of that night, of that guy, and of my weakness. I kept attacking the tattoo until my wrist was covered in bloody cuts. The cuts weren't deep enough to be dangerous, just deep enough to defile the symbol of my defilement. I finally threw the stone away. I felt calm again. Things would be OK. Sam was right about one thing. When it came to Seb and Pete, I had it all. I knew they would always be there for me. They nurtured my heart. They kept me sky-bound.

CHAPTER EIGHTEEN
Orion

August moseyed on by, as summer does. Eva and I went to several train bridge parties and by September claimed to be full-on *rockers*. The week before school started, we'd both got our long hair "feathered" into V-shaped layers that dipped down our backs. Which meant I had to straighten mine every morning to keep up the look. We'd also adjusted our wardrobe. Eva's mum had dug out her old sewing machine and helped us taper our well-worn Levi's jeans down the sides, so they were so skin-tight that when undressing, we had to peel them off inside out. We bought *biker*-themed tasselled T-shirts to go with our jeans. And we each had a leather jacket that had been hand-painted and customized just for us. On the back of mine were two dragons fighting, a white luck dragon and a blue devilish dragon. Eva had chosen a skull made of flowering vines for the back of hers. We both wore white-and-green Adidas leather sneakers, as they were *in* among Sunny's friends, and Sunny was the coolest girl ever. Eva's brother, Joe, nicknamed Eva and I "the rocker chicks" and Sunny "the mother rocker hen." Eva and I thought it very funny. Sunny, not so much. Joe quite enjoyed teasing Sunny. She pretended to get angry with him for it, but the twinkle in her eyes betrayed her. She was a terrible liar. Eva and I had bets on when they'd finally hook up.

School started uneventfully on the first Tuesday in September. Eva had met me on the seven-fifteen train that morning. Her mother had finally succumbed to Eva's tireless push for independent travel. She'd set aside her paranoid trust issues with public transportation and bought Eva a train pass. Eva boarded at Roxboro and met me in the last carriage, as planned. She was dressed in her tight jeans and new tasselled T-shirt, as was I in mine. It was too warm for leather jackets, so we'd both left those at home. The train crowd was still thin, as we had only just hit the first stop in Montreal. Eva made her way down the aisle without trouble and found me easily. I moved my sax case off the seat to give her room. Swinging her bag off her shoulder, she let herself fall into the seat beside me. She was obviously just as exhausted and unready for the first early morning of the year as I was. Eva looked at me through puffy eyes, yawned, smiled, and said sarcastically, "Yay! First day! Rock on, babe!" Then she leaned into me, put her head on my shoulder, and closed her eyes. I rested my head on hers and pushed play on my Walkman. Metallica's "Orion" ballad began like a slow-moving roller-coaster of mixed emotions. I loved this ballad. It reminded me of the way life moseyed along, through ups and downs, pushing us forward with a magical inner strength. I shut my eyes, only to open them again when the train stopped in Central Station.

Eva and I arrived at school with twenty minutes to spare before our first class of the day. The old pool club gang (and Gil) had gathered on the front steps. They didn't speak to me much anymore but had remained polite. I sensed disappointment, or disrespect, or something similar, from them toward me. As if I had become a contagious form of "troubled child" that they felt they should steer clear of. It made me sad, and there wasn't much I could do about it. I nodded to the boys as we passed them on the steps. "Hey, guys, how's it going?" They nodded back and smiled politely, mumbling some hellos. For a second, it seemed like Gil was going to say something more, but then he didn't. I felt a brief painful twinge in my heart and forced myself to ignore it. Eva must've sensed my pain, because she discreetly took my hand in hers and squeezed gently. Then, when they were out of earshot, she grumbled, "Arrogant assholes."

The same faces graced our grade ten classes as had our grade nine classes. There was no one new, and no one had left. Terrible Tammy and Dreadful Deidre sat in their usual spots in the back of the class, surrounded by the rest of the Terrible Twos, waiting to make a target out of some poor sap who had the ill fortune to glance sideways at them. After the day when Eva had spat in Tammy's face and we'd laughed at her rather than run, Tammy had made sure to keep her posse comfortably close by. We'd never caught her alone again. Apparently we'd discovered her weak spot. Without her gang, she was just a big lipsticked mouth full of gas but no muscle. Knowing this had given us power. Rather than retaliate against us, she had chosen to completely ignore us. Eva and I knew Terrible Tammy's secret, and she didn't want it shared. As a result, when we walked into class, our own eyes were free to roam wherever we pleased. Someday she may choose to retaliate, but she'd kept her silence for months, and she'd remained quiet on our first day in grade ten.

9

It was on the second day that things began to slip again with the Terrible Twos.

Maybe it was because of the superior feeling that they'd felt walking into school as *seniors* this year. Or maybe it was because Dreadful Deidre had decided to work harder on developing leadership skills. Or maybe they just didn't have another target at that moment in time and we'd do. Whatever the reason was, when we walked into Beats High on the second morning of the school year, an eerie feeling had entered the cease fire that Eva and I had enjoyed over the last few months. The Terrible Twos initiated their attack as we passed them at their lockers just before class.

It was Deidre's caustic smile that gave up their game. Out of habit and distrust, I glanced at them as Eva and I approached. I had developed this habit way back in grade eight in order to evaluate their mood and avoid confrontation. It had been a while since I'd sensed aggression toward us by them, but something had changed this morning. Four of the Terrible Twos were huddled around Tammy's locker, talking in low voices and laughing derisively. They stopped talking as we approached, and Deirdre flashed a wicked smile our way. I braced myself and instinctively put more space between them and me by moving closer to the wall on the other side of the hallway. I thought, *Fuck, here we go.* Eva was walking behind me and I wasn't sure whether she'd picked up on the renewed threat yet. But whether she had or not turned out to be inconsequential, as Deirdre eliminated any possibility for misunderstanding as we were walking past them.

Deirdre stepped in front of us, blocking our path, and the rest of the group joined her as we attempted to navigate around her. "Well, well, well, lookie here. It's the lesbo traitor and her cheap whore bodyguard. Or is it two lesbo cheap whores now? Who knows? A lot can happen over the summer, right?" Deirdre winked at Eva and Eva looked away, her anger turning her cheeks pink. Deirdre continued, "Oh, hit a sore spot, did I, Eva? Ha, she doesn't know yet, does she? Well, that's hilarious. What a sad love story. The poor secret lesbo wannabe lover doesn't even have the guts to make a pass at a common whore." Deirdre looked from Eva to me, smiling venomously. "You do know she has the hots for you, right? I mean, you don't actually think she's in it for the friendship?"

I glared back at Deirdre with furious contempt. There was a time when my fear of these girls had imprisoned me, but that time had ended over half a year ago. I was holding my sax case and now my hand was gripping the handle so hard that I was sure my nails had broken through the skin on my palm. If I had had super powers, the burning glare from my eyes would've melted Deirdre on the spot. In a fierce but calm and controlled voice, I said, "Step the fuck back, or I'm going to ram my sax right up where the sun don't shine. And I don't mean your ass."

Deirdre actually stepped back with a brief but sincere shocked look on her face. I stepped toward her, into the gap that had developed between us. Surprised, Tammy and the other girls glanced at each other and, not knowing how to respond, decided to give us space and also stepped back. Deirdre took back control over her facial expression and replaced the shock with her typical poisonous sneer. She remained quiet, glaring at me, considering her response.

That's when Tammy took over. "You think yer fuckin' tough? With yer stupid rocker clothes? Yer just a fuckin' poser. You both are. Fuckin' losers." She laughed and her Terrible Twos laughed along with her. Then they turned their backs on us and went back to ignoring us, whispering and laughing together in front of Tammy's locker.

Eva and I continued on our way to class. Eva was looking at the floor as she walked and not speaking. When we were out of earshot, I turned to her and said, "Hey, don't let those bitches get to you. They're a bunch of idiots. Nothing they say is true. It's all just crap. And no one believes them. Everyone knows they're full of shit. So don't worry about it, OK? Who needs them anyway? You matter to me. They don't. Fuck 'em."

Eva smiled and replied, "Yeah, OK. And, hey, you were wicked back there. I think Deirdre was actually speechless. You can be my *stupid rocker bodyguard* anytime." Eva laughed and winked at me jokingly.

Eva and I managed to get through the rest of the week relatively unscathed by Tammy and Deirdre. They were both careful to grace us with their evil eyes and sneers whenever they caught us looking at them, but they had refrained from direct confrontations. Telling them to go to hell had paid off—somewhat, anyway.

9

On Friday morning I was greeted with an invitation to an open-house party on Saturday. I opened my locker and the invitation fell to the floor between my feet. It was from a tenth grader named Vincent who was on the French side. I didn't know Vincent very well, but we sat beside each other in band class and he always said hi when passing in the hallway. He was friendly and nice, although awkward with girls, and he had a bit of a zit challenge going on. Eva had also received an invitation. Throughout the day, we'd learned that so had all the other tenth graders. It occurred to us that Vincent must either have a very big house and very lenient parents *or* his parents must be away and the size of his house was of little concern to him. We made an educated assumption that it was likely the latter. We agreed that it would be worth checking out.

As it turned out, Vincent lived in an apartment building of which his parents were the super-intendants. Vincent had been granted the privilege of revamping a huge concrete room in the basement of the building into an incredibly cool bedroom/clubhouse. The one thing we had been right about was that his parents were out of town for the weekend. The apartment building was located in easily accessible downtown Montreal, and Vincent's basement lair was thumping to the beat of partying teens by half-past nine. There were about sixty tenth graders at Beats and it looked like very few of them had missed the opportunity to check out Vincent's party. The room was filled with music, laughter, and a hazy, lazy pot-smoke fog.

Eva and I sat together on one of the old couches in Vincent's clubhouse bedroom, admiring it. Vincent had told us that the room had just looked like a big concrete garage before his parents had renovated it. They'd done an impressive job. Although there were still ugly metal stabilisation poles from floor to ceiling, the walls and ceiling had been soundproofed. On the walls, Vincent had painted stunning pictures of the four elements—air, fire, earth, and water. Each wall depicted a different element that Vincent had reinforced with a magical beast that complemented the particular element. There was a glorious sea monster representing *water*, an eight-armed elephant goddess representing *earth*, a magnificent flying dragon for *fire*, and an awe-inspiring stormy sky that depicted the essence of *air*. Vincent obviously had a lot of talent I'd been unaware of.

Someone turned the boom box off and whistled loudly into the crowd for everyone to shut up and listen. Vincent was standing on a homemade stage in the far corner of the room with his sax hanging from a strap that looped over his shoulder and around his neck. Three of his friends had taken up positions behind him. He had a backup of drums, electric guitar, and keyboard. When there was silence, he spoke to the crowd.

"You guys fuckin' rock! *Que la fête commence!*" Vincent shouted to the crowd.

We all shouted back, "Party on!" He smiled and shot his fist up in the air in a symbolic gesture that said we were all on the same team. He and his band then kicked off their first set with Supertramp's "The Logical Song." Vincent shared the vocals with his keyboardist. Transfixed, I watched him in awe. I couldn't believe that I'd never really *noticed* Vincent before. He was... *awesome.*

The guy sitting on the floor by my feet put his hand on my knee to get my attention, interrupting my hypnotic trance about halfway through the song. "Hey, Frankie, wakey wakey. Take the spliff. Pass it on." His voice was gruff and laced with unexplained laughter. He held up a joint and motioned for me to take it. I took it, took a toke, inhaling deeply and blowing rings as I exhaled. I'd learned that from Sunny. Then I relaxed back into the couch cushions. Life was happy. Life was perfect. Somewhere on another couch sat Terrible Tammy and Dreadful Deirdre, but I didn't care. My world was on this couch, and this world, on this couch, made me happy, and that's what mattered. I smiled at Eva and passed her the joint.

Eva leaned into me as she took a toke, then she passed it on, and we began to philosophize about the meaning of *time* and the time it may take us to get from our comfortable couch world to the last train of the evening. We'd decided to stay clear of alcohol that evening and stick to pot. We'd planned on catching the last train home, and there would be no time for the effects of risky mixing of the two. But at the rate joints were being passed around, we'd likely have to give ourselves plenty of time to get to the train station. It was only half-past ten and we were already in a state of pot-induced *who gives a fuck* bliss. The couch had become indescribably comfortable and I couldn't imagine ever removing myself from it. It would surely be a slow-movin' stroll to the train station. We comically discussed stealing skateboards, or hitching a ride on a newspaper boy's push-bike, or even flying there by kite (Vincent had a big one conveniently hanging from his ceiling that didn't look like it was in use).

Then, out of the blue, as we were giggling along with life, Eva kissed me, quite passionately, right smack on the lips.

My hand reflexively shot up in front of me and I pushed her back, away from me. "What are you doing?" Suddenly I became acutely aware of my surroundings again. I looked around, panicked, trying to guess who may have seen the kiss. "Eva, I—I... What was that? I mean, you're my, like, best friend. Why did you kiss me?" I didn't know what to say to her. I was shocked. I hadn't expected her kiss. I hadn't even considered her in that way. I had so many questions streaming through my mind. I had no idea how to react. Eva was my best friend.

Eva looked at me, stunned and hurt. She got up off the couch without saying a word and left the party. Her silence may have spoken volumes, but it had whizzed right on by me. I didn't get it. I was totally confused. I looked around nervously for possible witnesses. If the Terrible Twos got wind of this, my life (and Eva's) would turn to absolute shit. The guy at my feet nudged my leg again. I looked down at him and he said, "Hey, man, chill. She's into you. So fuckin' what. She's hot, man." Then he laughed and held up a joint.

I grabbed the joint and passed it down the line to the next person. Then slid down off the couch on top of Guy at My Feet, straddling him. I grabbed the collar of his T-shirt, pulled him toward me, and kissed him like he'd likely never been kissed before. Kissing led to some hurried, very brief fondling, and fondling led to extremely awkward sex in the bathroom. He was my second, and he also had had absolutely nothing to do with love. As he attempted to hold me up against the wall in the tiny bathroom, as they do in the movies, our pot-infused bodies kept sabotaging our imagined intentions. He was too stoned and weak to hold me up and I was too stoned and full of giggles to stay up. We ended up on the floor, with my head by the toilet bowl, while he humped me with my pants off and his only partway down. As my head banged against the toilet bowl, I started to wonder what the fuck I was doing there. He finally came, then rolled off me onto the floor and, from what I could tell, went directly to sleep. I nudged him and he grumbled something inaudible. My mind began to hurt. What the fuck was I thinking? I pulled my pants back on, stood up, and looked at myself in the mirror. My hair was a matted mess. I plucked a piece of soggy toilet paper from it, then turned on the tap and drenched my face with cold water. It was time to go home.

As luck would have it, Deirdre was waiting to use the bathroom as I exited. In about a second, she would discover the half-naked guy I had fucked sprawled on the floor next to the toilet. I thought, *Shit*, then I smiled sweetly at her and said, "Enjoy." At least there'd be no doubt in her mind concerning my sexual orientation.

9

I lay in bed Sunday morning, staring at the ceiling and fumbling over the events of the night before. I'd woken up early from that typical nightmare that I kept having, where I was trapped under some unseen force and unable to summon enough muscle power to escape. I had always assumed that unseen force to be Christien, but this time it had a different feeling. There was more to it. It was more than just Christien. Something more incredible was holding me down, something even harder to escape. I'd been sweating so profusely that my pajamas and sheets were thoroughly soaked. I lay there in my sweaty sheets, thinking about Eva.

Why had Eva kissed me at the party? Everything had been going perfectly. She was my best friend. I wanted her to stay. I wanted my best friend back. Where would we go from here, now that we'd kissed and now that I'd pushed her away? I loved her. But not in the same way that she might want to love me. I was so confused. Maybe I did love her in the same way as she loved me. I mean, to be honest, guys hadn't really come through for me. Maybe girls *was* the way to go. I tried to picture myself wanting a girl, you know, sexually. I assembled the scenario in my mind, kissing Eva the way Gil and I had once kissed, but the picture just wouldn't hold. It felt all wrong. Nope, I concluded, it wasn't in me. I had no physical desire for girls. Guys may generally be dickheads, but it was still them that I had the hots for. It made little sense. I remained confused.

The phone rang and I was startled out of my complicated state of sexual confusion. I picked up the receiver and said hello. There was a brief silence on the other end, then she spoke.

"Hey, Frankie. It's me, Eva. I'm... I'm sorry I left last night. And I, you know, didn't really mean anything with that kiss. I was super stoned. I guess maybe I should stay away from weed or something." Eva fell silent, waiting for my reply.

"Uh, yeah, uh, no problem. But, Eva? You know, I don't really care if you're into me in that way. I mean, I'm not into chicks like that, you know, but I'm OK with you being into chicks. Really. I'm fine with it," I said honestly.

There was silence on the line. Then Eva responded, "Yeah, uh, I am. You know, into chicks. But, I'm not really into you that way. I was just really stoned. And I kinda thought you might be into chicks too. I mean…you don't seem that interested in guys. You kinda keep your distance. And you broke up with a super great one. You know, uh, Gil. So, I sorta thought that you might not be into guys."

"Yeah. I'm not really into anyone. Guys are such dweebs. Gil and I had something for a bit, but it just didn't work out. Like I said, guys are dweebs." Eva laughed in agreement, and I continued, "Hey, Eva? I should warn you that Tammy and Deirdre might be out to get us on Monday. Or at least out to get me." I recounted what had happened after she had left the party.

Eva fell silent for a second and then said jokingly, "Well then, I say we concoct them a threesome story. You know, you, me and that guy in the bathroom. Give the pigs some more shit to roll in. As you said yourself, Fuck 'em!"

I replied, "Oh my god, imagine! Let's work 'em, babe, take those bitches for a ride!" We both laughed. All was good again. All was fixed. Eva was still my best friend and I loved her deeply. We proceeded to concoct hilarious hypothetical scenarios that had to do with our possible handling of the Terrible Twos.

CHAPTER NINETEEN
The Loneliness of the Long Distance Runner

September 1987

Have you ever had one of those moments when you look back to a specific point in time and think, *If I had only handled that pinprick in time differently, I could've changed the future*? For me, that pinprick in time happened on Monday morning, September 14, 1987, at 10:36.

The recess bell rang and I headed for gym class, strolling along passively through time. I stopped at the bathroom along the way and then continued on to the gymnasium. Eva had been at the dentist that morning and we hadn't seen each other yet. As I entered the gymnasium, Ms. Jones was struggling with a load of hockey sticks. I ran to help her and quite irrelevantly caught just one of the sticks as the rest of her load fell to the floor. Students filed into the gym, walking past us and over the sticks, on their way to the changing rooms. I helped Ms. Jones assemble the hockey sticks into a more organized pile. Ms. Jones was a friendly but odd gym teacher. Asking for help was not part of her rapport. She liked to do things herself, and as a result, I could tell you a few stories about some funny mishaps she's had with equipment. She smiled a thank-you at me when we were done and I headed to the changing rooms.

I entered the changing rooms and time turned from passive to decisive.

The changing room was a small communal room with benches along three walls. The light blue paint on the walls was peeling off, revealing a previous coat of pastel green. There were no showers, although oddly enough there was a drain in the middle of the floor, which made me think that perhaps the room had been a shower block at one point. I should've predicted what was coming. If I had predicted it, I could've thought through my reaction. But perhaps because it was a Monday morning or maybe because I just refused to concern myself too deeply about the Terrible Twos any longer, I swung the door to the changing room open and entered obliviously.

Eva was standing in the far corner of the room, facing five girls who were standing in a semi-circle around her. She looked both scared and defiant, like a panicked buffalo hemmed in by conspiring wolves. Eva was naked from the waist up and was covering her breasts with her hands. Tammy held Eva's bra in one hand and her T-shirt in the other, waving them in the air while she spewed out her typical insults. There were three other girls in the room who were not part of Tammy's gang, all trying hard to not involve themselves. For them, it was better to sacrifice one member of the herd than risk themselves as well. I understood their point. I'd been there, thinking along similar lines. The wrath of the Terrible Twos was cruel and relentless. But I'd stopped being a bystander a while ago, and I would never turn back. My drive came both from hate and love. I had both in my heart—hate for the way Tammy and Deirdre made others feel and an empathetic love for their targets. When I'd finally stood up to them in grade nine, I'd felt my heart strengthen, and each time thereafter my heart got a little stronger. To not stand up to the Terrible Twos would feel like a betrayal to my heart.

When Tammy spoke, even if you weren't facing her, you could hear the twisted sneer on her face. Her voice dripped with so much sarcasm that at times I imagined her lips melting right off her face onto the floor by her feet, and then her being sucked into her self-created puddle of vileness to never be seen again. I could only dream.

"What's wrong, Eva? You lookin' for somethin'?" Tammy dangled Eva's bra and T-shirt in front of her face. "This what you lookin' for? What are you gonna do for it?" Tammy turned to Deirdre and added mockingly, "What d'ya think we should make her do for it? Maybe a kiss? No, she'd enjoy that. Maybe we should just hold on to it. Or maybe the boys' locker room needs decorating?" Tammy and her gang sniggered. The three bystanders finished changing and quickly exited the room.

Eva looked panicked but also angry. It was that silent frozen kind of anger, the kind of anger that heats up like hot water does in a steam kettle. It wasn't quite at boiling point so hadn't started to whistle yet, but it was definitely getting there. Eva had an abundance of tolerance, and that incredible tolerance of hers had so far kept her anger below boiling point. She stood there, facing her tormentors, telling them silently through her glare to go to hell.

Then, without any warning signs, Deirdre grabbed Eva by her hair, pulled her close, kissed her full on the lips, and licked her cheek from chin to eye. Eva shoved Deirdre away violently and Deirdre fell to the floor. When it was apparent that Deirdre's pride had survived, the other girls broke out in derisive laughter.

Tammy threw Eva's clothes at her as she said, "Ya fuckin lesb—" I cut her off, yelling at them all to back off.

And, to my later regret, that's when I really let my tongue off its leash.

"So the fuck what? Eva likes girls! So fucking what? Does it really honestly affect you? Does it really matter that Eva is a lesbian? Because she's sure not a threat to you! There's no way in hell she'd be interested in such fucking bitches. Do any of you even have a fucking boyfriend? You can't even attract the guys. Why are you so worried about the girls? So just fuck off and mind your own fucking business!"

Everyone in the room had fallen silent. Eva picked up her T-shirt and threw it on quickly. Her face was red and her eyes moist. She pushed passed me toward the door. Ms. Jones opened the door, wondering about the yelling, and Eva ran out of the room passed her. I tried to follow but was stopped by Ms. Jones.

"What is going on in here?" Ms. Jones looked at each of us, trying to prompt a voluntary reply. We all looked at the floor. "I'm not sure who else heard your yelling, but I sure heard every word of it. It sounds like at least one of you owes Eva an apology."

It had sunk in quite suddenly that that person was me. My cheeks felt hot and my head hurt. I'd assumed that Tammy and Deirdre knew for a fact that Eva was gay as they were always teasing her about it, and I was sure they must've at least heard about what had happened at the party.

But Eva's reaction said otherwise.

I had just simultaneously outed my best friend and thrown her to the wolves.

❧

I found Eva lying on the grass under a Russian olive tree on McGill's campus at lunchtime. Her head was resting on her bag and she was staring up into the tree's twisted canopy. It was one of our favourite lunch spots. We liked it because of the evolving enchanted shadows the tree cast throughout the day. Eva had walked right out of the gymnasium before class started and I hadn't seen her since, until now. She hadn't noticed me approach and I paused for a moment before revealing my presence. So many thoughts and emotions stirred in my mind. I had crushed Eva. I had exposed her secret. And I might as well have yelled it out over the school intercom because the Terrible Twos would surely spread the word faster than a broken dam floods a landscape. What would I say? How would I fix this? I couldn't fix this.

I walked over to where she lay and sat down silently beside her. Iron Maiden's "The Loneliness of the Long Distance Runner" pulsed from Eva's earphones. Eva noticed me and closed her eyes. There were no words to express how sorry I was. I stayed silent and waited for her to speak. After a few minutes, she opened her eyes and looked at me. I could tell she had been crying earlier. Her eyes were still pink and puffy. Then she averted her eyes from mine, stood up, threw her backpack over her shoulder, and walked away.

❧

The rest of September was a lonely wander through remorse and worry. Eva was obviously in pain, but she refused to let me in. She wouldn't even look at me. She cocooned herself up in her own world and would not communicate with anyone. She walked, sat, and stood with a weight on her shoulders and her eyes on the ground. Tammy and Deirdre couldn't even break through the insulated layers Eva had wrapped herself in. Their insults fell on deaf ears, and their aggression was met with silent surrender.

I sat on the steps leading up to Beats's main entrance. Eva had likely headed over to her regular lunch spot under the Russian olive tree. Over the last few days, I'd sat there in silence a short distance from her, hoping she'd speak to me, but she didn't. She lay there with her earphones on and her eyes closed, listening to beats in her own world, so I finally decided to let her be. She could speak to me when she was ready. So I sat, alone, eating my sandwich and people-watching on the school's big cement steps, when Vincent sat down beside me.

"Hey, how's it goin'?" His smile was warm and empathetic. The last time we'd really spoken was at his party the weekend before. I smiled faintly back at him and signalled so-so with my hands. He added, "Yeah. I heard. Outing your best friend. Man, that's gotta feel like crap."

I nodded, "Uh-huh, probably feels worse for her." I looked at my knees, not really wanting to talk about it.

"But you know, word was already going around that she'd kissed you at my party. I mean, maybe you shouldn't be so hard on yourself. Anyway, I just wanted to tell you that 'cause you've been looking...sad, kinda." When I didn't respond, he continued, "Hey, some of us are going to the mountain on Saturday. Wanna come?"

Now I looked up at him. Vincent's inner crowd didn't include anyone I had issues with. Sounded like a good plan to me. I gave him a slow thank-you smile, "Yeah. That'd be great."

❦

On Saturday evening, I met Vincent and six others at the majestic, iron-winged Goddess of Liberty statue in Mount Royal Park. I hadn't been to this part of the park for years. My dad and I had spent much time exploring the place when I was a kid. Mount Royal is the name of the mountain in the centre of Montreal and the park encompasses most of it. The park had everything you could ask for in a city green space: wooded areas, grassy areas, ponds, lookouts, rocks (and statues) to climb, mounted police on horses, paths all over the place, and even a cemetery that was so beautiful that people wandered in for a visit just because. My dad and I would bring our kite and lunch, along with some food for the birds and fish, and make a day of exploring the park. It had just been the two of us, in a world of our own making.

The goddess was supported by the monument of George-Etienne Cartier, a symbolic figure at the heart of Quebec's unique culture and also one of Canada's fathers of Confederation. Vincent and his friends sat on the stone steps, just below Cartier. As I approached, the smell of pot wafted over. Vincent acknowledged me with a friendly wave. I didn't know the others very well, but I'd seen them around. Sylvie was in my band class, in the flute section. The other four were boys I'd only really talked to for the first time the weekend before at Vincent's party.

I sat down on the steps just below Vincent and Sylvie. Sylvie smiled. "*Salut,* Frankie! You play sax, eh? Like Vincent." I nodded, then she held out a pack of cigarettes. "Smoke?"

"Oh, *non merci*, but thanks." Then I looked at Vincent, who was holding a joint, and I smiled. "But I wouldn't refuse a toke." He mirrored my smile back at me and handed me the joint. The other boys were talking among themselves about the upcoming hockey season. From what I could hear, two of them played hockey on the same local team, but they both rooted for different NHL teams. The group of them were debating whether the Quebec Nordiques would be able to win their first game of the season against the Montreal Canadiens.

Sylvie reached into her bag and brought out a baggy of something that was organic but not weed. I studied it curiously from a distance.

Vincent looked over. "Awe, shroomies. You brought them!"

Sylvie winked at him. "*Bien sûr,* and it's the real thing. My dad just got back from BC." This time she winked at me, expecting I'd know what she meant. I remained confused and a little embarrassed that I indeed had no clue what it was.

Vincent picked up on my cluelessness. "Sylvie's got a hip dad. He takes his vacations picking magic mushrooms out west." Now he took his own turn at winking at me.

I'd heard of magic mushrooms, but mainly in the context of *Alice in Wonderland*. We'd discussed the book in English class, and we'd debated Alice's altered state of consciousness. From that conversation, a wider class discussion had evolved around drugs and addiction. Mrs. Ray, our English teacher, had clarified the difference between addictive and non-addictive drugs. By the end of that class, we'd had it drilled into us that cocaine and heroine were killers, while Alice's mushrooms were a more natural, safer high, as long as they were used in moderation. I've since wondered whether Mrs. Ray could've been fired for those comments if they'd got back to Principal Baldo. Maybe she did it because of her own ethical beliefs, or maybe it was because she knew some of us were dabbling already and she wanted to help us make better decisions. Who knows. Nonetheless, that spontaneous class conversation had a significant impact on what I chose *not* to put in my body.

"Ohhh, yeah. Wow, cool." I looked at Sylvie and nodded as if I knew exactly what I was talking about.

Sylvie knew better though. She looked at me curiously. "You've never tried it. First time, eh? Oh *mon dieu*, you're gonna love it. It's like...the key to..." She paused, thinking about how to describe it.

Vincent rolled his eyes and interrupted, "The key to a happy evening. Now get on with it." He smiled at me and said jokingly, "But no pressure."

Sylvie reached into the baggy and took a pinch of dried mushrooms. She looked at me. "*En veux-tu?* Want some?"

I shrugged. "Uh, yeah, sure." Sylvie handed me some, took some for herself, and then passed the bag around.

An hour later, we were all lying in a circle with our heads together on the grass up the hill from the statue, looking at the stars above. The sky looked like a huge deep blue ocean, throbbing with an unlimited depth of vibrancy and sprinkled with sparkling diamonds. I tried to catch a star between my fingertips and then broke out in uncontrolled giggles when the stars just "wouldn't stay still." Because of city lights, there were normally fewer stars viewable over the city, but the mushrooms seemed to have multiplied them tenfold. The night sky had become even more magnificent than I'd remembered it to be.

The longer I looked at the sky, the more it seemed like I was looking *into* the sky. My imagination had taken the wheel, and I was driving through space, dodging stars and orbiting planets, with the Muppets in the cockpit beside me. For effect, Vincent put on his best Kermit the Frog imitation and the rest of us followed suit with our own hilarious attempts at imitations of other Muppets characters. In the cockpit, Kermi was now accompanied by Miss Piggy, Animal, the Swedish Chef, Statler and Waldorf, and me as Beaker. We stood up and flew our spaceship over the field and up the hill through the trees, then back down to the goddess's stone lions that guarded the square she reigned above. The lions came to life, and we rode them like dragons through the sky, Muppets on their way to save the world from a mushroomless doom.

The whole trip was a ridiculously hilarious manifestation of our imaginations, and it was the most refreshing evening I'd had since our first day back at school. On that evening in the park, I felt connected with my peers on a level that contained none of the usual anxiety that filled my school days. I smiled silently to myself and hoped that I could share a similar feeling again with Eva sometime soon.

When we'd landed our spaceship back on planet Earth, Vincent lit a joint and passed it to me. We were all back where we started, leaning against Cartier's shrine with the Goddess of Liberty spreading her wings above us. I looked up at her, and Vincent followed my gaze.

"She's the real captain of our ship. We should let her fly," Vincent said in a half-baked dreamy line of thought.

Wistfully, I answered, "Yeah, too bad she's been soldered in stone to a man. Looks like she's trying to escape. Poor woman."

Sylvie laughed and said, "That's it. I'm freeing her!" She jumped up and started climbing up the Cartier monument toward the trapped goddess. We all laughed, but then, as we realized she was serious, we began to cheer her on.

Sylvie only got as far as Cartier himself, as the goddess stood on top of an unclimbable stone pillar. She put her arms around Cartier's neck and looked him in the eye, hard and long, and finally she said, "You typical fucker. Using a faceless representation of a woman to symbolize your glory, while taking all the credit for yourself. Fucking coward!" Sylvie then loudly and dramatically gathered a huge gob of saliva in her mouth and spat in his eye. We all broke out in laughter and continued to cheer her on. Then she looked down at us and said, "Oh fuck, that's high." She laughed nervously, "*Merde,* I'm afraid of heights, man. I think I'm stuck."

We spent the next half hour encouraging Sylvie's fear of heights out of her, coaching her every step until she finally had her two feet back down on solid ground. Then we smoked another joint and laughed until our buzz wore down, sometime around midnight.

Time travels differently when you're high, and I hadn't even thought of keeping tabs on it until it was too late. When I finally looked at my watch, it read 12:30 p.m. There was no way I'd be able to make the last train in fifteen minutes. Vincent offered me a place to crash at his place and I took him up on his offer. We found a pay phone and I called Seb. Pete answered. I tried to sober up and act normal, which wasn't as effective as I'd hoped. The conversation went something like this:

Me: "Hey, Pete. How are you?" I said as if it was half-past three in the afternoon. I tried hard to instil a sense of sincere interest in my voice.

Pete: "Uh, Frankie? It's twelve-forty. You should be catching the train right now. What's up?" Pete sounded concerned.

Me: "Nothing. Uh, you know, the metro broke down and, uh, well, I'm stuck and I can't make the train. Uh, can I sleep at Sylvie's place?"

Pete: "Sylvie?"

Me: "Uh, yeah. She's a friend from school. You know, on the French side. You met her once, at our concert last year. Remember?"

Pete: "Hmm. Do you want me to pick you up, Frankie? Really, I don't mind."

Me: "No, no, seriously, I'm good. I'll stay at Sylvie's."

Pete: "Mmm… OK. But I'll need Sylvie's number."

Me: "Her parents are asleep, though, you can't call now!"

Pete: "I can call tomorrow, you know, to thank them."

Me: "Oh. Yeah. OK. Well…" Sylvie was listening in and now she looked at me and nodded *no problem* and told me her number. I continued to Pete, "Yeah, it's 514-323-5555."

Pete: "Frankie? Are you high?"

Me: "What? No. What?"

Pete: (silence)

Pete: "Hmm. OK, then. I trust you. Stay safe. We'll see you tomorrow." Pete hung up.

I hung up the phone, turned to face Sylvie, and smiled as if I'd just talked myself out of jail.

,

Vincent and I parted with the others and headed through the park to his place. He lived just off Côte-des-Neiges, on the other side of the mountain, which proved to be a beautiful midnight's walk through the park along eerily quiet narrow roads and forest paths. Vincent was a good-looking guy. He was a head taller than me and had a slim, healthy build, with attractively unkempt golden brown hair and flecked eyes to match. I had taken little notice of him before his party. In band class, he'd always been a bit awkward with me, and that together with the incessant sprinkle of zits across his cheeks had blinded me. My blindness had been lifted at his party. I'd finally *seen* the real him. He was talented beyond anyone else I'd met at Beats, but he also had this inner kindness for people and he wasn't scared to let it shine through. He didn't care about the silly trivialities that created walls between students. He somehow lived outside those trivialities. He refused to acknowledge the walls that people built between them and others. He had friends in all circles. Mostly, he saw the best in people and they saw the best in him.

Vincent glanced at me as we stood on the top of the mountain under the huge lit-up steel cross. We'd taken a detour to see it. I'd never stood beneath it at night, but I'd seen it from a distance. It struck me as very typical for Montreal, the city of sin, to have installed upon the highest point in the city, a huge glowing reminder of the possibility of Sunday redemption: all you had to do was convert and your Saturday night sins could be washed away, until next Saturday when the cycle would start anew.

I relayed this idea to Vincent and he smiled. "Luckily I believe that sins are all subject to interpretation. Yup, I'm as clean as a freshly groomed cat. No sin that I need redeeming from." He winked at me.

We arrived at Vincent's shortly before three in the morning. It had been a long, chatty wander through the park. The sky had remained clear and the evening temperature hadn't dipped below eighteen degrees. We'd stopped at a 24-hour pizza place when we hit Côte-des-Neiges and now we sat eating pizza on the couch in Vincent's room, which was more like a teen's dream lair.

"Sooooo, any special girl in your life?" I'm not sure what gave me the confidence to ask Vincent this question, but there it was, I'd done it.

Vincent seemed surprised by my question. He laughed awkwardly. "Nope. Uh, I'm not really, uh, so great at that kind of thing."

The pizza box lay on the couch in between us, and I moved it to the floor. Sliding closer to Vincent, I put my hand on his crotch and leaned in for a kiss, closing my eyes as my lips quickly arrived within a few centimeters of his. But rather than having my lips caressed by his, as I'd so vividly imagined, Vincent's hands flew up in front of him and he caught me by the shoulders and pushed me away.

"What are you doing?" He looked confused, even disappointed. I became instantly embarrassed. I'd assumed he was also attracted to me, and, well, sex seemed to be the step that guys always wanted to take. I mean, that's what guys were interested in right? I bit my lip as I realized my mistake. His rejection had made me feel as if he didn't like me, as if I wasn't pretty enough for him. I immediately started to degrade myself in my head. A little voice in my brain chided me, *'Oh, come on, this guy has everything. Why would he want a nobody like you when he could have any girl? Get real.'*

When I didn't respond, Vincent said, "I—I... You're nice, you know, I like you. But I don't really know you. I mean, it's not like we've hung out much, you know? Let's just... take it easy, you know, be friends. I like you. I want to be your friend. OK?"

I felt really stupid. I thought, *I want to be your friend?* That seemed like a nice way of saying *not on yer life, loser.* I had begun to study my hands intently and I didn't look up. I was sure that my cheeks had rotated between multiple shades of pink. All I wanted was to be gone from that room, but I was stuck there.

Vincent reached out and put his hand on top of mine and I pulled my hand away. "Hey, I'll get you a blanket. It's late. Let's crash." He got up to find me a blanket.

I didn't sleep much that night. The little voice in my brain had grown louder and louder as the time ticked by. It kept telling me how much of an idiot I'd been, thinking that someone as kind and perfect as Vincent would want me. I felt like a fool. At one point I must've fallen asleep, because I was woken up by that dream again, the one where I can't move or scream, the one where I'm pinned down by forces out of my control.

The sun had come up and rays of light beamed in around the sides of the curtains. My watch read 7:13 a.m. when I crept out of Vincent's room, closed the door gently behind me, and headed for the train station.

CHAPTER TWENTY
On the Turning Away

On the first morning in October, Eva finally broke her silence with me.

I had to run for the train that morning. Pete had returned home from up north the night before and had made a mouth-watering, if not timely, fried breakfast that I couldn't resist nor refuse. I caught the train just as it had started its characteristically sluggish clinki-ti-clank roll out of the station. I jumped in through one of its permanently open side doors and walked down through the train to my usual spot in the last carriage. There were no other passengers in the carriage, which was quite normal for the morning trains. There was no way to board directly into the last three carriages as the station platforms were just not long enough. To get to the last carriage, passengers had to walk through the train, from carriage to carriage, to the end. People tended to sit in the most convenient spots, and the last carriage was far from convenient. It wouldn't fill up until we got much closer to downtown Montreal, and that's why Eva and I had chosen it to be our usual spot. Eva hadn't taken the train for a while now, but to me it would always be *our* usual spot. I sat down and plugged myself into my Walkman. Pete had brought Pink Floyd's *A Momentary Lapse of Reason* album home for me upon his return. I ejected Iron Maiden's *Caught Somewhere in Time* album and replaced it with Pink Floyd, then pressed play and gazed out the window as we rolled creakily onto the bridge, over the river, and into a new day.

A few moments after pulling out of Roxboro station, Eva sat down beside me. Part of me was afraid to look at her, afraid of being rejected. I'd tried to talk with her before but she had understandably stonewalled me each time. I glanced at her out of the corner of my eye without turning my head. She was turned to the window and looking directly at me. I slowly turned my head and looked back at her. Then she wrapped her arms around me and squeezed me into the biggest *I miss you* hug I'd ever received. I put my arms around her and squeezed just as hard. We both started crying. Through my sobs, I told her how sorry I was and how stupid I'd been. I told her how much I'd missed her and she hugged me even tighter. Eva hadn't given up on me. I felt like the luckiest girl in the world to have Eva as my best friend. That morning was my best morning ever.

Eva had found her strength again, and with that strength she'd developed an iron backbone. She kept up her silent treatment toward Tammy and gang, but now Eva kept her head high. Rather than silently crumbling every time they threw a barb her way or blocked her path, she kept moving, ploughing through the group of them as if she was riding a bike through an annoying but unavoidable cloud of flies. If Tammy and co. stood their ground and refused her passage, she'd stand still, cross her arms, and stare at them until they got bored and moved on. I tried not to involve myself too much, as I didn't want to screw things up for her again, but with all the corrosive insults being hurled her way, I was worried that it was only a matter of time before that iron backbone of hers would start to corrode.

❜

Eva and I spent the following weekend at my place catching up. On Friday, Pete made lasagna that put Seb's attempt in the summer to shame. Seb's lasagna had been more like a noodle soup with seaweed floating around in it. It had been so severely infused with thyme and oregano that I'd gagged on the first bite. And we were still undecided on what the other green stuff in it was. Parsley had been our best guess. The memory made Eva and me smile. When Eva took her first bite of Pete's five-star lasagna, she looked at me as she tried to keep her smile from turning into laughter. I was less successful and totally gave us away as my suppressed laugh began to expand within my chest and then suddenly burst through the dam I'd been trying to contain it with. Pete looked at both of us, amused and confused. He shot us his typical *uh-huh?* look, the one where he lowered one eyebrow and raised the other as he scrutinized the situation.

"Are you trying to tell me something about my lasagna?" Pete looked from me to Eva. He was a very proud chef.

Eva and I shook our heads but laughed harder. I managed a "Nope!" and Eva added in flustered embarrassment, "No, no, no! Your lasagna's really good!"

I just couldn't hold it in. "We're just really happy, you know, that *you're* the chef!" Eva and I roared with laughter. But now we'd got Seb's full attention.

Seb mockingly shook his finger at us. "Watch yourselves, or the only food you'll be getting from me from now on will be soggy anchovy omelette." Fearing he may just be serious, we swallowed our giggles and dug into our meals.

Sunny dropped by after supper. She'd been visiting Ani and was about to head home. She told us that Eva's brother, Joe, had finally dumped his bobble-head girlfriend that evening. We wondered how long it would take before Sunny and Joe finally became a thing. All Sunny ever talked about anymore was Joe.

Sunny and Joe had planned a party at the train bridge for Saturday night and she invited us along. It would likely be the last bridge party of the year as the fall evenings were getting colder. Eva and I wouldn't have missed it for the world, partly because it was a bridge party, but mostly because no one from our class would be there. We'd be able to relax and party freely. It would be our little vacation from judgment.

The last time I'd been out partying had been that time at the mountain with Vincent and his friends. It had been fun up until the moment I'd made a pass at Vincent. After that the evening had just turned into an embarrassing memory. However, strangely, when we'd returned to school that Monday, Vincent had acted like my pass had never happened. He'd come up to me and said, "*Salut,* Frankie!" with such enthusiasm that I'd briefly wondered whether he'd sprinkled some special herbs on his cereal that morning. He was normally much more awkward with me. I'd assumed that my attempted kiss would've pushed him away forever. It appeared that doing shrooms with me had had the magical effect of relieving his sense of unease. Vincent had even stopped to chat, seemingly not noticing my own awkwardness in the least. I remembered watching his lips move and his golden eyes twinkle as he dramatically told me about some funny run-in he'd had with an angry squirrel in the courtyard a few minutes earlier. The squirrel had chased him up the steps and almost right through the front door of the school. He had radiated joy while recounting the story. But I hadn't really been listening. Vincent bedazzled me. All I had wanted to do was attempt another kiss. My mind drifted and I had had to consciously reel in my thoughts. We spent little time together during the rest of September, but that was because of me. Being close to him made my heart beat too fast for my own good. Band class had become a great feat of concentration, as he sat in the seat directly beside mine. It terrified me that my lusty feelings for him might never be reciprocated.

As Eva and I prepared to leave for the party on Saturday afternoon, she asked me about Vincent.

"Sooo, what's up with you and Vincent? You look kinda silently chummy in band class." She smiled knowingly at me and I flushed slightly.

"What? Oh, nothing. Well. OK. Something. Kind of. But he's not into me, so it doesn't matter." I shrugged and looked away. She stood there looking at me, waiting for more. When it became obvious that she wasn't going to let it go, I let loose and told her everything. I hadn't told her earlier because I didn't really know what to say about it.

Eva listened, smiled, and then took the conversation along a different path. "Wow, magic mushrooms, eh? Joe's done them. Says they'd be too potent for me—I'd die laughing."

"Yup, we laughed all the way through the Milky Way with the Muppets in tow." My laugh turned into a snort, which rendered us both doubled over in giggles.

Then Eva piped up, "Hey, we should go to the mountain for your birthday. Halloween in the cemetery on shrooms! That would be so cool. We could celebrate both on that weekend. Maybe, uh, Vincent would like to join." Her smile was riddled with an inquisitive playfulness, but I detected sadness in her eyes.

"Mountain sounds cool. Vincent? I dunno. Maybe Sunny would like to come?" I responded.

Eva nodded enthusiastically. "Yeah, Sunny's fun. And maybe Joe and them?" I detected relief in her voice.

9

The sunset was breathtaking that evening. The sky glowed with wispy shades of purple and the sun slowly sank below the horizon like an impassioned drop of fire. Eva and I walked along the tracks under the beautiful sky toward the bridge, with Pinky running along behind us. People had started to gather on the other side of the bridge. Pink Floyd's trippy beats carried across the water. "Learning to Fly" was playing. This song spoke to something deep within me. My heart seemed to skip along in sync with its rhythm. I felt like a teenage misfit learning to fly with my wings clipped. Each time I succeeded in leaving the ground after something good had happened that lifted me up, some unforeseen force would grab me back and I'd crash land. And each time I crashed, I'd create a crater that kept getting bigger and harder to fly out of. The song didn't make me feel sad, but rather it made me feel connected. I was not alone in my struggles. I was one misfit among many. A whole community of us were learning to fly with clipped wings.

As we approached the bridge support post that was our regular meeting place, Eva turned to me. "Hey, you wanna just sit for a while?" She looked across at the riverbank on the other side. "There aren't so many who've arrived yet. We could just wait a bit?"

"Sure thing." I picked up Pinky, put her on my shoulder, and eased myself down onto the top of the concrete post. Eva followed.

We sat there on our post, under a magical darkening sky, watching the river meander by slowly beneath us, while the tunes from the party drifted up to us. When Pink Floyd's "Learning to Fly" came to an end, Sunny put on her latest homemade mix, featuring Stevie Nicks, Queen, Metallica, and Aerosmith among others. Bats wove between bridge supports above and below us. We chatted and laughed about nothing in particular. I'd missed laughing with Eva and was so glad to have her back.

During a moment of silence, I began to fiddle with my armband, like I often did while thinking. Hidden underneath it was my biggest secret and I was subconsciously drawn to it during lulls in conversations. I'd told Eva that I kept my tattoo hidden because it reminded me of Sam and I just wanted to forget her. But of course, this was a lie. The tattoo symbolized much more than Sam's frustrating friendship ethics. That little black butterfly was a constant reminder of a horribly painful secret that I just wanted to forget.

Eva noticed me fiddling with my armband and studied me hesitantly. "That tattoo... Is there more to tell about it? I mean, you're kinda distracted by it. And where did those scars come from?" I bit my lip. My arm had scarred when I'd tried to scrape the tattoo off just after my big fight with Sam. Eva had likely noticed the scars when I'd had my armband off overnight. She reached over and touched my wrist gently, pushing the armband down to peak at my little scarred butterfly. I pulled my arm away, more out of habit than not wanting to share. Then I removed the armband

and drew my fingers softly over the butterfly, examining it sadly as I'd done a million times before.

"Remember that time when Tammy and Deirdre put that note in my locker, welcoming me to the 'deflowered club'? And then they started picking on me, calling me a slut and stuff? I wasn't a slut. Well, not really. I mean, yeah, it was my fault, I got drunk, you know. But I didn't want to have sex. I didn't try to have sex. It just happened because I was stupid. And this older guy—he just, like, I dunno, got the wrong message or something."

"You mean you were raped," Eva said in a serious, matter-of-fact tone.

"No! I mean, kind of, in a way, I guess. That's what Gil said too, that it was rape. But I was stupid. And it's not like I ended up in hospital. I wasn't hurt much, just a little. Whatever. Anyway, that guy who had sex with me, he gave me this tattoo." I couldn't look at Eva. I was ashamed. I kept studying my tattoo. "I used to love butterflies."

"Oh my god. What an asshole. I'm so sorry, Frankie. I didn't know. I mean, I was hanging around with those fuckin' twats when they wrote that note. I didn't do anything. I'm so sorry." Eva reached out to me and we hugged. I'd stopped crying about the whole incident a short while ago and I mindfully forced my eyes to stay dry, but it felt really good to share my secret with Eva. Eva accepted me no matter what was hidden in my box of uncomfortable secrets and I loved her deeply for that.

When we'd stopped hugging, I laughed. "The next guy I slept with was that fuckin' stoner dude at Vincent's party. I've got such fuckin' A taste in guys, eh? Shoot me quick, before I go after the bum on the corner!" I laughed harder.

Eva smiled empathetically. Then she added sarcastically, "Me too, apparently. I don't go after guys at all. I'm a guy's worst nightmare—competition!" She started cracking up. "Sex, love, guys—they're all, like, *way* overrated. Chicks are where it's at! Well, chicks like us anyway. Tammy and Deirdre are more rabid vampire than cool chick. They don't count." Eva smiled and I laughed in agreement. Flirting, sex, love—they all seemed to exist solely for the purpose of keeping teenagers miserable. In my opinion, friendships were where it's at. Period. But of course things always proved to be more complicated.

"So what happened with that guy, you know, what's his name, the pothead in the bathroom at Vincent's party? Did he ever say anything to you after? He's a weird one. I think he's like *always* stoned." Eva glanced at me with a curious smile and then looked away again a bit nervously.

The memory of her kiss that evening flickered into my mind. That, together with the nervousness in her tone, made me want to change the subject. "Uh, nothing. He didn't even remember. Super stoner, for sure." I paused, thinking of how to switch directions. "Anyone special in *your* life?"

"Nah, not really. Don't think there are many like *me* around." Eva looked thoughtful.

I didn't really know how to respond. "Hmm. Yeah. Uh..."

"It's weird, you know. I mean, I guess I'm weird. I've just never been into guys. They're OK and all, I just don't...you know...like them like that. Never have. They kinda gross me out, thinking of them in that way. But I wish I could. I tried once, you know." Eva laughed. "There was this boy who lived next to us for a while a couple of years back. Rudy. He had pitch-black hair and eyes that were almost as dark, with long eyelashes and puffy lips. He was cute, in a puppy dog sort of way. Anyway, Rudy had a crush on me. He was always watching me and talking to me about strange things, like insect life cycles and shit. I think he just wanted to make conversation. I wasn't interested in boys, but I was curious about kissing, and I thought maybe if I tried it with him then I'd be transformed and would start, you know, *liking* boys after all." Eva emphasized the word "liking" with a "you know what I mean" look. "So one day after school, when his parents weren't home yet, I went to visit him. I sat on his bed and he was showing me all these Star Wars Lego ships he'd built as a kid. I dunno why—maybe he was nervous or something. He was a bit of a geek, though, so maybe that was it too. Anyway, he sat down beside me at one point and I just leaned over and gave him a big sloppy smackeroo kiss right on his lips." Eva cracked up laughing as she remembered and I laughed along with her.

"No way!" I chortled.

"Yes way! And it gets worse!" She laughed even harder. When she managed to gain some control again, she continued through intermittent giggles, "At first he was surprised. His eyes went all big and he didn't know what to do. But then he kissed me back and put his hands on my boobs, which was kinda weird but also felt good, you know, if I closed my eyes. So I closed them and just let myself feel the touching, you know, without having to see him. And, well, the touching felt good, so we went on like that—him touching me and me just feeling the touch—until he took my hand and put it on his naked *thingy*. Oh my god, Frankie, I was so shocked! I opened my eyes, stopped kissing him, and looked at it. He'd undone his pants and there it was sticking straight up, saluting the high heavens. It looked like an overdone breakfast sausage—you know, when a cooked sausage bursts out from its skin at the end? That's what it looked like. I put my hand over my mouth, trying to contain my laughter, but he saw through me. Poor guy was so insulted, he never spoke to me again!" Eva held her stomach as she fell into fits of laughter again.

"Holy shit, you're evil!" I said to Eva and she nodded in agreement as she laughed harder.

Our laughter died down and Eva said, "But that was it. I never risked kissing a boy again—didn't trust myself not to laugh." She smiled but then added more seriously, "I wish I could like boys. Life would be way easier. Now that everyone knows about me at Beats, none of the girls want to hang out with me. You'd think I was contagious or something." Eva noticed me staring sadly at her and she continued, "But it's not your fault. I mean, they were like that before. They kinda guessed it. That's why Tammy and Deirdre started to pick on me. They're such bitches anyway. I shouldn't really care. Hey, we wouldn't have started hanging out if it weren't for them being bitches." Eva smiled kindly at me.

"Yeah. Eva, I'm really sorry." I reached out, took her hand in mine, wrapping my fingers around hers. We sat there, holding hands, staring up at the night sky. The Milky Way swept over our heads and into the abyss. Someone at the party on the other side of the bridge had put the Pink Floyd tape back in the boom box and people were singing along to "On the Turning Away." It made me think of misfits serenading each other with a promise of eternal support and I smiled thoughtfully. I squeezed Eva's hand and asked, "Time to join the rest of the misfits?"

Eva smiled and nodded. "Yup." She looked over at the party. People were singing, laughing, smoking, and some were already falling over. "Looks like we have a lot of catching up to do. I hope Joe didn't drink our stash." She frowned slightly, the way sisters do when their brothers are being predictably annoying.

We climbed up from the support post and onto the tracks. I put Pinky down and gave her a few little pushes, encouraging her to walk home, but she just stood there staring at me, confused and not budging, waiting to follow. I put my hands on my hips like a frustrated mother and scrutinized her for a moment. Then I gave up. "Fine. But you're going in my sleeve and staying there, OK?" I picked her up and let her crawl into my lumber jacket.

CHAPTER TWENTY-ONE
The Edge of Seventeen

Halloween arrived on a Friday with an exhilarating thrill in the air. Seb and Pete had a special relationship with Halloween and they'd spent the previous evening turning the house into a devil's cavern. They'd planned a neighbourhood dinner party, in which the theme was the "devil's advocate." Although I had other plans for later that evening, Eva and I had agreed to split our evening and stay for dinner. We'd decided to dress up as our two favourite devil's advocates in *Alice in Wonderland*. I'd be the Mad Hatter and Eva would be the Queen of Hearts. We'd spent our lunch hours that week in the home economics room making our costumes from various bits and pieces that we'd picked up at the Salvation Army. They weren't perfect, but they were our creation and we were damn proud.

When I'd entered the kitchen for breakfast that Friday morning, I'd found a wrapped gift at my place on the table. Seb and Pete said that they'd decided that this particular gift couldn't wait until my birthday, as they wanted me to put it to use at their party that evening. To my utter thrill, I'd opened it to find a Polaroid camera inside. I'd never owned a camera before. It had been the most exciting gift ever. Seb and Pete rocked.

Before taking off for school, I ran back up to my room, put the camera on my bed, and fished through my drawer for the old wool Aran sweater that had belonged to my dad. It had been his favourite sweater and wearing it made me feel close to him. I threw it on as I ran down the stairs from my room to the kitchen, said goodbye to Pinky, Seb, and Pete, then grabbed my bag by the door and headed out to catch the train. It was a beautiful fall morning. The morning sky was light blue with wisps of white that, together with the frost in the air, made the sky shimmer like a moonstone. The ground was blanketed with frosty red and orange maple leaves that sparkled in the sunlight. I breathed in the crisp air as I left the house and felt thoroughly energized. I was late again, but I hadn't missed the train yet and today was not going to be any different. As I ran and began to sweat though, I contemplated (for the billionth time) asking for something with wheels for my birthday.

The day had started off so beautifully. As I ran to catch the train, I felt like a baby bird that had been learning to fly and had finally figured out how to soar. In two days I'd be fifteen. I'd survived the worst of my teen years. Life could only get easier from here. In a short two years, I'd be seventeen, done with high school, and free as an osprey to soar above the fray in places of my choosing. The prospect mesmerized me.

۹

Choir class was filled with an electrifying energy that morning, as we'd been practicing Queen's song "Save Me" for the upcoming fall concert. The song brought the class together in a unifying beat that seemed to speak to all our hearts. We sang it with inspired passion, as if it had been a sprouting seed deep within each of our souls that had now evolved into a single beautiful flower, with each of us representing a different coloured petal. I loved how Beats students became so powerfully united in music. United until the music stopped, we stepped out of class, and the flower shed its petals.

After class, Eva grumbled that she'd been summoned to a meeting with Principal Baldo during recess.

"Fuckin' Christ, Baldi wants to talk to me about my grades again. If I don't resurface before next class, send in the coroner 'cause it'll likely mean I've died a violent form of boredom." Eva looked pale and drawn. She sounded worn down.

"Hey, while he's talking, just daydream and nod. I do it all the time. As long as he can hear himself, he's happy." I smiled, trying to comfort her with a bit of humour.

When Eva didn't return to class after recess, I started to worry. Principal Baldo did love to hear himself speak, but he was just as infatuated with punctuality. He would keep a kid in his office, lecturing them until exactly two minutes before class started, then he'd abruptly finish his admonishments and yell, "What the hell you are waiting around for? Class is about to start!" Participating in a kid's lateness or absence from class was not generally a part of his rapport.

I excused myself from class under the *gotta go pee* pretext. Baldi's office was located in the admin corridor, beside the nurse's station. My plan was to visit the nurse, saying that I'd forgotten to bring pads and wondered if she had one I could have. Baldi's door was usually only closed if he had a student in his office, so I'd be able to deduce from the state of the door whether Eva was still in there.

The nurse wasn't in her station, so I walked right on by until I could clearly see Principal Baldo's door.

The door was open. I heard Baldi's chair squeak as he shifted sitting positions, but other than that it was quiet. He was alone in his office.

I paused in the hallway, wondering what do to from there. I briefly considered knocking on his door and asking what had happened to Eva, but that thought seemed so unrealistically stupid that it exited my mind almost as fast as it had entered. I'd have to find her myself. Maybe she'd been upset when Baldi had finished with her. The first place I checked was the 4½ floor landing, as that was where I went when I was upset. She wasn't there. She also wasn't in the washrooms on the third and fourth floors, where high school girls often went to cry. Then it hit me that she could be in the first floor washroom, as the elementary kids took their recess earlier than ours and that washroom could be depended on to be empty during the high school recess. I had often hidden there during my recesses in grade nine to avoid confrontations with the Terrible Twos. It was also the closest washroom to Baldi's office.

A feeling trickled through me as I entered the washroom through a short hallway. It was the kind of feeling that gives you goose bumps and makes the hair on your arms rise just a little. Like an unexplainable expectation, or prediction, of some awful news that is about to materialize out of thin air and disrupt happiness in any way it can. This feeling made me pause for a moment. I stood still in the entrance and listened.

I called Eva's name softly. "Eva? Are you in here? Eva?"

Silence.

That feeling prompted me to call again. "Eva? Hey, you here?"

A soft whimper broke the silence. I ran to where it had come from and opened the stall against the far wall, farthest from the entrance. It was a big wheelchair accessible stall.

Eva sat on the floor, with her back against the wall and her arms around her knees. She was resting her head on her knees, with her face turned away from me. Her hair was a mess and her T-shirt was ripped.

"Eva? Oh my god, Eva, what happened?" I fell to my knees beside her and tried to get her to look at me, but she wouldn't.

"Frankie, I..." She started to cry. "I... Deirdre..." She started to cry harder. Then she lifted her head and looked at me. There was a red-and-purple mark on the side of her face, like she'd been hit with something. I put my arms around her and hugged her until her crying subsided and she felt like talking.

Trying to control her sobs, she recounted what had happened. She spoke with reluctant speed, like a broken brake pedal. "I stopped to go to the washroom before my meeting with Principal Baldo. When I came out of the stall, Tammy and Deirdre were in here. No one else with them. Just those two. I thought it would be fine, you know, because I'd kinda got over them. So I just did as usual. I tried to just plow on by them, to walk past, you know? But they blocked me. They just stood there like fuckin' machines and refused to let me past. So I pushed Deirdre and told her to fuck off, you know. I told her I'd kick her ass if she didn't move. I felt good. I felt tough. I felt strong. I was sure they'd back off. But they didn't. It was like they'd been looking for me.

When I told them to fuck off, they got this weird look in their eyes, like they were pleased or something. I think I just gave them what they wanted. Oh my god, I'm such an idiot!" Eva started to cry harder again and had to take a few deep breaths before she could continue. "Deirdre pushed me back into the stall. I slipped and fell to the floor. I hit my head against the toilet and got a bit dazed. Tammy was telling her to hurry up, talking all low like and rushed. I think they were worried someone would walk in. I started to shout for help, and that's when Tammy really jumped in. She knelt beside me and covered my mouth with her sweater so I couldn't scream..." Eva's sobs grew and she covered her face with her sleeve. "Then Deirdre... Then Deirdre..." Eva's sobs took over until she couldn't speak at all.

I wrapped my arms around her in a hug. "It'll be OK. Eva, it's over. It'll be OK. I'm so sorry, Eva. They are so horrible. Oh, Eva." Tears were beginning to well up in my own eyes. I knew how horrible those girls could be.

Eva rested her head against the crook of my neck. She said, "They got me, Frankie. They deflowered me...with a...." Through barely controlled sobs, she glanced at the floor. A small glass coke bottle lay there, on the far side of the toilet. "They made me bleed, Frankie." She shut her eyes. Her body trembled with her sobs and she sank into me as if her muscles had dissolved into pulp.

❦

The last place Eva wanted to be at that moment was back in class with Tammy and Deirdre. We left out the side door of the building and headed for the Russian olive tree on McGill campus.

We lay under the twisted tree, side by side and holding hands. We stared up at its haunted canopy. Eva stopped crying and we lay there together, in silence, for quite some time. Then Eva turned her head and looked at me. She said, "Thanks, Frankie. You're the best." And she squeezed my hand.

I said, "Let's just skip the parties tonight, eh? Let's go to my place, hang out in my room. Seb and Pete will be OK with that. They're cool."

Eva thought for a moment, then replied, "No way, man. I am not letting those fuckwads get to me. Fuck those bitches! Let's party our asses off tonight." She sounded decided, as if something inside her had either broken or strengthened, but it was hard to tell which.

"Are you sure, Eva? I mean, I'm really OK with staying in with you. It's fun to hang out, you know, just us two. And maybe—maybe you need to recoup a bit, eh?"

"Fuck no. I'm fine. We are partying! OK?" She wasn't going to back down.

I nodded and smiled. "Yeah. OK. Let's party, chica!" I squeezed her hand and she returned my smile. I said, "Fuck 'em." Her smile grew, but her eyes were wet.

9

Seb and Pete's dinner party was anything but ordinary. The costumes had an exceptional homemade perfectness to them. They were far from perfect, and I suppose that is exactly what made them so perfect. The devil's advocate theme turned out to be interestingly subjective. Guests had interpreted it in all sorts of creative ways. Seb and Pete had turned themselves into Jekyll and Hyde. Ani came over dressed as Salvador Dali, twisted moustache and all. The Langleys had transformed into the *Cat in the Hat* crew, with Mr. Langley as the cat himself, the kids as Thing One and Thing Two, and Lynn Langley as the ultra-strict mother. She wore a wooden spanking spoon tucked into her well-pressed apron. The neighbour I had secretly nicknamed Al Capone showed up, quite ironically, dressed as the Pope. Other characters at the dinner party included the Joker and Batman, Fritz the Cat, and a couple of candy smugglers, whose pockets were overflowing with all sorts of sweet stuff. Our living room had metamorphosed into a gathering of conspiratorial social deviants with an excellent twisted sense of humour.

Eva and I sat on the living room floor next to the coffee table, taking photos of all my crazy costumed neighbours and snacking on some devil's eggs that the Pope had brought with him. Eva had been a bit withdrawn when we'd arrived home from school, but her spirits had lifted when our flamboyant guests had begun to arrive. As we sat together, recording history with my new camera, Eva seemed as happy as ever. Seb and Pete's Halloween music mix was playing and the floor vibrated with songs such as David Bowie's "Scary Monsters." We'd also received some compliments on our Queen of Hearts and the Mad Hatter costumes and were feeling quite proud. Originally, we'd planned to change before heading into town but had now decided against it. Too much work had gone into them to only wear them for a couple of hours. The clock struck seven, and we headed up to my room to fix our makeup before leaving for Montreal.

When we were done tweaking our looks, I picked my camera up off the bed, turned to Eva. and said, "Self-portrait, my fair Queen of Hearts?"

Eva smiled and put her arm around my shoulders. We held the camera out in front of us, our arms stretched as far as we were able, and snapped a close-up. The photo turned out blurry and made us look like colourful ghosts stuck behind a foggy mirror. Then we joined the crowd downstairs again and got Pete to take a better shot of us lounging devilishly on the step outside, feeding each other smuggled candy.

When we were almost ready to leave, Sunny and Joe called and cancelled on us. They'd planned on joining us at the mountain, but other arrangements that didn't involve us "young chick-lings" (as Joe liked to describe us) had become more important. Their change of plans was a drag as they were our suppliers, but it was nothing we couldn't adjust to. And, luckily, we managed to get Joe on board for the adjustments.

We caught the seven-thirty train. As we slowly pulled into the Roxboro station a few minutes later, we scanned the platform. Eva caught sight of Joe and let out a happy yelp.

"Yes! He came!" she said as she opened the window on the same side as the platform.

Joe jogged along beside us as the train came to a creaky stop. He held a little package up to the window and Eva reached out for it. He withdrew his hand just before she took the package. He said, "So dishes for a week, eh?"

Eva yelled at him, "Fuck off! I already said yes. Give it to me!"

Joe laughed. "Whoa, girl, show a little gratitude!" He pretended to put the package back in his shirt pocket and turned as if to walk away.

Eva replied, "I fucking am! I'm doing your fucking chores! Stop being an ass!"

After some more bickering, which Joe controlled entirely for the sake of his own amusement, Joe finally handed her the package just as the train began to pull out of the station. As he handed it to Eva, he jogged alongside our window again. He said, "I couldn't get shrooms. It's acid. Same thing but better. Let it dissolve on your tongue." Then, as the train was speeding up away from him, he shouted jokingly, "Be good! Don't do anything I wouldn't do!"

With the little package in her hand, Eva breathed a sign of exasperated relief and sat back, relaxing into the chair. The tiny envelope she now held was about the size of the palm of her hand. She held the envelope open and we both looked inside curiously. There were two tiny square pieces of white paper. They were each marked with a purple peace symbol.

Acid. Vincent had mentioned it that time we were tripping on magic mushrooms. He'd described tripping on acid as "phenomenal," like mushrooms but more hallucinogenic. Sounded good to me. Looking at these tiny squares of anticipated happiness made me feel electrified.

Eva smiled as she studied the little squares, then she looked at me. There was an edgy "fuck the world" excitement in her eyes. I'd seen the look before, in Sam's eyes when she'd showed up at my place after running away from the group home. Something deep inside my gut churned. I briefly considered sabotaging our evening, grabbing the little envelope, and throwing it out the window. But then the feeling diminished. Eva needed to be able to say fuck 'em. She needed to fight back. She needed to feel strong. And getting high on laughter tonight was her way of doing that.

Eva said excitingly, "This is going to be so wicked!" Then she closed the tiny envelope and put it in her heart-shaped blouse pocket.

❥

Eva, the Queen of Hearts, lay on the grass with an amazed smile on her face. She was looking up at a huge steel headstone that had been magnificently shaped into an old oak tree. A mischievous cat had been carved into its trunk and steel hummingbirds, butterflies, and fairies flew between its branches. There were coloured spotlights shining on the tombstone which made the tree look like it was in bloom—to us, anyway.

"Frankie! Did you see that? That one flew. I'm sure of it," Eva said, astonished.

I sat beside her, staring up at the tree's twisted branches. I replied matter-of-factly, "Of course it flew; it's a fairy."

We looked at each other, both trying to determine whether the other was serious.

I said, "Fairies are not, uh, usually real. But that one—" I pointed up into the branches. "That one! Do you see it? It's, like, totally, for sure, no doubt about it flying. Look at it! It's fluttering all over the place!"

Eva followed my gaze from one branch to the next, following the little purple fairy I had been pointing at. "Totally. Oh my god. The whole tree is moving, Frankie. They're all flying. And the branches. Oh my god. They're moving too! The tree's alive! Run!" Eva suddenly jumped up and I rolled backward onto the grass, surprised by her sudden move. She tripped over me and landed in a heap beside me, and we both burst out laughing with the ridiculousness of it all.

"Look! They're good fairies." As I saw them, the fairies were happily flying around under the tree's canopy, minding their own business. The tree's branches were pulsing, as if the tree had a heartbeat. Then the hummingbirds and the butterflies joined the party.

Eva looked abruptly concerned. "I dunno. Fairies are tricky little buggers, aren't they? That one's looking at me funny." Eva pointed to the fairy she was speaking of, but I couldn't see what she was referring to. We could only each see what our own minds concocted. Our trip was both social and individual: we both saw the fairies moving because we had decided together that they were alive; however, our interpretation of how the fairies behaved depended on our individual thoughts concerning fairies. I'd always thought of fairies to be mischievous but never a danger.

Then the cat on the tree trunk spoke and I stared at it, astonished. Its eyes glowed green as it looked at me and warned me in an annoyed tone, "Back off, missy. This is my dinner tree!" Then it snapped back into solid steel and was still again. Eva continued to look up at all the life fluttering around in the tree's canopy. She hadn't heard the cat.

"Uh... Hey, Eva? Maybe...let's, uh, let's go explore." This tree was becoming too lively for me.

We got up and made it only a few steps before we got totally absorbed in the long bluish grasses that had been planted around another tombstone. The headstone consisted of a stone mermaid sitting on top of a boulder. The grasses looked to me like ocean waves lapping at an island, with a mermaid sunning herself on top. The engraving on the stone read "From the Sea, to the Sea. Peace be to Captain Doherty."

I touched the grass, almost expecting my hand to get wet. I knew it couldn't be water, but that's definitely what my brain was telling me it was. I said to Eva, dumbfounded, "Wow. That totally looks like the ocean, eh?"

Eva laughed. "No man that's grass! But look—look at the—the mermaid just, like, said something to you. I think she's telling you to get your grubby fingers off her patch of sea." Eva was pulling my leg. She hadn't seen the grass the way I had.

Eva laughed and danced away from the mermaid along a walking path that led deeper into the cemetery. Although the grass was immaculately green on either side of the path, there were dandelions poking through the pebbles on the path itself, which made the path look golden. I skipped along after her. I felt like Dorothy, skipping along the golden path on the way to Oz. We giggled incessantly as we danced and skipped and tripped our way through the cemetery. At times, the wind would blow through the trees or a bat would swoop a little too close and we'd lose our shit and run the other direction, howling with terrified laughter.

As we resurfaced from a wooded part of the cemetery, we heard voices. We stopped and listened. The voices were definitely coming from teens. The chatter was mixed with loud laughter. And who else would be in a cemetery on Halloween?

Then I recognized one of the voices. "Hey. I think that's Vincent! And Sylvie!" Before Eva could reply, Vincent and his friends came into view from around a large headstone. I called to him, "Hey! Vincent!"

Eva had stopped giggling and had gone quiet.

"Frankie! Hey! So cool you're here! Gravestone tripping too?" Vincent sounded just as joyfully wired as we were.

"Uh, yeah! Halloween trippin', man!" Then I gave him an exaggerated wink. "Acid."

"Hey, us too. Totally tripping. Seen lots of crazy action in this place tonight. But no spaceships!" Vincent laughed and I laughed in return.

As we continued along the path with Vincent's group of friends, Vincent put his arm around my shoulders in a friendly, big brother-like way. Normally I would've melted, but I was way too giggly for any sort of passionate thoughts. My mind was stuck on having just plain fun in a carefree way, and passion had too much caring involved in it. I did, however, love Vincent's company and we quickly became absorbed in each other.

We headed for Mount Royal's big steel cross. We had no plan but to lie beneath it and bathe in its light. It was a thirty-meter high structure, with interwoven steel bars. I had once counted over a hundred and fifty lightbulbs on the cross.

When we arrived at the cross, Sylvie stood as erect as a soldier and said jokingly, "*Et bien!* Cleansing time! Bathe in the light! Let your demons fry!" Then, laughing, she crossed herself and lay down on the grass beneath the huge cross, immersed in its glow.

We all lay down beside her, staring up at the cross, watching the moths bounce repetitively off the lightbulbs. Eva was lying beside me. She hadn't spoken much since we met up with Vincent. I turned toward her to crack a joke about the moths. Her eyes were wide, and she looked startled, or maybe it was fear. My words caught in my throat. I asked Eva, "Eva? You OK?"

Eva jumped to her feet. She was looking down at the ground all around us. "You can't see them?" She looked both terrified and confused. She started jumping from foot to foot, as she was trying to keep her feet away from whatever she was seeing.

"See what?" I asked, in my confusion.

She yelled, "The eyes! The eyes! They're all over the place! They're all looking at me! Stop looking at me! Stop looking at me!"

In a very calm voice, Vincent said, "Eva, calm down. There are no eyes. It's only the acid. There are no eyes."

Eva considered Vincent's words for the briefest of moments and then reacted with full blown anger. "It's you! It's you! You're controlling the eyes!" Then she looked at me. "Get away from him, Frankie! He's the devil! He's tricking you! He's—he's..." Eva's yelling turned to incoherent mumbling and we all watched her silently, wondering how to handle this turn of events.

Vincent stood up and tried to reach out to her, but she pulled away aggressively and screeched at him, "Get away from me! Stop looking at me! Stop the eyes!" Terror filled Eva's expression, and she ran toward the cross and began to climb it like a ladder, from one bar to the next.

I sat there, staring at her for a moment, shocked. Then I jumped up, ran toward her, and grabbed her foot, just before she'd climbed out of reach. She shook her leg and I lost my grip. I called up to her, "Eva! Stop! There are no eyes! Come down!"

Eva yelled back, "They're everywhere, Frankie! They're mean! They're watching me!" Then she lowered her voice and continued, "I think they don't like me. They want me gone, Frankie." Eva had started to sob. "No one wants me. The eyes. That's what they keep saying. Can't you hear them? Frankie?"

I had no idea how to respond. "I... No, it's the acid, Eva. Please, come down. Please, Eva."

Eva shouted back at me, "You're one of them, aren't you? You're one of them!" And she began to climb higher.

Sylvie looked at the others and announced, "OK, I'm outta here. That one's gonna have the cops here soon." Sylvie got up and everyone except for Vincent and me followed.

Eva climbed almost to the top and hauled herself up into the crook on the structure's crossed section. She sat there for a moment, looking down at us. Then she stood up with a scary unsteadiness.

"No, Eva. Please! Sit down!" I shouted up to her desperately.

Eva started sobbing again. "Stop the eyes looking at me, Frankie! I can't take the eyes. They're saying things. They want to hurt me. If I come down, they're gonna hurt me."

Vincent looked at me. "I'm going up." He walked over to the cross and began to climb.

But Eva saw him and completely lost it. "Get off! Get off! Keep your eyes away from me! Get off! I'm gonna jump! Get off!"

Vincent stopped. "OK, Eva, I'm getting off." He climbed down, looked at me, and shrugged.

I looked up at Eva and asked, "Can I come up?" I took Eva's lack of reply as confirmation and began to climb up the structure. I climbed until I stood right below her. Eva was shaking and her eyes were damp and swollen from crying.

"Eva? Are you OK?" I asked, trying to think of something else to say.

"No! Get away!" She shouted at me. But then she softened her tone. "The eyes are right. I'm all wrong. Everyone knows it. Everyone knows it. The eyes are right." Tears resurfaced in Eva's eyes. "No one wants to be with me. I'm all wrong. I'm a fuckin' lesbo."

Now I started to cry. "Eva, I want to be with you. You're my best friend. Please, Eva, I love you. Come down."

I will never forget the look Eva gave me at that moment. It was like a wave of emotion that started in her eyes and ended on her lips. Pain, then anger, and finally resignation.

Eva said, "You're lying." Then she jumped.

OUTRO
Fumbling Toward Ecstasy
Breathe. Love.

July 1, 2018
Town of Sweet Spot, British Columbia

The white luck dragon tumbled down chaotically through a stormy sky, through heavy, rumbling black clouds that had blown in unexpectedly from a time long past. From somewhere in the distance, I shouted desperately at the dragon to fly. The terrified luck dragon flexed its muscles, tried to flap its wings, tried to howl and spit fire, tried to save itself, but its wings stayed still, its voice silent and its fire out. It just kept tumbling toward earth out of control, its eyes wide with fright. Then I remembered a secret we had shared a long time ago, a bit of protective magic that we had created together once upon a time. I closed my eyes and was suddenly on top of the luck dragon's back. My legs looped around the tops of its wings. I wrapped my arms around its neck and hung on tight as we fell head over feet together through danger. I looked up at the dragon's big leathery jaw and saw our silver piece of protective magic dangling from a rope around its neck. The soprano sax was almost out of reach, but I lunged and got it. I untied it, put it to my lips, and began to play. Sarah McLachlan's "Fumbling Toward Ecstasy" flowed out from deep within me, through the long graceful silver trunk of my sax and out into the open sky. The luck dragon reared and drew its wings wide, then it screeched and blew fire as we swooped back up into the storm, flew through the threatening clouds, and...onto my bike? What? My thoughts suddenly became scrambled. *Where am I? What's going on? Where's my dragon? Where's my sax?*

"She's conscious! Stop! She's awake!" The hands that had been touching me withdrew.

I was coughing up water, my vision was blurry, and I could only make out shapes, but I hung on to that voice. It sounded familiar.

Fiona! It was my daughter's voice. I tried to think, tried to piece the puzzle back together, to remember...something. Why was I here, lying in the recovery position, coughing up water on the river's edge, with Fiona and the rest of my Search and Rescue team panicking over me?

"Fiona? What's...what happened?" I looked at my daughter for answers.

"Mum! Oh my god, Mum, you're going to be OK, you're going to be OK, you're OK," Fiona said, fussing over me with her hands and consciously trying to calm herself as much as she was attempting to calm me. Fiona joined the SAR team a year ago, just after her twenty-seventh birthday. I'd been a member for ten years and had joined after we'd relocated from Montreal to the little town of Sweet Spot, BC.

My memory dribbled back in flashes. I'd fallen from the bridge. I'd been talking with a girl. She was going to jump.

Suddenly alarmed, I sat up and asked Fiona, "Where's... uh...where's..." I flipped through my memory files for her name but couldn't find it.

"She's OK. She's OK. She fell too, but we got her. We got her. We got you both." Then Fiona collapsed back onto the ground beside me. Holding her chest, she breathed a sigh of relief. Then she laughed and said, "We even saved your bike." She laughed harder, more out of relief than for any other reason. She motioned to Dan, the kid on our team, and said, "You can thank Spidey for the bike—he noticed it leaning against this end of the bridge and was worried about a train, and he speed-climbed *that* to get it." Fiona pointed at a steep slope with lots of brush and big boulders that lead up to the tracks. "Should've seen him. Like Spider-Man with his ass on fire." She laughed, then continued, "And why the fuck did ya leave your bike on the tracks?"

That was definitely unlike me. Why did I leave it on the tracks?

"I dunno," I replied, truthfully dumbfounded. I was wet, bruised, tired, and just glad everything had turned out OK. The rest would come to me eventually.

I could hear the whoop-whooping of a chopper as it touched down in a nearby clearing.

A few minutes later, the pilot came running over to us, followed by his two passengers, and fell to his knees beside me.

"Frankie, I'm so glad you're OK." Sean leaned over and hugged me. "We're going to move the girl first. She'll be OK, but she's a bit more broken up than you." Sean was my life partner. We'd been together for fifteen years. We were both musicians, but that had been a coincidence.

I'd met Sean through my work as a nature photographer. Following Pete's advice, I'd hired him as my pilot during one of my photography expeditions in northern Quebec. We had spent a week together following a pack of wolves, and by the end of the week we had already begun to plan our next trip. Sean looked both worried and relieved. He was the most level-headed and calm person I knew, but the tension around his eyes gave him away.

I nodded and replied, "Yes, I'm fine. Go. Don't worry about me. I'm OK, Sean. Uh, Vanessa. Her name's Vanessa."

He nodded, kissed my forehead, and replied, "I love you. Tim'll be here shortly. He'll fly you back, and I'll meet you at the hospital. I need to borrow Fiona for a few minutes. She'll be back in a mo."

As Sean turned to leave, the two people behind him came into view. Eva collapsed onto the ground beside me. She had tears in her eyes and her voice was all shaky. "Fuck, Frankie. Holy fuck. You're OK. That was some fuckin' fall." Eva let out a nerve-wracked laugh, then wrapped her arms around me and hugged me like she was never going to let go. Eva's wife, Mia, sat on the other side of me and joined the hug, sandwiching me in between the two of them.

Eva and Mia lived in Spain and were spending their summer vacation with us. They had met at university many years ago and had married as soon as the law permitted it. Eva had been a sociology student and Mia had been studying kinesiology when they met. In Eva's second year, she'd participated as a subject in a physical rehabilitation study and Mia had been on the research team. Eva was left with a limp after her leg got mangled due to getting caught in the cross's structure as she tried to jump off it. With Mia's help, her limp was now almost nonexistent.

After a couple of minutes, Eva and Mia released me from their embrace, and with sighs of relief, we all collapsed back onto the ground beside each other. I gazed at the summer sky. A few clouds rolled on by, but other than that the sky was as peaceful as ever. I'd been very lucky. Other than some big bruises, deep scratches. and a headache, I felt fine. My memories of what had happened on the bridge began to trickle in more clearly.

Vanessa. That was the girl's name, the one on the bridge. I sat there thinking about the events that had just unravelled, trying to remember. I'd been biking on the mountain trails not far from the train bridge when I'd received a text from SAR saying that there was a situation on the bridge. I'd stopped riding and responded that I was in the vicinity and would meet the team at the location. From there things got a little blurry. I could remember parts but not the links between parts.

I remembered biking toward the train bridge along the Victor Turner trail through the trees. The bridge reminded me of the one that lead to Seb and Pete's place on Ile des Voyageurs. It had long iron beams that extended well above it in two big arches, and the whole structure was supported with tall pillars. Vanessa was sitting on top of one of the iron arches when I arrived. She must've been no more than sixteen. I remembered my feeling of panic as she stood up when she saw me. She'd shouted down at me, "Leave me be! I'll jump, I swear it!" I'd been struck by how much she looked like Eva. She had the same ginger hair, same body type. Seeing this Eva look-alike up there wanting to jump reminded me of Eva's attempt on the cross. I'd had to actively push the thought out of mind to refocus and calm myself. That's when I must've left my bike on the tracks.

My next memory bubble is of me sitting on top of the iron beam beside Vanessa. Vanessa was still standing, her legs shaking. I tried to convince her to sit, but she wouldn't. Through sobs, she blamed herself for a classmate's suicide. She'd told me how she'd been involved in some kind of joke where she'd shared an embarrassing photo on Snapchat of a girl making out with another girl. Things had spiralled downhill from there. One girl was now dead, and Vanessa was standing on a bridge over a river trying to convince herself to jump.

I remember feeling conflicted as I listened to Vanessa's story. Eva had also tried to kill herself after being targeted because of her positioning on society's sexual compass. And Seb and Pete had kept their own sexual orientation secret for years, even from me, because of fear of how people might react. They'd finally revealed their secret after I'd given birth to Fiona, at the age of seventeen.

The pregnancy had been the result of a quick tryst I'd had with some guy at a party, after my relationship with Vincent fell apart. The decision to go through with my pregnancy had been the most difficult one I'd ever had to make. I'd ultimately made up my mind as I sat in the waiting room of the Montreal Children's Hospital. Seb and Pete sat on either side of me, each holding one of my hands. I was waiting for my turn to have an abortion. Seb had turned to me and said, "Frankie, this is your decision. We will be here for you no matter what you decide. We love you, Frankie. We are here for you, always, OK?" That's when I made my decision. I squeezed their hands, looked at each of them, took a deep breath, and I said, "Guys... we're having a baby." Then Seb and Pete both wrapped their arms around me and we all cried. I had felt so relieved, and so loved.

When Fiona arrived into our complicated but perfect family, Seb and Pete had been ecstatically over-joyed as they stood beside me in the birthing room and they'd instinctively embraced each other and then kissed right smack on the lips, in front of everyone. As I watched them reveal their love to the world, a light bulb had flickered on in my head. Suddenly everything made sense. Why I hadn't clued in earlier was a mystery to me.

Listening to Vanessa describe her role in the bullying of a gay girl made me feel nauseous. But at that moment in time it was Vanessa who was at risk. She was up on this bridge because she understood what she had done was wrong. And the guilt and pain that she had suffered because of her own stupidity had been so intolerable that she thought that the only way to correct things was to end her life. Her pain reminded me of the guilt I'd felt when Eva had tried to kill herself. I knew I'd contributed to Eva's pain when I'd made her life so much more unbearable after I'd outed her to the Terrible Twos. I'd thoughtlessly done something hurtful that I couldn't take back, and that hurtful thing had rippled its way through the future in ways I couldn't have predicted. Although my action was unintentional, I could still relate to Vanessa's feeling of guilt.

The next thing I remember was Vanessa attempting to sit down. We'd made a connection and she'd changed her mind about jumping. Now she just wanted to talk. I moved toward her to support her, to steady her as she lowered herself into a sitting position. I could see the rest of my SAR team arriving below us on the river's edge. Fiona and two others had started the trek up the steep rocky hill toward the bridge. They were carrying backpacks that I assumed were filled with rescue gear. I had felt comfort in knowing we'd soon have a rope and harnesses to help secure our way down from the top of the arch. I just needed to keep

Vanessa steady as she sat down. Her legs were so shaky. Sitting would be much safer. The last thing I wanted was for her to slip. But then she did just that.

Vanessa slipped,

and I was brought down with her.

All went dark.

My luck dragon roared.

And I woke again on the river's edge

into the present

fumbling along

through drizzle and rainbows

composing my tune

to life's beats

and always onwards.

ABOUT THE AUTHOR

Check out Jane Powell's website for interesting facts about her and her endeavors:
www.janepowell.org

PLAYLIST
See *Sky-Bound Misfit Playlist* on Youtube for chapter theme songs.

DISCUSSION QUESTIONS

1. This story is told from Frankie's point of view. How does her view evolve as she ages?

2. The author uses music as one of her tools in telling this story. What do the songs tell you about Frankie?

3. Frankie's way of handling her bullies changes significantly throughout the story. What influenced these changes within her? Do these changes make it easier for her? If yes, in what way? If no, why not?

4. The events in this story took place in the 1980s. Are similar events still taking place today? How have such events evolved since the 80s?

5. Sam reacts to life's challenges differently than Frankie. Why is this? What path is Sam heading along and

what could change its direction?

6. There are various forms of discrimination in this story. What are they and how do they affect the characters?

7. How do students' reactions to Eva's sexual orientation affect her experience with the world around her? How does she handle the situation? What could have happened that could have made things easier for her?

8. There are several forms of sexual harassment and assault within this story. What are they? How do they differ? And how do they affect the characters' relationships?

9. The school staff plays a role in the way Frankie, Sam and Eva experience the world around them. What role do each of the staff members play? Do they differ from each other? If so, how?

10. What role do Seb and Pete play in telling the story? How would Frankie's story be different if they hadn't have been part of it?

11. What about Frankie's mother? Is her absence significant? If so, how?

12. Frankie's father disappears from the story quite suddenly. If he hadn't disappeared, how might the story be different?

13. Frankie thinks of the main bullies in the story as 'two dimensional'. What do you think about this view?

14. Frankie, Sam and Eva experiment with alcohol and drugs. Experimentation in the 80s was not uncommon among teens in Montreal. However, what other

reasons may have driven them to experiment? What role did alcohol and drugs play in the way they handled challenges.

15. What do Frankie's dreams tell you about how she's feeling along her path in life?

16. What insights does the ending give you into Frankie's life beyond teen-hood?

17. Would you read a sequel to this book? If so, what or who would you like it to be about?

CPSIA information can be obtained
at www.ICGtesting.com
Printed in the USA
LVHW042153040319
609507LV00001B/79/P